A NEW LOVE FOR CHAR

"I thought you were my friend," she said.

"I thought you trusted me," he countered.

"How did I not trust you?" she asked.

It was getting hard to hold the same position, but he'd be a son of a gun before he backed down from her. Just like with Goldie, he had to show her that he was serious. He'd been easygoing about it for way too long. Now was the time to state his intentions and pray that God was on his side.

"I told you I loved you. And you said I didn't . . ."

Books by Amy Lillard

The Wells Landing Series
CAROLINE'S SECRET
COURTING EMILY
LORIE'S HEART
JUST PLAIN SADIE
TITUS RETURNS
MARRYING JONAH
THE QUILTING CIRCLE
A WELLS LANDING CHRISTMAS
LOVING JENNA
ROMANCING NADINE
A NEW LOVE FOR CHARLOTTE

The Pontotoc Mississippi Series
A HOME FOR HANNAH
A LOVE FOR LEAH
A FAMILY FOR GRACIE
AN AMISH HUSBAND FOR TILLIE

Amish Mysteries
KAPPY KING AND THE PUPPY KAPER
KAPPY KING AND THE PICKLE KAPER
KAPPY KING AND THE PIE KAPER

Published by Kensington Publishing Corp.

A NEW LOVE
FOR CHARLOTTE

AMY LILLARD

ZEBRA BOOKS
KENSINGTON PUBLISHING CORP.
www.kensingtonbooks.com

For he satisfies the longing soul, and the hungry soul he fills with good things.

—Psalm 107:9

Chapter One

"And sometimes I even check things that I haven't turned on," Charlotte said as she poured him a cup of the fresh coffee.

Paul Brennaman sat back in his seat at Charlotte's kitchen table and waited for her to pour her own cup and ease down into her chair. He tested the brew with a small sip. Perfect.

"Do you think . . ." She paused as if reluctant to say the words that followed. "Do you think I'm losing my mind?" She waited patiently, nearly browbeaten, for him to reply.

"Of course not," he assured her.

Still, she didn't breathe.

"Really, Charlotte. You've been through a lot." And that was just taking into account everything that had happened to the woman and her family since they had moved to Oklahoma.

Paul had been neighbors with Charlotte Burkhart, her mother-in-law, and her daughter since they had moved to Wells Landing from Yoder, Kansas. That was over a year ago. Now Jenna had moved out and married Buddy

Miller. They both lived on the camel farm with Titus and Abbie Lambert and Abbie's parents, Emmanuel and Priscilla King. It was an interesting setup. Not just because Titus and Buddy milked the camels and sold their product for a small fortune to the English, but Buddy and Jenna had . . . special brains. He supposed that was the best way to put it. Buddy had something that folks called Down syndrome. It wasn't harmful, just made him process things a little slower than some. And he had a different look to his cheeks and eyes. But you couldn't ask to meet a nicer young man. Jenna had sustained damage to her brain in a swimming accident when she was a pre-teen. The lack of oxygen had left her with the mind of a much younger girl, but as far as Paul could see, she got along just fine. Yet he understood that it was easier for him to acknowledge this, standing on the outside. When Jenna and Buddy had first wanted to date, neither one of their families had seemed keen on the idea. In fact, the Millers—Gertie, Buddy's *mamm* in particular—had seemed downright opposed to the idea. Somehow, the young couple had managed to bring their parents around, and now every time Paul saw them, they seemed nothing but happy.

Buddy helped Titus with the camels, and Jenna helped Abbie with her toddler girls, a more identical pair of twins he'd challenge you to find.

Then Charlotte's mother-in-law, Nadine, had gone and fallen in love with Amos Fisher. Not that it was a bad thing. Amos was a good man. He seemed to be kind enough and Paul suspected he would take good care of Nadine, but between moving to a different state and losing her daughter to marriage and eventually her mother-in-law to the same, Charlotte's confidence had taken quite a hit.

Finally, she exhaled. "If you think so."

He wanted to reach across the table and cover her hand with his, but he managed to refrain. It wasn't the nature of their relationship, though the more time he spent with Charlotte, the more time he wanted to spend with her. During the last couple of months, just since the weather started to turn nice again, he and Charlotte had become good friends.

"I do." He cleared his throat. "After Marie died, I did the same thing."

Charlotte's eyebrows raised. "You checked the stove to see if it's off and the water to make sure it wasn't turned on every time you left the house?"

He nodded with a rueful twist of his mouth. "My worry was the windows and the barn. I don't know why I thought I needed to check the barn, since the horse was with me. We only had one horse at the time, but I had to make sure the barn was locked up."

His words made her smile. Well, he hoped it was his words that brought that curve to her lips. He wanted it to be. And what he said was the truth. When his wife had passed away suddenly, he had felt lost and adrift, much like Charlotte felt now.

"Maybe you would feel better if you had Goldie back here," he continued.

Goldie was the golden retriever that Charlotte had gotten from Paul's son Obie. Obie had been raising golden retriever puppies for many years now. And he raised some of the finest dogs in Wells Landing.

Charlotte sighed and stirred a spoonful of sugar into her coffee. "She's so rambunctious."

Paul suppressed a chuckle. "She'll get better as she gets older."

Charlotte shook her head. "She's almost a year old. And she doesn't mind worth anything."

"Training a dog takes patience," he confirmed.

"And that's why I sent her over to the Lamberts. I figured Buddy could do a better job with her than I ever could."

Paul could only nod. When it came to animals, Buddy Miller had the patience of a saint.

"And when I saw how she and PJ played together," Charlotte continued. "Well, I'd feel bad taking her away."

"I understand," Paul said. But he didn't really. It seemed as if Charlotte was making excuses for not having the dog underfoot. He knew as well as any man that dogs came with all sorts of temperaments and personalities, and it just seemed that Goldie was a little more wound up than most. Mix that with the fact that he was pretty sure Charlotte had only gotten the dog because she was missing Jenna, and not because she truly wanted one. . . . Well, it made for a bad combination.

Not that he thought Charlotte was a bad person. She was struggling, that was all, and trying to do her best to make up for the losses in her life. He couldn't find fault with her for that.

"Maybe you should do what Amos did," Paul suggested.

Amos Fisher had decided that he wanted a dog, so he had gone out and adopted one from the animal shelter. He had gotten an older dog. Amos had said he didn't want one that barked at every little sound and ran around crazy like puppies were prone to do.

At the sound of Amos's name, Charlotte pressed her lips together.

It wasn't that she didn't like Amos. Everyone liked Amos. But Paul knew that Amos was taking Nadine away from Charlotte. Just one more loss in her life that she had to face.

Amos had recently traveled back to Missouri to spend some time with his people there. He had been gone when Charlotte and her family had moved to Wells Landing. But when he'd come back, he had fallen instantly in love with Nadine and now the two were a steady couple. Everyone was talking about when they might get married, though they had made no intention known. It was just a matter of time. Everyone in Wells Landing knew it. And when Nadine got married, Charlotte would be truly alone. Jenna was married to Buddy and living with the Lamberts. Once Nadine was married to Amos, they would live in his trailer on the piece of land where he was starting to build a big, beautiful house for her. And Charlotte would be left alone to rattle around the house that he was certain she'd thought she would stay in with her family forever.

"Change is hard," Paul said.

Charlotte flipped her prayer covering strings over her shoulder. Only recently had she been going around with them untied. Paul had noticed, but he wasn't sure if anyone else had. Certainly, when it came to small details like that, most Amish were very attentive. He just couldn't figure out the nature of her rebellion. If he could even call it that. He wasn't sure anyone cared whether her strings were tied or not. And he certainly couldn't figure out what rebelling would do to stop this slow trickle of loss in her life.

"Don't I know it." Then, as if she realized who she was talking to, she let out a quick breath and reached across the table toward him.

Her hand touched his so briefly; then, as if remembering her place, she pulled away. Not quick enough that the softness of her skin didn't register against his own.

"I didn't mean that," she said.

He hoped she was talking about her words and not the small, elegant touch.

Regardless, Paul nodded. He had been through a lot in his life. He had lost his wife to cancer and one son to the sunshine of the Pinecraft Amish community in Florida. But he had gained a few things along the way. His son Obie had married Clara Rose Yutzy and started a family. They had taken over the family house, so Paul and the other two boys lived in a trailer behind the main house. It was good enough for him. He didn't need much, and he wanted Obadiah and Clara Rose to have plenty of room for their family. Obie's twin brother, Zeb, had come back from Florida for a time, then married Ivy Weaver. Zeb had moved her and her grandfather down to Florida with him. Paul supposed he could chalk them up as a loss in life. He hadn't seen his son in years; then Zeb had returned only to leave again. But Paul would rather think that he'd gotten a friend in her grandfather and another daughter in Ivy.

There were gains to be seen, marks for the "pro" column, if only he looked hard enough. And he figured it was worth the effort.

From where they sat in the kitchen, he heard the front door open and close.

Charlotte immediately stiffened. "Nadine," she said quietly. Paul was used to the change in her manner. Poor Charlotte couldn't see what was in front of her through the losses that clouded her way. And she had lost a lot, but Paul had learned long ago that focusing on the bad things just seemed to make it worse, so he would rather focus on the good.

He wasn't able to reply as Nadine swept into the kitchen, a smile on her face. At sixty-five, she looked much younger, but he supposed love would do that to a person. He just wished he could do that for Charlotte.

Charlotte's back stiffened as Nadine greeted Paul. It wasn't that Charlotte had done anything wrong. But she knew something was wrong inside her. Regardless of Paul's assurances.

She didn't like to talk about it, or maybe she didn't want to face the truth. There had already been too many changes.

"You're back, I see," Charlotte said unnecessarily. Immediately, she wished to call the words back, but it had been that way lately. It seemed as if her mouth ran before she even thought about what she was saying. And that was not like her at all. She would always stand up and speak her mind, but never in such a hurtful manner. She felt a lot like Velma Byler, an old woman in their church district who saw fit to grumble about everything from the weather to the color of the sky. She walked with a cane, and though the Amish were considered to be nonviolent people, Velma had a tendency to "accidentally" whack people in the shins with that hard cherrywood walking stick.

Was that her fate? Was Charlotte destined to be the next Velma Byler? The thought deepened her sadness until she thought she might drown in it. Every day was a struggle. And she hated it. And she hated that she hated it. And that made it worse. So bad that getting out of bed was a chore. Getting dressed was a chore. Fixing her hair, walking down the stairs, cooking breakfast, sitting down at the table to eat. Everything felt like too much effort, and the longer she felt that way, the worse it seemed to get. She had no idea how to get over it.

"You really should come with us sometime." Nadine moved to the coffeepot. She retrieved a mug from one of the cabinets and filled it with the fresh brew.

Charlotte tamped back her annoyance. She had no right to be annoyed. She had made the coffee for people to drink, and Nadine certainly fit into the category of people. But somehow it annoyed her all the same. It seemed the only person that didn't annoy her these days was sitting across from her.

Paul.

He had been her rock, her sounding board, as the English say. He had listened to her rant and fuss and cry and try to work through all these problems that seemed to be piling on top of her one by one. It might've been okay if they had been loose in their structure, but it seemed as if they had been set by a brickmason one by one, offset for strength with mortar in between. Even the visual that it presented was crushing.

"Fishing?" Charlotte said as Paul said, "I'd love to."

Charlotte looked to her friend. "You want to go fishing?"

"Of course. I love fishing."

"How can sitting on the edge of the pond with a pole in the water just waiting for some poor creature to come bite the end of it be considered a good time?" The moment she said the words, she wished she hadn't spoken. She had gone fishing before. Why was it such a bad time now? Maybe because sitting and relaxing in that manner made her feel like she wasn't working on the problem at hand. She didn't know. She only knew the bubbling anger and resentment that seemed to own her these days.

Nadine started scooping sugar and powdered creamer into her coffee, and Charlotte had to bite back her protest. Nadine had drunk her coffee with three sugars and four creams ever since Charlotte had first met her. It had never bothered Charlotte before now. But it seemed things had changed. It did bother her. A lot.

Thankfully, she stopped the words of protest before they escaped her lips. But she knew Nadine had seen her frown. She wanted to apologize but couldn't bring the words to her lips.

"It's relaxing," Nadine said. "You should try it some-time. Really. It might make you feel a little . . . better."

"I feel fine, thank you." But a bigger lie she didn't remember ever telling. Even when her husband, Daniel, had died, and everyone asked her if she was okay. Even then, she'd told the truth. That she was struggling but managing, that she missed him but knew he was in God's hands. The pain had been so intense, the hole his death left in her life immense, but she'd had Jenna. Her daughter had needed her, and she had continued on. So what was different about now? What made the loss of Jenna, not even to death but merely to marriage, and the impending loss of Nadine in the same manner . . . what made this harder to deal with than the permanent loss of the man she loved? It just didn't make sense.

"So," Charlotte started, not liking the sharpness of her tone, but once it was out there, what could she do? "Have you set a date?"

Nadine took a tentative sip of her coffee, then flipped one hand in Charlotte's direction. "We're in no hurry." And that was something Charlotte couldn't understand either. Why weren't they in a hurry to start a new life together? She was certain it would be better if they went ahead and got married now instead of dragging it out indefinitely. It would be better for her at any rate. Kind of like ripping off a bandage when it was stuck to the skin too tight. Of course, sometimes that took a lot of the skin and some of the hair with it, but wasn't it better to get it done in one fell swoop? Maybe then Charlotte could bounce back to herself.

"We just haven't made a decision yet." Nadine set her coffee cup back on the table and gave Charlotte and Paul a secretive smile. At least Charlotte felt like it was secretive.

It was common for older couples starting their second marriage not to make such a big deal out of things, to keep their dating a secret and only announce the wedding just a couple of months before. But as Wells Landing grew, so did the population and the number of weddings. There were only so many days in a week and only so many weeks in the wedding season. Sometimes couples announced their wedding a year in advance in order to secure a date for their nuptials. But truly what decision needed to be made? She knew as well as Nadine and Amos that they would get married. And once that happened, Charlotte would be left truly by herself.

She didn't even have her dog now. Maybe she should bring Goldie back from the Lamberts'. It wouldn't be long before Nadine was gone and Charlotte was left alone in the house to rattle around with no one but the buggy horse for company. Perhaps she should move to a smaller place. But the thought of that was worse than thinking about being left in this house all by herself.

While she had been mulling over every little detail of her life and obsessing over the fact that she would soon be abandoned by those she loved, Paul had finished his coffee. He stood and stretched his legs, the action surprising Charlotte. It was something he did every time he got ready to leave. She just wasn't sure why he was leaving just yet. Maybe her attitude was chasing him away. She really needed to do something to figure out what was causing her surliness so she could get over it already and go on. She would add it to her prayers tonight. Maybe even this afternoon.

"You're leaving?" Charlotte asked.

"I need to get back to the house. Thanks for the offer to go fishing, Nadine. I'm going to take you up on it."

"I'll make sure you do." Nadine smiled.

A little zing of jealousy zipped through Charlotte. Nadine and Paul were happily talking about fishing, doing things together, but as friends. She and Paul used to have similar chats. What had happened to that easy banter in her life? She had no idea, but the problems that were weighing on her were beginning to become tiresome, a burden she needed to figure out what to do with, and soon.

She walked Paul to the door and stood on the porch, watching as he started off across the field that separated their houses. It was nothing but wildflowers and various weeds, but come the fall, it would be baled as hay. Yet now, in April, it was nothing but ground covering.

She sensed, rather than heard, Nadine step out onto the porch next to her. "Are you okay today?" Nadine asked.

Charlotte cleared her throat. "Of course." Another lie. The problem was growing and Nadine knew it as well as she.

"You don't seem like yourself lately."

I've not felt like myself lately. But Charlotte bit back the words. It wasn't something she could admit out loud. It was just something she was going to have to fix inside herself. "Change in the weather, I suppose."

Nadine made a noise in her throat, almost a protest but not quite. They both knew that other changes on the horizon were giving her these problems. But Nadine wasn't ready to come right out and say anything. Not yet anyway.

"Everything's fine," Charlotte said, though they both knew it wasn't the truth.

Chapter Two

"Will you come on?"

At Nadine's impatiently asked question, Charlotte bustled from the kitchen after checking the stove for the third time that morning. Which wouldn't have been a problem except they had cold cereal with milk and a piece of fruit for breakfast. The stove hadn't been on since yesterday. They hadn't even made coffee. And yet she felt the need to check it three times as if something were missing in her life.

Halfway across the living room, she came to a screeching halt, then doubled back to look at herself in the mirror in the downstairs hallway. It seemed no matter how much baby lotion she used, her hair still held a frizzy look. As if it echoed her thoughts, standing on end, frazzled, unable to sit still. She smoothed back some of the strands, noticing now, even more than yesterday, the overwhelming gray. Her hair had been dark her entire life, and she had wondered if perhaps she would go prematurely gray sometime in her twenties, but that never happened. Now, at forty-three, she seemed to be graying by the hour. Not that it mattered. It shouldn't matter. Except those gray hairs represented the passage of time that she couldn't recall. What had happened? Where had it all gone? And with Nadine soon to marry Amos Fisher and Jenna already married to Buddy Miller, Charlotte felt left behind. That was the only way she could describe it.

"Charlotte!" Nadine called from the front door. "We need to get out of here or we're going to be late."

Charlotte ignored the wrinkles fanning out from her eyes and the skin that just wasn't quite as firm as it had been before and hurried toward the door.

"I'm sorry," she said breathlessly as she rushed out of the house. She stopped on the first step, almost unable to control the urge to run back inside and check the stove even though she had just checked it. But had she looked to make sure it was completely off, or had she just looked at the burner? She couldn't remember. Why couldn't she remember? And why did it matter? If it had been on, it had been on all night. It was gas. Surely they would have figured it out by now.

"Get in the buggy. I checked the stove myself. Every-thing's okay." At the sound of Nadine's softly spoken words, tears sprang into Charlotte's eyes. Maybe she was losing her mind after all, and Paul just didn't want to tell her. But she didn't want to accept that either. Paul was her best friend. He had held her steady through these crazy times, and she wouldn't know what to do without him. She surely hoped that someone that important in her life would always tell her the truth.

"I'm sorry," Charlotte said again. How many times had she apologized? And somehow, even as she felt she needed to hush, she wanted to say the words again. Maybe she should set up a jar and make herself put a dollar in it every time she apologized. Like one of those English families that were trying to stop their kids from using ugly words and had a 'swear jar.' Maybe she could just put in a quarter, but she wasn't sure how it would work exactly. What was she going to do with the money when she was done? It didn't matter—she knew she needed to stop apologizing for every little thing, however she managed to accomplish it. She felt stuck in the mud like a tractor that had lost its traction, back tires spinning, trying, trying, trying to go somewhere, but unable to move forward or even backward. She sighed, then hopped up inside the buggy. "Did you get the food?" she asked, then started to get back down.

Nadine stopped her with one hand on her arm. "I've got everything. You just need to take a breath and calm down. It's all okay."

She knew Nadine understood too, but somehow Nadine's understanding and Paul's understanding were two different things. Nadine was trying to be supportive. Paul had lived through it as well, and suddenly Charlotte wished that she had taken him with her to church. Maybe they should have run by and picked him up. It wasn't as if he lived far away. And then she would be able to ride home from church with him and at least have some company because chances were that once the service ended and they ate their afternoon meal, Nadine would most likely ride home with Amos. And that left Charlotte dangling, whipping in the wind, hanging alone. Kind of like one of those fly strips they used to keep on the back porch.

Had she really just compared herself to a fly strip? She surely needed to get a hold of herself, and quickly. She was either apologizing or snapping someone's head off, and neither could continue. She was going to chase away the people that she did have around her if she didn't remember how to treat them. No, that wasn't right. She knew how to treat them. She just couldn't seem to make herself bring forth those manners that had been instilled in her when she was a child. It was as if someone else had taken over her body, pretending to be her while acting up and trying to push everyone away.

"I don't mean to," Charlotte said.

Nadine nodded, but didn't take her eyes from the road ahead. Still, she reached out a hand and patted Charlotte on the knee in a reassuring manner.

Charlotte could never say that she and her mother-in-law had ever been particularly close. But in the recent months since they had moved to Oklahoma, she had felt the nature of their relationship change, especially with the worry over Jenna and her play at independence. Not to mention all the other changes in their life. Charlotte felt that she understood Nadine a bit more now than she ever had, even though they had been in each other's lives for decades.

"This too shall pass," Nadine said.

"I know," Charlotte murmured. The question was when. And would she be able to survive until then?

She was being dramatic, but she didn't like not feeling like herself. She didn't like feeling like she was putting everyone aside, away from her. Times like these, a person needed family more than anything, yet she seemed determined to push everyone away or at the very least keep them at an arm's distance.

They rode quietly for a while until they pulled into the driveway at Margaret and Jason Lapp's house. The Lapps were what Charlotte would call "fancy Amish." The house wasn't pure white, but more of a creamy color. It had vinyl siding, and she was certain they had more grass in their yard than anybody else in Wells Landing. Well, the Amish of Wells Landing anyway. They drove the nicest tractor in town, and it had never seen a field. They raised horses for a living, but not like the ones that Andrew Fitch raised. These were thoroughbred horses, built for racing. Charlotte supposed that raising horses to race was different from betting on the horses themselves, or that must have been Jason Lapp's argument to the bishop. If he had even been questioned about such matters. Whatever happened, Jason was allowed to raise his horses, and his son, Thomas, was surely going to follow in his footsteps.

Nadine pulled the buggy to one side and handed off the reins to the young man whose job it was to unhook the horse and pasture it for safekeeping while they held service. Charlotte hopped down from the buggy, surprised to feel her heart beating heavily in her chest. They were just going to church and yet she felt like she was about to walk off a cliff. What was wrong with her these days? But her thoughts kept circling back to one thing: she was missing something. It wasn't like Paul had suggested yesterday. It was different. *Jah*, she was missing Jenna, and she was missing Nadine, even though Nadine wasn't quite gone yet. Charlotte knew a time would come very soon that Nadine would be gone. Nadine, like Jenna, would abandon her, and she would be left alone. The thought dried up her mouth, made her stomach cramp, and had her heart beating a little faster than it should.

Why was she so afraid of being alone? It wasn't like she had health issues or was scared to be there by herself.

She had lived plenty of time by herself. Okay, maybe not. She had married Daniel and moved from her parents' house to the house they'd shared until he died. By then, she'd had Jenna, and then the two of them had moved with Nadine down to Oklahoma. Perhaps that was the problem. She had never had time for herself. She had never had a time when she wasn't responsible for somebody else, and she wasn't sure what to do with it. It felt odd, wrong.

She stopped halfway toward the house. They had gotten there just in time for the service. Folks were milling around, and people were starting to go inside the large barn for the service. The Lapps were one of those families who had a special building just for church. They stored stuff in it during the year, but it was mainly for church. Not many folks in Wells Landing could afford such a luxury. It was nice to attend church in such a spacious place, but it was a little unnerving as well.

She shook her head at herself.

"What's wrong?" Nadine circled back to her.

Charlotte forced a smile. "Nothing, nothing. I'm sorry. I'm fine." There she went, apologizing again.

Nadine gave her a quick smile. It was fast but genuine, completely unlike the one that Charlotte had used. Then Nadine took her hand and tugged Charlotte toward the house.

"Come," she said. "Give it to God."

And that was exactly what she tried to do. During the service, she did her best to relax her mind, unclench her jaw, and allow her thoughts to just be. She needed to give it to God. Even as she listened to the bishop talk about the perils of the modern world and where the Amish fit into it, Charlotte did her very, very best to give it all over to God.

Why was that such a hard thing to do? She trusted God in so many instances in her life. When bad things happened, she said prayers of solace. When good things happened, she said prayers of thanks. When nothing happened, she said prayers of need. Now it was almost like too much had happened. She had said prayers of peace, yet peace wasn't coming to her.

The bishop, Cephas Ebersol, continued his sermon, and she was certain it was most likely a very well-thought-out sermon, even if it was "off the cuff."

The Amish preachers spoke about what was on their minds that morning; it wasn't something they practiced throughout the week like other Christian pastors did. Or so she had been told. Amish church leaders decided on the very day of the sermon what God wanted them to speak about and they spoke immediately on the topic. It meant that the church leaders, the bishop, the deacon, the minister, and the preacher, all had to know their Bible, know their community, and be able to put all that together on such short notice. And yet, even with all the focus and energy that Cephas was using, Charlotte could hardly pay one bit of attention. Instead, she stared at her fingernails and silently prayed for . . . something.

Church was almost over, and somehow she had made it through three hours of sitting, listening, and trying to focus enough to pray. She looked up from her lap, and her eyes immediately went to a man directly across the way.

She had never seen him before. Or maybe she had and just didn't remember. But she certainly didn't think he belonged in their church district. Wells Landing was not a tiny community, but it certainly wasn't as large as some. Most everyone knew everyone else in all three of the districts, though she wasn't as familiar with those who lived in the other two districts. The Amish community there was a little spread out, not lumped all together, and travel by tractor from some places was difficult. This man, he must be from a different district. One of Bishop Treager's districts.

It was a common practice for the Amish to visit each other in their churches on Sunday. Sometimes they even went on an off Sunday to a nearby district to have church a second time, two Sundays in a row. One of the other communities in Wells Landing held church the same day they did. Bishop Vernon Treager served two districts, one only half the size of a regular church district and not big enough to support its own elders. Instead, they used the bishop and others from the neighboring district. Thus, church was held on opposite Sundays.

It seemed a little odd to Charlotte, but it wasn't unheard of. Some things just were.

But surely that was the reason that she didn't know the man seated across from her. Plus, she had been in Wells Landing for just over a year. With all the work she had been doing with Jenna and keeping up the house and baking and Goldie, she hadn't gotten around to meeting everyone.

But this man she wanted to meet. She couldn't say why, she simply did. Want to meet him.

He had a nice face, she decided. Kind brown eyes and

a warm smile. But mostly there was something different about him.

She looked away when he noticed her stare and turned his gaze toward her. Her own gaze slammed into that of Paul Brennaman. Sweet, understanding Paul. Maybe he knew the man and could introduce them this afternoon. But somehow she knew she wouldn't ask him.

Charlotte went through all the motions for the remainder of the service. She sang when she was supposed to sing, knelt when she was supposed to kneel, and prayed when she was supposed to pray.

As usual, the men set up the tables using the benches they sat on for church. It took only a minute to do, and while they completed that transformation, the women got the food out and ready to eat. It didn't take long, but it seemed to take forever. She wanted to meet this newcomer to Wells Landing. Or whatever she could call him. The man with the nice brown eyes.

Once everyone was served and everyone had eaten, the cleanup began. This seemed to take another long while, though she was certain it didn't take any longer than necessary. The Lapps had plenty of room in their bonus barn. That made it go quicker since, as a person helped, they weren't bumping into a dozen bodies all trying to do their part of the work.

It couldn't have been later than two when everything was done. It was a beautiful day outside, and folks had started gathering. Some of the women had found Margaret's lawn chairs and plopped them down under the large oak tree in the front yard. The men, of course, had gathered around the corral and the pasture checking out the new horses that were now a part of the Lapp farm.

Charlotte had to admit that the horses were beautiful, their coats gleaming in the sun as they pranced around the paddock, showing off for the men who were watching. But Charlotte only had eyes for one man.

She grabbed Amos by one arm and turned him toward the line of men standing at the fence. "Do you know him?" she quietly asked, hoping only he could hear. She wouldn't want to start any undue rumors. She just wanted to meet the man.

Though she would say that he was about the most handsome man she had ever seen. He seemed to get more handsome as the afternoon wore on.

Amos stroked his beard and tried his best to follow the line of her finger to where she was pointing. It didn't help that she was pointing from about waist high. "Andrew Fitch?"

Charlotte shook her head. "Next to him."

"That's Danny Fitch, his cousin."

Charlotte bit back a sigh and pointed again. "On the other side."

Amos stroked his beard once again. "I don't believe I do. But I was gone for a while and people move in and out sometimes. But I bet Paul does."

Before Charlotte could utter one word of protest, Amos was headed off to find Paul. And Paul was the last person that Charlotte wanted to ask. He was her friend and would ask way too many questions. She didn't want or need all that. She just wanted to know the man's name.

"What's going on?" Paul said as he walked toward her, Amos on his heels. The sunlight glinted off the gold in Paul's hair, giving him the effect of a halo. She almost shook her head at her fanciful thoughts. "Who is it?"

"That's what I was hoping you would tell me."

Paul squinted toward the line of men still admiring the expensive horseflesh strutting about in the green, green pasture. "I do believe that's Glenn Esh." He paused a second before asking, "Did he upset you?"

Charlotte shook her head and hoped that, if anyone asked, she could blame her heated cheeks on the bright spring sunshine. "I've never seen him before. I just wanted to know his name."

"Glenn," Paul said with a quick nod. Then, louder: "Glenn!"

The handsome man turned, and Charlotte's heart beat a little faster in her chest as Paul motioned him to join them.

He was tall and polished in a way that most Amish men weren't. It wasn't something she could readily describe; it was more of an air about him. He carried himself differently. She had a feeling he was fancy Amish just like the Lapps.

From the touch of gray at his temples, she figured him to be nearing fifty if he was not already there. Just as she had noticed inside, his eyes were warm brown, caring with just a little sparkle of mischief.

"Paul," Glenn greeted as he neared them. He stuck out a hand to shake. Charlotte watched as they exchanged their greetings.

"Glenn, this is my . . . good friend, Charlotte Burkhart. She and her family moved down here from Yoder, Kansas."

"Charlotte." Glenn nodded in her direction, and Charlotte felt a warmth course through her. He really was a handsome man.

"Nice to meet you." She tried to smile, but her lips

quivered a bit. What was wrong with her? She needed to get a hold of herself.

"Glenn lives in Vernon's district," Paul told her.

She was proud of herself for guessing that correctly.

"But I am thinking about buying a house over on this side of town." He shrugged as if everyone moved from one side of Wells Landing to the other on a regular basis.

"So good of you to join us today. Are you staying for supper?" she asked.

If Glenn was surprised by her boldness, he never let it show. Paul, on the other hand, blinked hard as if he couldn't focus on what was happening. He should be used to it by now, but it seemed that it had slipped his mind of late.

She had always been a little . . . forceful. When she was younger, it had gotten her into a little trouble. Nothing too big. But it was safe to say that she and her father's switch were well acquainted.

"I'm eating with the Cephas Ebersols this evening."

Charlotte smiled. "And I'm sure he's showing you around."

He nodded. "Tomorrow. Then I have a driver taking me back home. That way, I can stay late and not worry about it getting dark on me before I'm finished looking around."

"Then you'll have to come to supper at my house tomorrow night. My mother-in-law, Nadine, and I would love to have you."

"That's very kind of you. Thank you."

She saw Paul shift out of the corner of her eye, but she wasn't looking directly at him. She could only see Glenn Esh. He was the answer to what had been bothering her lately. She and Jenna and Nadine had moved down to Wells Landing for a fresh start. Charlotte had believed that they would have their fresh start together, but then Jenna up and got married. Now Nadine was about to move out and leave Charlotte all alone in the house she'd thought they would all live in for the rest of their lives.

But maybe the way for all of them to start over was to find love, get married, and have a life outside of one another.

And in that instant, she knew it. She was going to marry Glenn Esh.

Chapter Three

"He's an interesting man, don't you think?" Charlotte asked Paul after Glenn had moved away. Being as he wasn't a regular part of their church, everyone wanted to talk to him, visit with him, and find out more about him in general. Some members she was certain knew him better than others and wanted to inquire about his family and his plans to move to their district.

But if he was coming to supper tomorrow night . . . she needed to get up early tomorrow and start cleaning. She needed to sweep and mop the floors and dust the living room. Especially dust the living room.

"*Jah*, interesting," Paul said. He kicked at a clump of weed in the Lapps' otherwise perfect yard.

"Is something wrong?" she asked. And air out the couch cushions. That was a must.

"Of course not," Paul said. "What could be wrong?"

"I don't know," Charlotte returned. "That's why I'm asking you." The list of chores in her head was growing even as she conversed with her friend.

Goodness, she had a lot to get done before supper tomorrow.

"I thought I might come over later. Take a look at that loose board in the barn loft."

"That sounds suspiciously like work on a Sunday." And what were they going to eat? She'd have to check the freezer. A roast would be nice. Mashed potatoes. Gravy. Yum.

"Nah. I thought I'd just walk over and give it a look-see. Then tomorrow I can come over and fix it. It won't take no time if I already know what I'm up against."

She was never going to be able to get everything done unless she started this afternoon. And she couldn't start this afternoon if she had Paul underfoot watching her.

It might be against their *Ordnung* to work on a Sunday, but this was a special circumstance. Kind of like when dairy farmers and such had to work on Sundays, tending their animals. Kind of.

"I think I need a rest this afternoon." She would have to be certain to ask forgiveness for all the lies she had been telling lately, but this too was a special circumstance. Surely God could understand and forgive that.

"A what?" Paul's forehead puckered in confusion.

"A nap."

He frowned. "You've never taken a nap on a Sunday afternoon before."

"That was because I've always had too many responsibilities, Jenna and Nadine. Now that they are both off with their new loves, I can have a little more time for me."

She was surprised when he didn't roll his eyes at her statement, even though she sounded like one of those signs she had seen in the general store advertising the latest new bath beads. *To indulge yourself.*

"Tomorrow, then?"

"How about Tuesday?" She didn't have to say it. Tomorrow she would be getting ready for her dinner with Glenn. Well, hers and Nadine's. It wasn't like Glenn was coming to supper and she would be there all alone. That wouldn't be appropriate at all.

"*Jah.*" He nodded slowly.

"Is something wrong?" she asked.

He shook his head. "I'll see you Tuesday."

She watched as he quietly walked away. She stared after him for a moment, a little concerned, but trusting of her friend. Surely if something was wrong he would tell her. Maybe he was reluctant to say what was on his mind. She knew Paul well enough to know that he would let her know when he was ready. And until then, she had to get her house ready for tomorrow's supper.

For once, she didn't mind riding home alone.

Paul was out in his yard when she pulled her buggy past. She waved, and he smiled and waved in return. Maybe she had just imagined his melancholy attitude after church. She had been thinking a lot about Glenn and the dinner she was going to prepare. Maybe she had been so wrapped up in coming events that she hadn't been paying good enough attention to the now, as they said.

She would have to watch that in the future. She might be marrying Glenn Esh, God willing, but she still wanted to remain friends with Paul Brennaman.

She pulled her horse to a stop in front of her house, then unhitched the mare and led her to the barn. She thought of Paul as she poured the horse a bucket of oats and started to brush her down. Paul had been such a good friend to her. Just about the time that Jenna had gotten married. Maybe that was the first time that she had seen him. Really spoken to him.

It had snowed that day, great huge white flakes falling from the sky as if their very existence depended on it. Within hours, there had been a foot of snow, so unlike the normally mild Oklahoma winters. She had been told when they moved to Wells Landing that Oklahoma weather was completely unpredictable. Near-blizzard conditions on the day of her daughter's wedding was proof positive of the very same.

Not many guests had been able to attend. If it hadn't been for the new preacher, Aaron Yoder, who lived on the other side of her, across the field in the opposite direction from the Brennamans, then Jenna and Buddy might not have been able to get married on their planned day. But Aaron had tromped through the snow and saved the day. Most of the guests—Buddy's immediate family, and those who had come early to help them set up—had been there through the night.

Jenna and Buddy couldn't have cared less if people didn't attend. They were just happy to be finally getting married. But the one guest there who was not family was Paul. He had trudged across the field separating their houses to see her daughter get married. The gesture had touched her heart, and they had become fast friends.

Sure, they had known each other before, but that one unselfish act from Paul had put everything on a different level between them. Now, she wouldn't know what to do without him.

She finished with Sunshine and turned her out into the

small pasture the previous owner had built adjacent to the barn. Charlotte loved to look out the kitchen window and see her horse grazing there in the spring green grass.

With one last look at the horse, she made her way to the house. She wouldn't have time to gaze out the window and simply watch her horse today. Not if she was going to have the house ready for Glenn to come over tomorrow.

Never before had such an idea occurred to her so quick and clear. She had seen him and she had known instantly what God was trying to tell her. Glenn was the man for her. He, God, had brought her family to Oklahoma so they could all start over, find love. And build the new lives they all so desperately needed. Even if they hadn't realized that they had wanted it until now.

Charlotte made her way through the house and grabbed the broom from the back porch. She'd start by sweeping and moping, though she might have to sweep again come tomorrow. That was just the way with the Oklahoma wind. She had pretty much settled herself to sweeping every day, sometimes twice in the warmer months, depending on how long the windows were open. She'd mop afterwards and start dusting.

And baking! She couldn't have Glenn to supper without something wonderfully tasty for dessert.

She leaned the broom in one corner of the living room and made her way to the kitchen. She knew most of her own recipes by heart, but for the life of her, she couldn't think of anything special enough to serve her future husband (God willing). She had her mother's recipe book. Maybe there would be something worthy in there.

She fetched the book from the top cabinet over the

fridge—one of the benefits of being tall—and made her way back to the living room. She needed to clean, but she could take a break long enough to find a marvelous dessert for the meal.

It only took a couple of minutes to locate what she wanted. Red Berry Meringue Roulade. She had only made it once before, long ago, but it was impressive to look at, delicious to eat and not extremely difficult. In fact, it looked harder to make than it really was. That was exactly what she needed. A dessert that appeared to have taken more effort than it really had. Otherwise, she might not get the house clean enough to make a good impression.

And she did want to impress Glenn. God may have intended for them to get married soon, but it was her job to give God a hand whenever she could. It wasn't enough merely to sit back and wait for the blessings. A person had to get out and grab a few for herself. And that was exactly what Charlotte planned on doing.

"You're in a good mood tonight," Nadine said hours later when she came home from fishing with Amos. What the two of them saw in waiting for a fish to bite a hook was beyond her, but they enjoyed it. Normally, Charlotte was a little miffed when Nadine stayed gone all day, lolling about over nothing, but not today.

Today was different. She had worked the afternoon away, knowing that God was forgiving her for the tasks she had completed on His day. Tomorrow, she would get up early and go into town. Her first stop would be the butcher counter at the grocery store to get the best and juiciest roast available. Then she would come home, put it on to bake, low and slow, while she finished the house, recleaned the things that had gotten messed up in the time since she had cleaned them last, and started on the remainder of the supper.

Charlotte looked up from the notebook where she was writing the grocery list of what she would need for the supper.

Rolls! *Jah!* They had to have fresh baked rolls. And fresh butter.

She added a trip to the Hershbergers' dairy in order to get the fresh butter from them instead of the store. Their butter was so much better than the kind that came in prestamped wax paper and a cardboard box. The supper—the *night*—had to be perfect. She might know that she and Glenn were destined to be together, but he might not know yet. Everything had to be perfect to keep any doubts away from his mind.

"The house smells nice," Nadine commented as she made her way to the kitchen.

"Umm-hmm," Charlotte murmured by way of an answer.

"Have you eaten?" Nadine called.

"*Jah*," Charlotte said, still not taking her eyes from the grocery list. "I had something earlier. Just a snack."

That was the tradition on Sunday evening. Just a snack, nothing too much. It was, after all, Sunday.

Nadine came out of the kitchen with a couple of slices of cheese and a handful of crackers. "Have you been cleaning house?"

Charlotte looked up at her mother-in-law and debated the benefits of lying. As far as she could tell, there were none other than not getting a chastising look or even a dressing-down for not following the Lord's commands. And Charlotte would have to come clean with Nadine soon enough to explain how Glenn was coming to dinner tomorrow night.

Charlotte shrugged as if none of that were a big deal. "Just a little. Sometimes I get bored." She did her best to make her tone sound offhand, as if cleaning house on a Sunday because your mind needed occupying was acceptable and not at all like cleaning house on a Sunday because you were expecting a special guest on Monday and you wanted to get a jumpstart.

"Read your Bible," Nadine said.

Charlotte nodded, knowing better than to fuss. She needed to let the subject drop and as quickly as possible. Normally, when she got bored, that was exactly what she did. There was nothing like the Lord's word to refresh the spirit. And perhaps that was some of her problem lately. Maybe she hadn't been turning to the good book enough. "I'll read some tonight."

Nadine settled down into the chair at a right angle from where Charlotte sat on the couch. "What you got there?"

Charlotte paused for a moment, trying to gather her thoughts just a bit. "A grocery list. We're having a dinner guest tomorrow, and I want to make sure the menu is acceptable."

"A guest?" Nadine asked. "Who?"

"His name is Glenn Esh," Charlotte said. "He was at church today. The tall man with brown eyes." Dreamy brown eyes that seemed full of God's love and a hearty spirit.

"A man?" Nadine said. "Who else is coming?"

"No one else is coming," Charlotte said. "Except you."

Nadine shook her head. "I won't be here. I'll be at the seniors' meeting with Amos."

The seniors' meeting! Charlotte had forgotten all about the Monday-night seniors' meeting. And she had no excuse other than she was a little bit awestruck having just met Glenn Esh and realizing that he was the man she was supposed to marry. Nadine and Amos had been going to the Monday night seniors' meetings for almost six months now, maybe even longer, yet one look from those beautiful brown eyes of Glenn Esh's and Charlotte forgot all about it.

"You can't have dinner with him alone." Nadine dusted the cracker crumbs from her hands and waited for Charlotte to answer.

Charlotte frantically searched her mind for some solution to the problem, but the only one she could see was . . . "Please," she said, looking at Nadine.

"You want me to stay home so you can have dinner with this man."

"Please," Charlotte said again.

Nadine crossed her arms. "Reschedule."

"I can't."

"Why not?"

It was unlike Charlotte to beg for things or even plead with people. She knew folks called her forceful and maybe a little intimidating, but she had been larger than most her entire life and somehow it had just become ingrained in her nature to get what she wanted. She didn't think folks should find fault with her if people gave her what she wanted. Who was she to go against that? But this was different. "You'll laugh at me if I tell you," Charlotte said.

"How do you know I'll laugh?"

Because it seems crazy to me and I'm the one who believes it. But she couldn't say that to Nadine. "I have a feeling about this man," Charlotte said instead. That didn't sound quite so far-fetched. It was one thing to have a feeling about someone and another to tell someone outright that you were destined to be married.

"What kind of feeling?" Nadine asked.

"A good one," Charlotte said. Then she ventured a bit further. "I think I'm going to marry him."

Nadine was on her feet in the second. "What?"

"I knew I shouldn't have told you. I knew you would laugh."

Nadine shook her head. "I'm not laughing. I'm just trying to figure this out. What makes you think you'll marry this man? You just met him."

"It's just a feeling I have," Charlotte said with a sniff.

"A feeling?"

"A good feeling," Charlotte said. She didn't know how else to explain it. She wasn't sure she could make anyone else understand. She just knew that she and Glenn Esh were meant to be together. It all started with a good dinner tomorrow night, and for that, she needed her mother-in-law.

"I'm cooking," Charlotte said by way of enticement. "And making dessert."

Nadine's shoulders dropped just a bit. Until that moment, Charlotte hadn't realized how tense the woman looked. They may not have been close the whole time Charlotte had been married to Daniel, but since moving to Wells Landing, they had gotten a bit closer. Especially since Nadine had started standing up for herself a bit. Charlotte didn't mean to, but she tended to run over people. She supposed it was just her nature, and if people allowed it, what was she supposed to do? But when Jenna had started dating Buddy, Nadine had started standing up for her. Then, when Nadine had started dating Amos, she'd started standing up for herself. It was something Charlotte could admire. But she didn't need Nadine bucking her on this one.

"Amos can come too," she said. "In fact, I would like him to come. I think you would like Glenn, and I would like to get his thoughts on the matter."

Nadine's mouth dropped open. "You're going to tell Amos your plans to marry Glenn Esh? When Glenn is here?"

Charlotte scoffed. "Of course not. That would be silly. I just want to know what Amos thinks about him." Charlotte might be a little awestruck and half in love, but she knew as well as the next person that God's signs and signals could easily be misconstrued, misunderstood, and misinterpreted. She would like to get Amos's point of view on the matter—man to man, so to speak.

"What if Paul comes over?"

It seemed like a logical idea. After all, Paul was the one who had introduced them. But it just seemed wrong somehow to involve him in her plan to make Glenn see what she already knew: that she and he were meant to be together. Paul was her friend, and for some reason, that just didn't seem right. Not that she could explain that to Nadine either.

"I'd rather not," was all she said.

Nadine eased back into her seat and pressed her lips together. "They're not doing anything much fun tomorrow night," Nadine said. "We're not going bowling or anything. So, I guess it'll be all right. I'll have to run over tomorrow morning and tell Amos. Make sure he's okay with the whole deal."

"Tell him I'm making a very special dessert," Charlotte said. "That should get him."

Nadine chuckled. "Dessert gets Amos every time."

Chapter Four

"Are you having church here next time?" Jenna asked, twirling in a circle as she looked over the house. Charlotte had gotten up early, before the chickens as they say, and begun to clean once again. As soon as it had been light and she'd known for a fact that the stores would be open, she had gone into town on her tractor and picked up all the things that she needed for this very special supper.

Now, the roast was dressed and waiting to go into the oven, and she was busily working on the dessert. The curd was made and cooling a bit before she put it into the refrigerator to chill.

"No," Nadine said, but didn't comment any more as Jenna followed her into the kitchen.

Charlotte was only half-aware of their talking and conversation. She was too busy slowly adding the sugar to the meringue she was whipping. It needed a precise hand.

"Is there anything I can do to help?" Jenna asked. "What are you making?"

"Dessert and no," Charlotte said, not taking her eyes from the bowl in front of her. She would hate to have to start all over. And making the meringue was the most difficult part of the process.

Once she had gone to a cooking class at the community center. They'd had electricity, of course, and she had fallen in love with the stand mixer that could whip up meringue in an instant. The mixer held the bowl while the beaters twirled about of their own accord. All she had to do was gently add the sugar and other ingredients. It was the only time she wished that she were allowed to use electricity. Ever since that day, she'd wondered what was wrong with it. She had decided that it was a slippery slope and many wouldn't be able to stand the call of other appliances, radios, televisions, and other such things that were deemed inappropriate by her church. So the old-fashioned way was what she used.

"Dessert for what?" Jenna asked.

"Supper tonight."

Jenna looked from the curd to the swiss roll tin already lined with the parchment baking paper. Then she dipped a finger into the mortar where the remainder of the crushed fruit for the dessert waited. "Yum."

"Get your fingers out of that, Jenna Gail," Charlotte warned.

"Who's coming? The bishop?" she asked. "No, wait. The president? Or even better, the king of England?"

"England doesn't have a king," Nadine said.

Charlotte looked up to give her mother-in-law a sharp look, then went back to the task at hand. "Are you saying I'm making a special supper?"

"Sure looks that way to me," Jenna said.

"Glenn Esh," Nadine replied.

Charlotte sent her another stern look, but Nadine wasn't

paying her much mind. "The man who was at church yesterday."

"There were a lot of men at church yesterday," Jenna said with a laugh.

"The one who was visiting," Charlotte explained. She switched out the whisk for a large metal spoon and started folding in the rest of the ingredients.

"Tall, brown eyes, nice smile," Nadine added.

So Charlotte hadn't been the only one to notice Glenn. Even those who were in love and decades older could see how special he was.

"Doesn't he live way on the other side of town? Like almost into Taylor Creek?"

Taylor Creek was the town where most of the Mennonites lived. It was about the same size as Wells Landing but had a fantastic rec center where the teenagers could play volleyball and hold holiday parties.

"*Jah*," Charlotte said. "But he's thinking about moving into our district. And I just want to welcome him."

Jenna gave a low whistle, then an impish grin. "That's some welcome."

"Your mother," Nadine started, but Charlotte cut her off.

"Not the time," she said. She didn't want Nadine to tell Jenna that she expected to marry Glenn Esh. This was just the first of many suppers and times that they would have together. It was too soon for that. Jenna wouldn't understand. For now, her daughter simply needed to believe that she was only trying to welcome the man to their side of the community.

"My mother what?" Jenna asked, looking from one of them to the other.

"Is just being neighborly," Nadine finished, her voice just the tiniest bit sour.

"That's right," Charlotte said. She tapped her spoon against the edge of the bowl and moved toward the lined baking pan.

"That sure is a fancy way to welcome someone." Sometimes Jenna was too smart for her own good. Or maybe it was that Charlotte underestimated her. Whatever it was, Jenna could be as astute as the next person despite her brain injury.

"It's good to make people feel special," Charlotte explained, smoothing the meringue, then gently sliding the pan into the preheated oven.

"Will you make me feel special next?" Jenna asked with a grin.

"How about this?" She lifted the lid on the German chocolate cake she had baked the night before.

"Very special." Jenna's eyes lit up. "And what about the yeast rolls?"

Charlotte slid a piece of cake onto a saucer, then handed it to Jenna. Then she grabbed another two plates, one for Nadine and one for herself. "Who said I made yeast rolls?"

"No one, but I can still smell them."

Jenna had an incredible sense of smell, at least where dinner rolls were concerned.

"I'll have to make you some later. Those are for supper tonight. Or better yet, I'll get you the recipe and you can make them yourself."

Jenna took a bite of the rich cake, then shook her head.

"Something wrong, love?" Nadine asked as Charlotte stood to retrieve the notebook where she had all her own recipes written down.

"I'd rather Mamm make them," she said, as Nadine chuckled.

"Nice try," Charlotte said, returning to the table notebook in hand. "You're a married woman now. You need to be doing these things for yourself." It was the first time she could remember that thinking about her baby having a husband and living off on her own didn't make her stomach cramp.

"And your family," Nadine added.

Now that made her stomach act up. Not really cramp but definitely clench. It was one thing that she dreaded more than anything, Jenna having a baby of her own. Would she be able to care for a newborn? Charlotte shouldn't worry about things that hadn't happened yet, but sometimes she did. She had worried about Jenna since her accident. She felt as if God had given Jenna back to her and Charlotte couldn't take that gift for granted. And she didn't want Jenna Gail to either. As she had been growing up, Jenna had been grateful. Only since they had moved to Wells Landing and she had met Buddy Miller had that attitude changed.

It had been hard for Charlotte to accept the changes. Everyone said changes were hard, but now that she had met Glenn, she understood why Nadine and Jenna had gone to every length to secure their love. It was worth it. It wasn't just about not being alone; having someone who truly cared for you was the most important thing in life. And she had only just realized it.

She ate her piece of cake and wrote down the recipe for her daughter.

"Why didn't Buddy come today?" Nadine asked.

Jenna wrinkled her nose. "One of the camels is giving

birth soon. He didn't want to be far from home when that happens."

"I thought all the stock were girls," Nadine asked.

"Me too," Charlotte echoed.

"They are, but apparently there are times when a camel needs to have a baby, just like with cows. I don't understand it all, but when Buddy and Titus get to talking . . ." She shook her head. "You don't want to know."

Nadine laughed and scraped the edge of her fork along her plate to get up any wayward bits of cake, coconut, and frosting.

"And you don't want to see the miracle of life coming into the world?" Nadine asked.

Jenna pulled a face somewhere between horror and disgust. "I've seen it, and I've decided that I would rather let them handle it. I'll come in when the baby is all cleaned up and standing on its own four legs."

The thought shouldn't have been reassuring to Charlotte, but it was. She didn't want Jenna rushing into anything she wasn't ready for. And as much as she and Buddy had both proclaimed that they were ready for marriage, Charlotte couldn't help but wonder if they really were. Or pray that God would delay things for them until they had the chance to adjust to the changes in their lives. But there was nothing she could say to her daughter. She had tried several times, but Jenna wasn't willing to listen. Charlotte could only hope that Titus's wife, Abbie, and Priscilla, her mother were there for Jenna when she needed them to be, since Charlotte herself couldn't be.

She tore the page she had written the recipe on from her book and handed it to her daughter. "Well, it sounds like he works hard and you should honor him with some fresh rolls."

"And that's why you're doing this for Glenn? Because he works hard?"

Charlotte stopped. She didn't even know what Glenn did for a living. Not that it mattered. She knew she was going to marry him, as sure as she knew that the sun would set in the west in a couple of hours. What he did for a living was secondary. God had brought Glenn to her and she had to trust that, from there, everything would fall into place. "Partly, I suppose."

But she was saved from having to answer further as a knock sounded on the door.

Nadine looked to the clock on the wall just above the sink. "That must be Amos."

He was early, but that was just his nature. They had all gotten quite used to it over the time that he had been in their lives.

"I'll get it." Jenna hopped up from the table and skipped from the kitchen.

Charlotte stood and followed after her.

"Am—" Jenna started as she flung open the door. However, it wasn't Amos Fisher who stood there, but Paul Brennaman.

"Hi, Dawdi Paul," Jenna greeted him. She stepped back and allowed him to enter.

"Jenna Gail," Charlotte said from the doorway of the kitchen. "He's not a *dawdi* to your dog."

"I don't see why not. And he's *dawdi* to your dog as well."

Paul just smiled. "I don't mind," he said. "I'm sure I've

been called worse by the Englishers who get behind my tractor on the old two-lane highway."

"What are you doing here, Paul?" Charlotte asked.

"It's not Amos?" Nadine asked, coming in behind her.

Charlotte stepped farther into the living room, allowing Nadine to pass by her.

"Hi, Nadine. I thought I would come by and take a quick look at that board in the hayloft."

"I told you it could keep," Charlotte gently admonished. It didn't need such immediate attention, but that was Paul, ever vigilant when someone he cared about needed him. And she knew he cared about her. They were practically best friends, if such a relationship could exist between a man and a woman who weren't married. The English said it could, but well . . . they weren't English.

"It's no trouble. Unless I'm interrupting something." He shifted in place and twisted his hat in his hands.

"Not at all." Charlotte motioned him toward the front door and followed him out, Nadine right behind.

"Amos should be here in a minute," Nadine said.

Paul nodded toward the drive, where Amos was chugging along on his tractor. "There he is now." He stopped and waited for Amos to park. "Are y'all going to the seniors' meeting tonight?"

"Not tonight." Nadine shifted her gaze to one side, and Charlotte resisted the urge to roll her eyes at the woman.

"I invited Glenn Esh over for supper tonight."

Why did everything turn so still? It was as if everyone was reading way more into the invitation than they should be. Or maybe they were reading it right—that she was out to snag him as a husband—and were surprised at the swiftness of her moves. Early bird and all that. But she had made up her mind to marry Glenn Esh, and that was just what she was going to do. Once it was all said and done, her family would be happy for her.

"He's looking at houses in the area, and I thought it would be a nice gesture to have him for supper."

Paul's expression was slightly blank, but pleasant. Like a mask. "That's very neighborly of you, Charlotte."

She nodded. See? Paul got it, but he was her best friend.

"Hi there, Paul," Amos greeted him as he came toward them.

"Paul is checking on a loose board in the hayloft," Nadine said. "Can you give him a hand?"

"Sure."

"Can you show them?" Charlotte asked. "I need to check my dessert." And start the roast, finish sewing her dress, and clean up some of the mess she had made cooking before Glenn arrived.

"Of course. This way, men." Nadine raised one hand and marched toward the barn.

Charlotte started back toward the house, then spun around once again. "And Paul?"

He stopped, turned to face her. "*Jah*?"

"*Danki*," she said. "I appreciate your help."

"You're welcome. Always," he said. Then he started toward the barn, but not before she saw the flash of sadness in his eyes.

She should ask him about it. And she would. Just not right then. Right then, she had to get supper started. What might turn out to be the most important supper of her life.

* * *

"I don't see why you're making a new dress for one supper," Jenna said an hour or so later. The dessert was ready to be assembled, the roast was in the oven, and the loose board in the hayloft was repaired.

Charlotte had had to fix the men something to drink, and she'd had Jenna run it out to the barn for them while she hurriedly cut out the pattern for the new dress she wanted to make. She should have started it yesterday, but she hadn't realized that everything she had looked so shabby until she was trying to make sure that her favorite dress was clean for the evening.

That was when she'd noticed that nothing she had seemed appropriate for someone as fancy as Glenn Esh. It never bothered her to go to church at the Lapps' and they were fancy, but this was entirely different. She needed Glenn to see her as a complement to himself, a part of his life that he hadn't known was missing until he found it. Found her. Or, rather, she'd found him.

But it was all part of God's plan, and surely He would help her see it through.

"If you sew those two pieces together, half of your dress will be upside down." Jenna frowned at her. "Are you sure you're okay?"

Charlotte sighed and started unpinning the parts that she had just then pinned into place. "I'm fine, of course. What could be wrong with me?"

"Here." Jenna took the two pieces of the dress from Charlotte and shooed her away from the sewing machine. "You go do whatever's needed to that dessert, and I'll do this before you end up with something the bishop won't let you wear even at the house."

"*Danki*," Charlotte said.

"You sure are acting strange," Jenna said as she settled down into the seat Charlotte has just vacated.

Charlotte didn't answer as she moved to the kitchen counter to start assembling the dessert. "I just want everything to be perfect tonight."

Jenna was silent for a moment. And still. Charlotte didn't need to look to know that her daughter was holding the pieces of the dress up but hadn't yet tucked them under the presser foot to sew. "You like him."

And this was the part she had dreaded. Even though she wasn't sure why. "*Jah*," she finally answered on a heavy sigh.

"Really?" Jenna practically squealed. "And he likes you?" She jumped to her feet and flung her arms around Charlotte.

Charlotte took a moment to enjoy the spontaneous embrace, then pulled her daughter's arms from around her neck. "Don't go getting ahead of yourself," she chided. "We're having supper together. Just a neighborly gesture." She hoped it went more places after that. But for now, that was all it was.

Jenna grinned like crazy, then sat back down at the sewing machine. "I'm going to make this with all the love I can. Surely that will help. Even if just a little."

And a little was a lot as far as Charlotte was concerned. She hadn't known she had wanted this, a man, a husband to share the rest of her life with, but now that she did, she was impatient to put it all together.

Chapter Five

"He's here," Nadine called from the living room.

Charlotte took one last look at herself in the mirror and tried to be content with what she saw. She wished that perhaps she didn't have quite so many strands of gray in her once dark, dark hair. But her eyes were nice. And the charcoal dress that Jenna had sewn together for her complemented the green in her eyes. And maybe took a little bit of starkness from those streaks of white that littered her hair just at the edge of her prayer covering.

Amish men weren't supposed to notice things like that. Looks weren't supposed to be all that important. Not at all what made a good marriage, but she was smart enough to know that biology was biology. They might not study much science in Amish school and not any past the eighth-grade, but she knew that some sort of attraction had to exist before a man and a woman. . . .

"Charlotte!" Nadine called once more. This time, it sounded like she was at the foot of the stairs.

"Coming." She shouldn't be so nervous, but it seemed as if her entire life depended on this supper. This one meal. Suddenly she wished she had invited Paul. She could use his support. His kind face across the table from her, encouraging and caring.

She needed to go check on him tomorrow, make sure that he was fine and that the sadness in his expression had washed away with the time that had passed.

But for now, she had a supper to put on and a love to win over, and the rest of her life to plan. No pressure.

Glenn Esh was coming to supper. Paul should have known something was up yesterday at church when she was asking so many questions about the man.

Well, he sort of had. And that was why he'd decided to walk over and fix the loose board in her hayloft. He'd thought maybe, after the job was complete, they could sit on the porch and talk for a bit and he could tell her what had been knocking around in his head for the past few weeks. That he had started to think of her as more than a friend.

Maybe even more than more than a friend.

He shook his head at himself as he walked across the field that separated their houses. Over the last couple of weeks, she had become special to him. A kindred spirit, the English would say. The Amish would call it God's divine plan.

They had lived next to each other for over a year now. His son Obie had sold her a dog, sold her son-in-law a pup before he was even her son-in-law. Paul couldn't say they had been close to each other. Then, after the wedding—Buddy and Jenna's wedding—something had changed. Their relationship had shifted. At least for him, it had, and he had begun finding excuses to walk over to her house. When he had run out of proper reasons, he had popped over for no reason at all. Charlotte hadn't seemed shocked or offended so he'd kept it up, thinking that eventually it would be the right time to tell her that he thought he was falling in love with her.

The idea was shocking to him. He had never expected to start to care for her other than as a friend. Charlotte wasn't the squishy romantic kind. In fact, she could be a little hard, with sharp edges and an even sharper tongue, but he understood. She had been formed by the tragedies in her life. Some folks saw her as immovable, but he knew that she was simply protecting what was hers. What she had built after loss and strife. And he loved her all the more for it.

But he was starting to see that perhaps he was a fool.

"Paul Daniel's been asking for you," Clara Rose called from the front porch. "He's holding up his snack until you come in."

The words brought a smile to his lips, and he adjusted his path to take him to the main house instead of the trailer that he shared with his sons, Benjie and Adam. Paul usually ate an afternoon snack with his grandson, Paul Daniel. Today he'd been too caught up to even give it a thought, but his namesake hadn't forgotten.

"I'm coming."

Clara Rose held the door open for him, waiting there on the porch for him to finish his trek across the yard.

Clara Rose had been married to his son Obie for a few years now—four or five, Paul had lost count—and was soon to have another grandchild for him in the fall. God willing. She'd lost one baby since having Paul Daniel. Though she hadn't been very far along and Paul himself most likely wasn't supposed to have known that she had been pregnant at all.

"Where've you been?" Clara Rose asked, as he stepped into the house.

"I went over to fix a loose board in the hayloft at the Burkharts'." He pulled his hat from his head and hung it on the peg by the front door.

"Sure seems to be a lot of loose boards and such across that field."

Paul sighed. "What is it, Clara Rose?"

She shrugged and smiled. "Nothing. Just saying."

"I—" Paul started, then shook his head and made his way toward the kitchen.

"Whatever it is, I don't have to tell Obie." Her voice had turned soft and serious, a far cry from the teasing tone that had been present only a heartbeat before.

"There's nothing to tell," he said, stopping outside the actual door to the kitchen. His grandson waited inside, most likely seated in his high chair, with apples and peanut butter, their favorite snack, on the tray before him. "She's having supper with Glenn Esh tonight."

Clara Rose nodded. "I see."

"I suppose you do, but . . ." He trailed off with a shrug of his own, then pushed through the swinging door into the kitchen itself. As always these days, the kitchen was bright and clean, and smelled of whatever tasty thing Clara Rose was cooking. Today, it smelled like chicken soup. His Marie's recipe.

"Daw-dee!" Paul Daniel cried. He clapped his chubby hands and laughed at the sight of his *dawdi*. Paul Daniel was the spitting image of his father, Paul's son Obie, and his twin, Zeb. Hair as dark as a raven's wing and crystal-blue eyes the color of the ocean in the poster that graced the window at the travel agency in town. The same color as the water in Pinecraft, where Zeb had moved off to years ago.

Paul smiled at the boy in return. Having Paul Daniel took him back in time to when Obie and Zeb were that age. That better time when Marie had still been alive and the world had seemed endless. But Marie had died shortly after Adam had turned ten and the world hadn't seemed as full of possibilities after that.

He had managed. They all had. But he had missed his wife, her caring ways and sweet laughter. And he'd thought that he would never love again. But seeing Paul Daniel, so like his own sons in coloring and disposition, made him long for those better times.

At least that's what he thought the reason was. He had never imagined that he would love again, and all of a sudden, he was falling for Charlotte Burkhart. Perhaps the last person he would have suspected.

Charlotte seemed to be the exact opposite of his Marie. Marie had been tiny and petite with the same dark hair and blue eyes she had passed on to his boys. Marie had never frowned. Never. Not even when the cancer had taken her breath from her body. She had gone to the Lord with a smile on her face. That was just the kind of person she had been.

Paul slid into the chair at the table closest to Paul Daniel. The boy scooped up a bite of peanut butter on an apple wedge and offered it to Paul. He bit into the fruit, barely missing those chubby little fingers. That close call was on purpose. Paul Daniel giggled in return and ate the rest of his apple slice himself. It was the game they always played.

"You're quiet today," Clara Rose mused.

"I am?" he asked, though he knew that he had been lost in his thoughts for a while now. He couldn't help it. He couldn't help but think about Glenn Esh at supper with Charlotte Burkhart tonight.

"Does this have anything to do with our neighbors?"

Paul took his time chewing up the bite of apple and peanut butter and tried to think of the best answer. One thing he could say about Clara Rose—she might be young, but she was quick. Even though she had almost missed her chance and married the wrong man, Paul knew she was smart.

"*Jah.*" The one word hung in the air between them. It was one thing to harbor feelings for Charlotte Burkhart inside, keeping them locked up into himself, and quite another to share them with his daughter-in-law.

"I see." She laid a protective hand over the swell of her belly. There wasn't much of a bump there, but Paul knew from his own experiences with Marie that losing one child tended to make a woman more careful when the next pregnancy came along. Marie had lost two babies in the course of their marriage, but she never dwelled on it. She focused on the blessings they had in the twins and with Benjie and Adam.

"I would appreciate if you didn't say anything," Paul said.

Clara Rose frowned. "I won't, of course, but why?"

"I think she's got eyes for Glenn Esh. Or maybe he has eyes for her." Paul shook his head. "I don't know. He's coming to her house for supper tonight, and I figure that's as good as done."

"Seriously? One supper and you think it's over?"

For a moment there, Paul had forgotten who he was talking to. Clara Rose had gone as far as her actual wedding day before admitting that she was in love with another man. And then it had been Thomas Lapp who had set her free and not the other way around. Clara Rose, Paul was certain, had felt she was being noble in upholding her promise to Thomas, but Thomas had known, as they all did, that Clara Rose and Obie belonged together. Paul couldn't say the same thing about him and Charlotte. No one had said as much, even though Clara Rose knew that he was interested in Charlotte.

"It's different," Paul finally said.

Clara Rose chuckled. "It always is." She stood and made her way to the stove to stir the bubbling pot of chicken soup he had smelled when he'd first walked into the house. "The question is, what are you going to do about it?"

"That was a fine meal." Glenn stood and patted his trim waist as if he had gained ten pounds from eating the one supper she had served him.

Charlotte didn't mean to sound prideful, but it was a good meal. If anything would impress Glenn, it would be her skills in the kitchen. She hoped like everything that those skills would keep him from concentrating so much on her graying hair and the fact that she stood a good two inches taller than he did.

After all, that sort of thing shouldn't be all that important.

In fact, it shouldn't be important at all unless you were vain. Or English. Or maybe fancy Amish. Not that she knew first-hand. But just in being fancy, it seemed as if they held things at a different standard. And she liked Glenn Esh. She wanted to marry him. So she said a quick little prayer that she hadn't come up lacking in his eyes.

What was she thinking? Of course she hadn't. She was going to marry him, and she surely wouldn't marry a man so shallow.

"How about a game of cards?" Charlotte suggested.

"No!" Nadine and Amos said at the same time.

Charlotte sighed. That was the thing about Nadine. She was fiercely competitive when it came to such games, and Amos was too laid-back to care all that much. It made for an interesting game to watch, but not much fun for the two of them to play when they were partners.

"Do you think Jenna would mind if we work some on the puzzle?" Charlotte asked Nadine.

Since Jenna had moved out, she and Buddy, along with the Lamberts and occasionally the Kings, came over every Wednesday for puzzle night. It was a good way for the family to get together and spend time just being. Charlotte was glad to have that time with her daughter. She was proud of her. She thought Jenna had chosen herself a good man as a husband, but she missed her all the same.

Truth be known, she had thought Jenna would live with her forever. And though she was happy that Jenna had found love, Charlotte couldn't help but miss having her daughter underfoot.

"I don't think Jenna would mind at all if we worked

on the puzzle. It's not like we can have it finished tonight."
They'd just started it a couple of weeks ago.

"What kind of puzzle?" Glenn asked. "It's been years
since I put together a puzzle." He smiled and seemed to
genuinely like the idea.

She told him about their weekly meetings and showed
him the puzzle board that Amos had made for them. It
was a large board with a lip all around to keep the pieces
from getting knocked to the floor. The whole setup was
on a swivel pedestal so it could be turned from side to
side as they needed to move it to place a particular piece.
And the best part of all, it could be covered so they could
eat without having to move the half-finished puzzle.

"That's a real clever setup," Glenn said with a nod.

"*Danki*," Amos said.

Glenn turned to him, eyebrows raised in apparent in-
terest. "You made this?"

"*Jah,*" Amos said.

"Your design?" Glenn continued.

"*Jah*." Amos shrugged.

"Have you thought about selling these?" Glenn asked.

Nadine stepped in before Amos could answer. "We're
not talking business tonight, gentlemen." She looped her
arm through Amos's and led him to the table. "Y'all can
talk tomorrow if you think it's necessary, but tonight
we're having fun."

"Here, here," Charlotte said.

They all gathered around the table. Charlotte began
to separate some of the puzzle pieces using one finger to
push them from side to side, but she was all too aware
of Glenn sitting next to her. He was studying the puzzle.
It was the only way she could describe his look while

everyone else flicked through pieces and picked up a
particular color to work on. They were all looking for
the pieces while he sat back in his chair, cupped one
hand thoughtfully over his chin, and simply stared at the
puzzle.

"What is it?" he finally asked.

Charlotte turned to him, slightly confused over what
he meant.

But it seemed Amos wasn't having those problems.
"It's a puzzle," he said with a chuckle.

But his laughter ended in an exclamation of pain and
Charlotte knew that Nadine had stomped on his foot
under the table.

"It's something Jenna started," Nadine explained.
"Once we open the puzzles, we put all the pieces in a bag
and hide the box covers so . . ."

"So you don't know what it is?" Glenn asked.

Charlotte smiled in relief. "That's right." She could see
how the average person coming in and not understanding
their puzzle night would get a little confused. Not everybody completely ignored the box in favor of having a
discovery once the puzzle was put together. But Glenn
got it. He understood.

"That's . . . different." His words were not encouraging.

"*Jah*, well, that's Jenna," Charlotte said. She supposed
her daughter felt confined at times and found adventures
where she could. Puzzle night was a perfect example.

He nodded again thoughtfully. "I suppose." He leaned
forward as if studying the puzzle pieces in earnest. Then
he pressed his lips together, made a tsking sound, and sat
back once more. "It doesn't seem quite as sporting without the box."

Charlotte turned to stare at him, but not before catching Amos's look of incredulous surprise.

"I think it's more sporting, actually. You have to pick a color to work on, then hope you get it right. Then as you go along, you get to see what the picture really is."

"You saw the box, when you bought the puzzle."

"*Jah*," Charlotte said. "We did. But we bought several puzzles at one time and emptied each one into a separate Ziploc bag. Then we put them on the top shelf in the closet. We threw the boxes away and mixed up the order of the bags. No one has any idea what is on the picture until we get really into the puzzle." Why was he so confused? It was a puzzle.

Glenn waved a hand toward the half-finished puzzle. "Surely you can tell that it's a plate on the shelf with some flowers."

"Well, *jah*," Charlotte said. "But we don't remember all the details. And we still have to get all the rest of the flowers in place. The plate has such an intricate design on it. It's just a little more fun if you can't look at the box every time you find a piece and you don't know where it belongs."

She wanted to give him the benefit of the doubt, but it seemed as if he was taking puzzle night to heart.

He sighed heavily.

Charlotte watched him, all too aware that everyone else was as well. Then he shook his head and sat forward as if caving in to their bizarre rules. "Okay," he said. "Let's do it."

Charlotte released her own breath, not realizing until that moment that she had been holding it. Why? Because she felt as if Glenn was passing some sort of judgment over how they ran puzzle night, and if he was not satisfied, then all her hopes and dreams and plans would be for nothing.

But that wasn't how it was going to be. Soon, he would come to realize, as she already had, that they were meant to be together and it was all part of God's plan for the two of them.

"Is it just me or was that weird?" Nadine asked an hour or so later. The English driver had come to pick up Glenn and Amos had already hopped on his tractor and headed back to his place, leaving Nadine and Charlotte alone once more. Nadine and Charlotte had been alone together at the house many times since Jenna had moved out and sometimes even before, but tonight Charlotte had been dreading it. Because she had known this conversation was going to happen, that Nadine would ask this question, and Charlotte wasn't certain how to answer it.

"What do you mean?" Okay, so she was just stalling for time but she really was as confused by Glenn's comments as her mother-in-law appeared to be.

"Well, the puzzle box for starters," Nadine said.

Charlotte took the dish rag over to wipe down the edge of the table and put the lid back on their puzzle board before answering. "He's just one of those logical people."

She didn't look up, but she knew that Nadine had turned to face her. And she could well imagine the look on her face. Eyebrows raised, mouth slightly open. "Logical?"

Charlotte snapped down the lid to their puzzle box, then continued to wipe down the table as if her life depended on it. "Yeah. Logical. You know how some people are just better at math than others."

"You're saying that he's not creative. It's not that he's weird; he's just not creative."

"No, I don't think he's weird." But she was lying to herself a bit on that one. It was strange, but one thing she had learned in her forty-five years was that people were different and their brains worked differently. Jenna had showed her that, and Buddy as well. Some people's brains just operated in a more logical manner. Not as playful as others. And it seemed that Glenn had gotten one of those logical, non-playful brains.

"So you enjoyed having him for supper?" Nadine pressed.

Charlotte stopped scrubbing the table. "You didn't?"

"I didn't say that."

She didn't have to. "He's a little different, I suppose. But we had a nice conversation at supper, *jah*?"

Nadine nodded. She couldn't argue with that, Charlotte knew.

"He's fancy," Nadine said unnecessarily.

"*Jah.*"

"And you still like him? After tonight and all?"

Charlotte sighed. "You've been talking to Jenna."

Nadine shrugged. "She may have mentioned something when she was leaving earlier."

Charlotte held her breath lest she sigh like a teenager at her first singing. How did she explain to Nadine that she needed love and a future as well? How did she explain without having to say the actual words? She didn't want to say them out loud, for they seemed a little sad. She didn't want to seem lonely. She wasn't lonely. Not yet.

But she would be when Nadine finally married Amos and moved into his trailer with him. Charlotte would be left behind to rattle around in the house all by herself, just waiting for the times when Paul walked across the field to share a cup of coffee. In her imagination, he only did this a couple of times a month, leaving her to spend the rest of her time alone.

She released her breath and managed to keep her sigh to a containable level. "I do like him," she finally said. Then she stiffened her backbone and lifted her chin. "I'm going to marry him."

Chapter Six

"Paul!" Charlotte exclaimed as she opened the door the following day.

He took off his hat as she stepped back for him to enter. "Good afternoon, Charlotte."

"What brings you out today?" she asked.

He smiled, the conversation going just as he had imagined it would. "Just thought I would come over and check on you. See how your supper went last night."

"It was good," she said, leading the way to the kitchen. "You want some coffee?"

"That would be fine, thanks." *Jah*, the conversation was going exactly as he had imagined that it would, except he felt as if he were playing a part in a children's Christmas program, reciting lines that the teacher had written to get the maximum effect from the audience. In a way, he supposed he was.

"Have her tell you about the puzzle," Nadine said, bustling in from another part of the house.

"I thought you had a date with Amos." Charlotte's voice had turned sour.

Paul glanced at one of them, then the other.

"I hardly call a trip to the grocery store a date, but *jah*, he should be here soon." Nadine propped her hands on her hips as if daring Charlotte to continue.

It was a strange relationship between these two, Paul thought. He could see the love and respect simmering just below the surface, but for some reason neither one wanted to show it to the other.

"Speaking of," Nadine said as she turned to him. "Would you like me to bring you anything home from the store? Since I'm going," she continued.

"Thanks, but I believe Clara Rose is going to pick up what we need this afternoon."

Nadine nodded in a way that said it was her pleasure to help, then made her way to the front door. She opened it but turned before actually stepping outside to wait for Amos. "Ask her about the puzzle," she said. Then she stepped onto the porch and shut the door behind her.

Charlotte sighed.

"Tell me about the puzzle," Paul said. "If you want to."

Charlotte sighed again, as if to ask, *Do I really have a choice?*

She did as far as he was concerned, but she nodded anyway. "Do you want a piece of cake?" she asked.

"Sure." He was always up for a slice of whatever Charlotte had been baking. Except that recently he had noticed that the greater stress in her life, the more she seemed to bake.

She set a plate of dessert in front of him, and Paul's mouth fell open. He couldn't help it. "That's a cake?"

He enjoyed the smile of pride that curved her lips upward. "It's called a roulade."

"Fancy." He was teasing and she knew it, but the word

just brought to mind Glenn Esh. A fancy dessert for the fancy Amish. It all seemed to fit. In as much as he wanted to hear about the puzzle, he wasn't going to ask her again.

"Did you know we have puzzle night every Wednesday?"

Paul had taken the first bite of Charlotte's fancy cake and couldn't concentrate on anything other than the goodness that was in his mouth. Fruity, chewy. Delicious. "This is good," he said, breaking his mother's cardinal rule of talking with his mouth full.

Charlotte waved away the compliment as if it was to be expected. Or maybe no big deal that she made such an elaborate dessert. "It's better when it's fresh and crunchy." He couldn't imagine it being any better than it was right then. Hands down, the best dessert he had ever eaten. He was surprised that he didn't drop his fork and demand that she marry him right there on the spot. He didn't though. "Puzzle night," he prompted, then took another bite of the delicious dessert as he waited for Charlotte to continue.

"It started when Jenna moved in with the Lamberts, you know, to help with the babies."

Paul nodded. "This was before she and Buddy got married. I remember."

"Well, it's hard for me," she admitted. "I guess I always thought that Jenna would stay with me. It was something I prepared for since the accident, that she would most likely live at home. That I would have her with me always."

He stopped eating and watched her closely, concerned by the break in her voice. But she sniffed once and pulled herself together so quickly he wondered if he might have imagined that stutter at all. "Because of this, we decided to have puzzle night every Wednesday. The families all getting together. Everyone is invited and anyone can come."

"We have a game night once a month," Paul said. It was as good an excuse as any for the boys to spend time with their brother. He may only live a few feet away, but life got ahead of everyone and pulled them in different directions. Benjie was courting Amanda Byler, and Adam was just now starting to run around. It was good to get everyone together from time to time to remind themselves that they were all a family.

"Then Jenna Gail said it wasn't much fun to look at the puzzle box and put the puzzle together."

Paul swallowed the last bite of his dessert and wondered how shocking it would be if he licked the plate. Somehow he refrained and instead nodded at Charlotte. "Let me guess. She threw all the boxes away and now you guys have to put the puzzles together without the benefit of knowing what it looks like beforehand."

He must've shocked her. Charlotte's eyes widened showing every bit of that beautiful green that was beautifully complemented by the plum-colored dress she wore today. "That's right," she said. "You think that's weird?"

Paul set back in his chair. "Of course not."

She continued to stare at him as if she wasn't quite sure where he had come from.

"What's wrong?" he asked.

She shook her head. "Nothing."

"Did Glenn think it was weird?" Paul asked. "Is that what this is all about?"

Charlotte released a heavy breath. "*Jah*. He thought it was weird, and I don't know. Maybe it is weird."

"Maybe he's just fancier than us," Paul said. Which was the truth. And things were different in all sorts of families. But he couldn't help feeling just a tad of triumph that he had gotten the exercise correct and Glenn had thought it strange. But still . . .

She seems to like Glenn. And there were all the questions that Charlotte had asked about the other man.

"Did you have a good time though?" Paul asked.

Charlotte nodded, her face relaxing and a smile taking over her features. "Oh *jah*," she said. "We had a wonderful time."

"And with a dessert like that." He nodded toward his empty plate.

"You like that?" Charlotte asked with a smile.

"Let's just say you could make that for me every day for the rest of our lives and I would not complain even once."

Charlotte laughed, and he loved hearing the sound from her lips. It seemed these last few weeks she had smiled and laughed less and less, and he was grateful to be able to give some of that back to her.

"So tomorrow night is puzzle night?" Paul asked.

"*Jah*," she said. "You want to come?"

"Is Glenn coming?" He could've bit his tongue saying the words. Here she was inviting him to a family puzzle night and he was worried about Glenn Esh.

She shook her head. "I don't think so. I didn't invite him outright. There was an open invitation, but I don't think he'll come. I don't think he enjoys puzzles the way my family does."

Paul nodded. Just another piece to show that she and Glenn Esh were not as compatible as she wanted them to be. But he knew one thing about Charlotte Burkhart— she had to discover these things for herself. Him pointing them out to her was certainly not going to help. It would just cause her to dig in her heels and strive harder for the goals she had set for herself.

"Speaking of which," she started. "I have an appointment next Wednesday and I need a driver. The last girl I had—" She shook her head, but didn't finish the statement.

"I think I know who you're talking about." She was a young girl, better suited to driving the English than the Amish, but she apparently thought there was more money in driving the Amish than in working for Uber. When he had ridden with her last, she had kept offering him a charger for his phone, a phone he didn't have, and asking what his favorite radio station was. She was nice enough, he supposed, but he would rather sit in the back and have her drive him where he needed to go rather than try to make his ride more comfortable by English standards.

"Can you get me a driver or help me get a better one?"

He nodded. "What time do you need to be there? And where are you going?" Again, he spoke before he thought. "I mean, I don't mean to be nosy. But I will need to be able to tell them where you're going, what time you need to be there, so they can figure out what time you need to leave. That sort of thing."

She nodded. "I have a doctor's appointment in Tulsa."

Concern ran through him. "Is everything okay?"

"Just a checkup."

He nodded, thankful that everything was okay and

trusting that if it wasn't, she would tell him. They had become close in the last few months. "Just give me the time and I'll make sure you have a driver here." She smiled at him again. He loved the sight.

"Thanks, Paul."

He smiled in return. "Anytime."

Charlotte stood at the window just inside and watched as Paul made his way across the field that separated their houses. Behind her Eileen Brennaman lived with her husband, Paul's brother. And on the other side of them, Aaron Yoder, the new preacher. As she watched Paul walk home, she realized she was surrounded, and yet somehow she felt all alone.

The sack she had given him swung at his side as he made his way through the tangle of grass that, in the fall, would be cut for hay. Inside the sack was the rest of the roulade she had made for supper the night before. She figured any man who had enjoyed the dessert as much as he had should have all that was left of it. His enjoyment had made her smile. It was one of the pleasures of baking, to bring smiles to people's faces when they had a wonderful treat set before them. Of course it helped her in times of stress. When things turned topsy-turvy in her world, baking was an anchor. Creating something new and tasty from ingredients scattered across her kitchen was a miracle in itself. Baking was like magic. Though she could never imagine doing it for a living. She baked on a whim, what she wanted when she wanted, and she liked it that way.

Paul disappeared over the hill, and she turned and made

her way back to the kitchen, picking up the cookbook she'd found at a garage sale the week before. It was one of those spiral-bound books that the ladies' auxiliary of a church had produced for some fundraiser or another. The First Presbyterian Women's Auxiliary Favorite Recipes Cookbook. It was a fun book, kind of random. One page would have a dessert and the next page would have something savory like a roast, but it was fun that way, kind of like putting together a puzzle without the box.

She wasn't sure why that bothered her so much, that Glenn didn't understand her family's take on puzzles. But it did. She couldn't put her finger on just why.

Charlotte flipped through the recipe book until she found one that sounded interesting. Turtle brownies with praline pecans, candied walnuts, and toasted coconut for topping.

She told herself she wasn't stressed, even as she lined up the ingredients from the cabinet on the counter. She wasn't stressed at all. This was just for fun.

"What are you doing, Dat?"

Paul was standing in the back of the trailer looking first one way and then the other as his son Adam came out onto the porch. Like all his brothers, Adam took after his mother with dark hair and crystal blue eyes. It was a beautiful combination, and Paul loved that when he looked at his boys he saw Marie there. She might not be in this world any longer, but a part of her still remained.

"I'm thinking about building a house."

Adam stopped in his tracks. "A house?" he asked. "A *house* house?"

"What other kind of house is there?" Paul returned.

Adam frowned. "Why would you build a house?"

Now there was the question. Why would he build a house? Or maybe it was why wouldn't he build a house?

Except Paul wasn't the kind of person who needed a lot. He never had been. When she had been alive, all he had needed was Marie and his family. And when Obie had married Clara Rose, Paul had known they were about to start their own family. He'd had no problems moving out of the house and into the trailer with Benjie and Adam and allowing the new family room to grow. If he'd lived in a traditionally built Amish home, he would've had a *dawdi* house to move into, but since they didn't, the trailer would suffice for the same. But now he had started to think. Maybe he did need a house. Not a *dawdi* house attached to the main house or a mobile home out back, but a real house on its own.

"You don't think we deserve to have a house?" Paul asked.

"Deserve?" Adam studied him closely. "What's gotten into you?"

"It just feels like something I should do. You two boys will be here for a little while, then one of you can take over the house when I go."

Adam shook his head. "The trailer works just fine. I've got a while before I get married, and Benjie even longer. We have all we need right here." That was Adam, so much like Paul himself.

But whereas he hadn't needed much in his life before, somehow, he felt the need for those things now.

To prove to Charlotte that he had all the things in life a man should have. At least what a man thought he needed. Perhaps then he could get married. One day anyway.

"It would be nice though, right?"

Adam shrugged again. "*Jah*, I guess."

"We could have it face the east," Paul said. "Your *mamm* always wanted a house to face the east. She said it was good for growing plants in the front yard, flowers and such."

Adam glanced over to the house where he had lived once upon a time with his mother. "I remember the flowers." But the house where Clara Rose and Obie lived faced west. It didn't get the morning sunshine. Marie had always wanted to grow petunias and sunflowers right there by the house, but she never could make them grow in the shade cast in the western exposure. He wondered how Charlotte felt about such things.

There were flowers planted around the Burkhart property, but Charlotte had told him that Amos had planted them when he was courting Nadine. Paul and Charlotte hadn't been such good friends then, though he could recall seeing the flowers. He supposed Charlotte liked flowers and their house faced the south, another good sun exposure for growing according to Marie.

"What is all this really about?" Adam asked. "Are you going through some midlife crisis?"

Paul laughed. "Where did you hear something like that? And what is it?"

"At the store." Adam worked part-time at the Super Cost Saver grocery store in town. Paul supposed he was exposed to all sorts of conversations. "It means that you're at a point in your life where you feel that there's something lacking. The English do it all the time."

"I'm not English," Paul said. But he did feel that something was lacking and he supposed he was in the middle of his life, if he lived to be ninety. "And I'm not having a midlife crisis," he denied. Though the thought nagged at him. He seemed to be having some kind of crisis. Midlife or not. Maybe it was just being in love with someone who seemed to be in love with someone else. What was a man supposed to do with that?

"A house," Adam said again.

Paul smiled and clapped him on the back, pushing all thoughts of midlife and other crises from his mind. "Just think about it."

Adam shook his head in that incredulous way only a sixteen-year-old could. "You can think about it," he said. "I've got to get to work."

Paul nodded. "Be safe," he said as his son walked away.

Adam looked back only once as Paul turned and faced east once more, the sun warming his back. *Jah*, a house facing east would be best. But was it really time to build a house? Maybe. After all, Amos was building a house for him and Nadine to live in. Of course Amos and Nadine were getting married soon. Nothing had been said, but it was plain as the nose on Paul's face. What was the point of Paul building another house to live in alone? And that's surely what would happen if Charlotte continued to pursue Glenn Esh.

When she'd first moved to Wells Landing, Charlotte had seemed a little standoffish. Paul had immediately wanted to get to know her better, but he couldn't seem to scale the walls she put up between her and the world. Only in the last few months, since Amos and Nadine had become something of a couple, had Charlotte allowed him in enough to become her friend, and that, it seemed, was all they would ever be.

Charlotte shifted uncomfortably on the paper-covered exam table and wondered how much longer it would be.

The nurse had come in, made her pee in a cup, and taken some blood, her blood pressure, and her weight, heaven help them all. And then she'd left again, stating that the doctor would be in shortly. Now despite the thin boxy shirt she wore and the equally thin sheet she had to cover her bottom half, she was sweating. Was it really that hot in there? Or was it just her? She didn't know. She picked up a magazine that had some movie star completely unknown to her on the cover and started to fan herself with it. She was ready to get this appointment over and done with. Truth be known, she was a little early for her yearly appointment at the gynecologist.

After her scare last year, when she'd thought she'd been going through the change so early, she thought it best to get checked out, just to be on the safe side. What if it was something more than nature? She couldn't let something like that go unattended. So she had made a secret appointment and been told that everything was fine. She hated to admit that Nadine was correct. The interruption in her cycle had been caused by stress. The stress of Jenna moving out saying she wanted to marry Buddy Miller and all the other changes that had come at that time in her life. Now that it had been a year, things seemed to be fairly normal. Not that her cycles had ever been completely faithful. Still, things had returned to normal for her. Last year, she had managed to fake her way through the trip that she and Nadine and Jenna had made to the doctors' office, and here she was back for her annual appointment alone.

She fanned herself one more time, then tossed the magazine onto the chair next to the exam table. It was a stool really, with wheels on the legs so the doctor could roll around with ease.

Maybe they should get chairs like that for the dining room table. It might be fun for puzzle night. The thought brought a smile to her lips.

A knock sounded at the door, softly; then it slid open and there stood her doctor.

"Charlotte," Dr. Bass greeted her. She was a small woman, tiny and blond, and somehow made Charlotte feel like one of those fictional women from the Amazon, huge and towering. It should have made her feel strong, but somehow it just felt awkward.

"How have you been?"

Charlotte twisted her fingers together, then stopped, rested them in her lap, and tried to act like everything was perfectly normal. Because it was. Wasn't it?

"I've been fine."

The doctor nodded and opened the file she'd brought into the room with her. "I just took a look at your test," Dr. Bass said. "And just want to inform you that you are indeed going through perimenopause."

"Menopause?" This couldn't be. She'd just had her time. A month or so ago, wasn't it? She couldn't remember. She had done her best to stop worrying about such things after her appointment with Dr. Bass last year.

"I know this is kind of a shock," the doctor said. "After

all, you are fairly young. But it's not unheard of. And this is the beginning stages. What we call perimenopause. It could go on for a couple of years. You never really know, but you are there." She smiled and shut the file. "Congratulations."

Charlotte was numb. *Congratulations.* She supposed some women considered it a badge of honor that they had passed over the threshold to the other side of womanhood. But she just couldn't help thinking about all of her failings with Jenna. And, on top of it all, she hadn't liked being pregnant, she hadn't liked not liking being pregnant. It had nothing to do with the baby and everything to do with the losses she had suffered trying to have a baby. She had suffered miscarriage after miscarriage until finally she could barely get her hopes up enough even to tell Daniel that she was pregnant again. She must've been close to five months along before she actually admitted to him that they could have another baby. Possibly. She'd never made it to five months before, so that in itself was a miracle. And, now, to know that she would never have that joy again. Not necessarily being pregnant, but that joy of holding a tiny infant that was hers and hers alone. Knowing that God entrusted to her with a beautiful creature that needed her. A beautiful creature that He wanted her to raise and love and cherish and teach. It was the greatest honor anyone could have. The greatest honor of a woman. And she had only been blessed the one time.

"I'll have the receptionist give you some information on everything," Dr. Bass was saying.

Charlotte had missed the first part of whatever it was. She'd been too wrapped up in her own thoughts. Dr. Bass hadn't noticed. Charlotte supposed she had been nodding in all the right places.

"If you have any questions, just call. I know that it will be a little harder for you, but we're always here if you need us. Just call the emergency number if necessary, and I'll return your call. Got any questions now?"

Questions? Did she have any questions? That was a question. Her thoughts tumbled around inside her head like two squirrels fighting in the spring. She didn't have any questions, she supposed, except for what now? What was she supposed to do now?

Chapter Seven

She just wanted to be alone. Charlotte paid the driver with cash and half a pan of the brownies she'd made the day before. He was a nice man. Young, but unlike the girl driver, he seemed to know what the Amish were all about. He didn't offer chargers for electronics, or music or even talk radio. He had allowed her to initiate conversation. He had spoken clearly and respectfully, and otherwise allowed her to have her own thoughts on the trip to Tulsa and again on the way home. Now she just wanted to go inside sit on the couch and process everything she'd been told today.

She made her way up the porch steps and into the home she shared with Nadine. Most likely, Nadine was out with Amos, and Charlotte would have the wonderful coveted time alone that she usually dreaded. But this afternoon was different. She had a lot on her mind. The doctor had said congratulations, as if menopause were some rite of passage. Maybe to some. Not to Charlotte. It felt like a part of her had died.

It's God's plan, she told herself. This was all God's

plan, and she had to see it through. Yet what was a person to do when God's plan and their own didn't seem to balance? Not that she had expected to have another baby at her age. Still, she'd wanted the option. What if she married Glenn and he wanted children? Now she couldn't have any. It was one thing to choose not have a baby and another to have that option taken away.

She collapsed down on the sofa, then jumped as Nadine spoke behind her. "There you are. Did you have a nice visit with Paul?"

It was the excuse she had used to go to the doctor. She had told Nadine that she was going to Paul's to visit, and instead she had gone to Paul's, been picked up by the driver, gone to Tulsa, gotten terrible news, and been driven back home.

"I thought you'd be out with Amos." She had counted on it.

"He's off with one of his buddies from the shed company." She waved one hand in the air as if that somehow explained it all. "You know he likes to spend time with his English friends."

That she did. Charlotte settled back into the cushions as her thoughts swirled around inside her mind.

Nadine came around the couch and sat down in the rocking chair next to Charlotte. "Something wrong with you?"

"No," Charlotte lied. "Why would anything be wrong with me?"

Nadine frowned. "This wouldn't have anything to do with the doctor's appointment, would it?"

Charlotte's heart sank. "How do you know I had a doctor's appointment today?"

Nadine shrugged. "Messaging at the phone shanty."

She'd thought she had picked up the paper with the reminder written on it that Eileen Brennaman had taken down for them, but she supposed she had left it there. How careless.

"Would you like to talk about it?"

Charlotte shook her head. "There's nothing to talk about."

She didn't need to tell Nadine what was happening. They'd had a conversation just last year on the very thing. At the time, Charlotte had been convinced she was going through the change, only to find out that she wasn't. Now she wasn't convinced and the doctor was. What did she make of that?

"Seems to me like maybe there is." Nadine's voice was soft and caring and almost did Charlotte in. Somehow, though, she managed to keep her tears at bay.

"It's hard," was all she managed to say.

Nadine nodded. "Harder for some than others."

"I just thought I would have more time."

Nadine smiled, the curve of her lips wistful. "Don't we all?"

"I guess, when people get to my age, they start thinking about their grandchildren, holding those babies and loving those babies, teaching them, showing them the way. But Jenna . . ."

"Jenna will make a wonderful mother. Someday," Nadine said. "You have to trust the Lord in this one and know that He has a plan for her and Buddy. I know it's hard to think of them as parents. They seem so young, even younger than their true ages, but they'll be just fine. And if you let yourself, you'll know it as a fact."

"But—"

"Hup." Nadine shook her head. "There is no but here. Some things are simply beyond our control."

That was the crux of it. Charlotte didn't like not having things in her control. Some might say that she didn't trust God, but she did. And she also trusted herself to do what was right and what needed to be done, to help God to fill the plans that He came up with for all of them. There was nothing wrong with that. *Jah*, she had heard whispers behind her back, especially back in Yoder. They all said she was a control freak, but she ignored them, just like she ignored any that she heard around town these days. What was so wrong with wanting a neat and orderly life? What was so wrong with being careful and cautious and not leaving too much to chance? She had let Jenna go off swimming, and Jenna had come home but just barely. She had come home changed altered forever by the accident that had nearly taken her life. Charlotte had vowed that day not to let the little things slip through her fingers any longer.

But this was truly out of her control.

"God grant me the serenity to accept the things I cannot change," Nadine started.

"The courage to change the things that I can," Charlotte continued.

"And the wisdom to know the difference," they finished together.

"I suppose I should embroider that on a pillow," Charlotte said.

Nadine chuckled. "I could paint it on the wall in the dining room."

"I'm not sure it would help." Charlotte frowned.

"Don't say that," Nadine admonished. "You have a good heart, Charlotte Burkhart. You just have to keep reminding yourself that God is in charge."

"I know that," she said.

Nadine nodded. "*Jah*, you know it. Now do you believe it?"

"Look who's here," Nadine exclaimed shortly before supper.

Charlotte was in the kitchen, cleaning up after their evening snack. They didn't eat a big meal on Wednesday, preferring instead to snack with their company as they worked on the puzzle. But Charlotte needed the chore. She had been moping around for the better part of the afternoon, unable to shake the melancholy that weighed her down. She had tried. She even wanted to, but she almost felt as if she needed to merely get through the day, go to bed early, and hopefully reset as she slept. Maybe, when she woke in the morning, things would look different.

She could hope anyway.

She wiped her hands on a dish towel and moved so she could see the front door through the cut out between the kitchen and living room.

She had thought perhaps Buddy and Jenna could be surprising her with a visit, and though she loved when Jenna came over, tonight she wasn't sure she would be able to enjoy the company of others. Or that they would enjoy hers.

Tonight! It was Wednesday. Puzzle night.

She closed her eyes and said a prayer of strength.

She was going to need all of it the good Lord could see fit to send her way. But she couldn't call off the weekly meeting. Not for something like this.

"It's puzzle night, right?"

She opened her eyes at the sound of that voice.

"Paul?"

He was standing at the front door, a bakery box balanced in one hand. He frowned. "Do I have the wrong day?"

She shook her head and gathered her thoughts. "No." She came around through the kitchen doorway and into the living room. "No. Come in."

"I brought some new treats from Esther's."

"*Danki*," Charlotte said.

"We can have it for dessert," Nadine suggested.

"Actually, they are savory meat pies and quiches. I've never had a quiche before," Paul said, looking at the box as if the secrets it held were priceless. "But it sounded good when Esther was talking about it." He turned to Charlotte. "And I know how you love to bake. I thought something salty would be better than a dessert."

"Absolutely." Nadine plucked the box from his hands and made her way to the kitchen.

"She said to heat them for fifteen minutes on three hundred," he called after her.

Nadine made a noise that seemed like acknowledgement, and Charlotte was left alone with Paul.

"I'm glad you came over," she said. And she meant it. She had wanted to be alone tonight, but it wasn't going to be the case and somehow having Paul there would make it all bearable.

"Who else is coming?" Paul asked.

"Jenna and Buddy will be here shortly, I suppose. Usually Titus and Abbie come and leave the babies with her mother and father. Or the other way around."

"Priscilla and Emmanuel come and leave Titus and Abbie at home with the babies?"

"Exactly."

Nadine came out of the kitchen. "They're not coming tonight."

"Who's not coming?"

"No one. They called and said that they weren't feeling well and everyone was staying at home tonight."

"Everyone?" Charlotte asked, her concern rising.

Nadine shrugged. "That's what the message said."

Charlotte turned back to Paul. "I guess it's just us." Her smile wavered a bit as a knock sounded at the front door.

"And Amos," Nadine said, making her way over to let him in.

It was a setup, Charlotte realized as Amos stepped into the house. He hung up his hat and came over to join them.

She just couldn't figure out whose idea it had been. Nadine's? Jenna's?

Nadine.

Had to be.

"Come sit down," Nadine told Amos. "I just put some pies and quiche into the oven for us to have while we work."

Amos shook Paul's hand. "So that's what the pies were for."

Paul nodded. "I'm not surprised to see you here, but you threw me for a loop when I saw you at Esther's."

"I've been working there awhile now," Amos said. "Keeps me out of trouble."

"Just barely," Nadine quipped.

Everyone laughed. Even Charlotte. Though she was still trying to figure out how all this had come about. Was Nadine against her getting to know Glenn Esh better? Was that why she had invited Paul?

Or had Charlotte invited him? She couldn't remember. Though she was glad Paul was there.

"So you made the pies?" Nadine asked Amos.

"Better than that," he said. "Adding something savory to the menu was my idea. Not everyone wants sweets all the time. I thought it might be good for a change."

"And Esther went for it?" Paul asked.

Amos grinned. "One hundred percent."

"I wonder if Glenn will show up this week," Charlotte mused, carefully watching Nadine's expression. It wavered but only a bit.

"I don't think so," Nadine replied.

"Did he call?" Charlotte moved toward the table as the timer on the oven went off.

"There's the pies." Nadine bustled away before answering.

Seemingly oblivious to the turmoil in the room, Amos pulled out a seat and started getting the table ready for the puzzle night.

Paul looked from the kitchen door through which Nadine had disappeared to Charlotte. Something wasn't quite right.

"Is everything okay?" he whispered to Charlotte.

She nodded, unable to say anything more. She didn't want to reveal too much in front of Amos.

Just then, Nadine bustled back into the dining area with the goodies that Paul had brought.

Charlotte settled down in her seat, wondering if the day she'd been having was real or a dream.

Glenn Esh. He was all Charlotte seemed to be able to talk about. Why? What was so special about Glenn Esh? For the life of him, Paul couldn't figure it out. And he was having just as much trouble with his thoughts as he was with the puzzle. Or maybe his thoughts were causing him to have trouble with the puzzle. Who knew? He did know that he was confused and unable to concentrate for more than a moment before he lost his place in trying to put together the pieces that matched up to be a blue and white Dutch plate.

"That does it for me." Amos sat back in his seat. It was after eight, and the sun was quickly setting. Soon, it wouldn't be dark until nine-thirty, but it was April and still spring in Oklahoma.

Paul sighed and sat back from the table as well. He may have gotten a couple of pieces joined, but he had yet to connect them all together. Sort of like his feelings for Charlotte. They were a little scattered, and the more she talked of Glenn Esh and how wonderful he was, the more scattered they became.

His *dawdi* would have told him that he was trying too hard. And maybe he was. But right when he was ready to tell Charlotte his true feelings for her, she had gone and fallen in love with Glenn Esh!

How was a man supposed to overcome that?

Slow and steady wins the race. That was something

else his *dawdi* often said. He'd been slow, all right. Now he supposed all he could do was be steady.

Like tonight. He had been there when Glenn hadn't. Though he had a feeling that Nadine had had more to do with that than mere chance.

Paul helped clear the table and stacked the dishes in the sink. Amos offered to wash them but was shooed away by Nadine. She claimed that she would wash them later, but for now, Amos needed to be getting home before it got too dark to see—even with headlights on his tractor.

Paul hung back as Nadine walked Amos to the porch. Charlotte was at the sink, running a pan of water to soak the dishes in. He poked his head into the kitchen doorway. "Let me help with those," he said.

Charlotte turned off the water and dried her hands on a dish towel. "No need. Nadine will wash them later. It's her turn." Charlotte smiled, and he realized that she had hardly smiled all evening. She had been pleasant enough. Just not very happy. Because Jenna was not well?

If Jenna truly was sick, then there went his theory of Nadine having a hand in the guest list for the evening.

Or maybe he was reading way too much into the entire thing.

Love was making him a little batty.

"Are you all right tonight?" he finally asked.

Charlotte's smile stayed firmly in place. "*Jah*. Of course."

But he knew that wasn't the truth. "Everything go okay at the appointment today?"

She nodded and turned back to the sink, but not before he saw the quiver of her lips.

He stood rooted to the spot, unsure of what to do. Her expression told all—everything hadn't been fine at the doctor's appointment. If it truly had been, then she wouldn't be upset. But he couldn't ask her any questions. That was just too personal.

"You know I'm here for you if you need me," he said.

She took a deep, shuddering breath, then turned to face him once more. "I know. And I appreciate that so much, Paul."

He nodded.

"I really am all right. I'm just overreacting to nothing."

He nodded again, slower this time. "Okay," he said. Then he added, "Just remember that God is in charge."

She stared at him a moment, seemingly dumbfounded by his words. They weren't all that special. Just another one of those things his *dawdi* was always saying. Or had said when he was still alive and on the earth. But Charlotte looked for a moment as if he had whispered the secrets of the universe.

Then she looked out the window at the blackening sky. "Oh, dear. It's gotten so dark. Let me get you a flashlight for your walk home."

In an instant, she was moving past him, out of the kitchen and into the hallway. He heard the closet door open, and he followed behind her.

She turned and handed him the handheld light. "This should do it."

"*Danki*," Paul said, taking it from her. "I'll bring it back to you tomorrow."

Her smile turned softer around the edges and her eyes darkened just a bit from mystical jade to the deep green of good summer grass. "I would like that," she said. And he could tell that she meant it. Every word.

Then tomorrow would come, and she would be back to treating him as only a friend.

One day, he hoped that she would see him as more than that. And when that happened, he wouldn't have to say good-bye and leave. He would be able to stay. But that was a lot of what-ifs and a ton of dreams. None of which seemed like they would ever come true.

"Good night," he said.

Charlotte held herself together from the sheer strength of Paul's presence next to her. *God is in charge.*

Had he really said that to her?

Had he said it to her only a few hours after Nadine had told her the very same thing? Coincidence or something more? How was she to know?

Charlotte pushed the whirling thoughts from her head and walked Paul to the front door. Amos had long since driven off, and Nadine was nowhere around as they stepped out onto the porch.

"Thanks for coming and bringing such wonderful snacks," Charlotte said. Somehow the words seemed too formal for the occasion. This was Paul. Her best friend, if there was such a relationship between a man and a woman. Her Paul, so to speak. And she was talking to him as if he were a stranger.

"Thanks for having me. I had a good time."

"Me too."

He paused then, stood in the waning light and watched her.

She thought he might say something. He seemed ready to; then he turned and made his way down the porch steps. "I'll see you tomorrow," he said, without turning to face her. The flashlight swung at his side, casting a streak of light as he made his way.

She watched him until he disappeared over the hill and into the night.

God is in charge.

Those words echoed around in her head long after Charlotte had gone to bed. Nadine had said them. Paul had said them. And they'd both felt she needed to hear them. Why?

Did Charlotte believe that God was in charge? Absolutely. Was she good at giving over control to Him? Not at all.

She threw back her covers and knelt down by the bed for the second time that night. She had heard the hall clock strike midnight. She had been lying awake for hours thinking about Nadine and Paul's identical words, arguing them over in her head and all it had gotten her was a sleepless night.

What is it you want? Nadine would ask.

"I want a second chance," she whispered.

A second chance at what? Nadine's voice had turned deep and masculine. But it wasn't Paul.

"Life," she returned in a whisper. "No, motherhood."

She had failed Jenna, allowed her to get hurt. She had done the best she had known at the time, but it hadn't been enough. She was older now. She would love nothing more than to have a second chance to bring a child into the world, hold her, comfort her, and raise her to adulthood whole and healthy.

And more than anything, she needed to know that she could do it. She needed to know that she could be a good mother. A mother who didn't fail her child.

You'll never get that chance. The voice had turned back into that of Nadine, softly chastising and pressing. *It's time to move forward.*

Move forward. Wasn't that what she was trying to do?

Jah. She was. She was moving on with life. And then this trip to the doctor . . .

It could be worse, the voice said, deeper this time. It echoed inside her head. It was gentle but firm. Loud enough that she had to pay attention to it.

It could be worse. It could always be worse.

That thought should have brought her some peace, but it didn't. All she could think about were the chances she had lost and the time that had passed. The Bible told them that for everything there was a season. And she knew this to be true. She'd just thought she would have a bit longer.

She stirred a bit of milk into her coffee and sighed. Who was she trying to fool? Certainly not herself. She might not ever be truly in a position to have another child. But, again, it was the choice being taken from her that had set her back, had her questioning all her life decisions.

But no matter how unlikely things might seem, God was in charge. God knew she wanted a second chance. God could give it to her. It was as simple as that.

She turned as Nadine pushed through the back door. In her hands, she held a dead hen. "Look at this," she said.

Charlotte made a face. "I can see it. But why did you bring it into the house?"

Nadine looked down at the bird, then gave a little shrug. "I came in to get a bag. Who knows how long it's been dead."

So they wouldn't be able to salvage the meat. "You think a fox got her?" Charlotte got up and retrieved a garbage bag for Nadine to place the bird in.

"Her and four others." Nadine made a face. "It's too bad."

"We didn't have this problem when we had Goldie around," Charlotte said.

"Nope."

"I guess I should call Titus and Buddy and have them bring her back over," Charlotte mused.

"Might be the best idea," Nadine said. "Unless you want to buy new hens every other week and hope the foxes get tired of raiding our chicken house."

"I'll get my shoes," Charlotte said. "And go over to the phone shanty and give them a call."

"Perfect idea." Nadine grinned and handed her the sack containing the dead hen. "And while you are at it, you can help me clean up all the feathers."

"Here," Charlotte said half an hour later, once the chicken house and surrounding yard were almost cleaned up from feathers. The chickens themselves were still a little flustered, looking around and seeming easily spooked after their close brush with death the night before.

She handed Nadine the trash bag they had used to pick up what they could of the mess. "I'm going to the phone shanty and calling Titus." It seemed the only thing that could be done. Getting the dog back would surely deter the foxes from coming too close, but Charlotte wasn't sure how Nadine would feel about having the dog back.

Goldie was a hyper dog. Granted, she was a puppy, or she had been when Charlotte had decided that she needed a dog. She couldn't say that it was the best decision she'd ever made. People should want a dog for companionship and unconditional love, to be stewards of the earth. Not because they were afraid of being left alone. Still, she kind of missed the pup.

"And I'm calling Glenn Esh to see if he can come to supper tonight," she added at the end.

"Do you think that's a good idea?" Nadine asked.

Charlotte made her way over to the water pump to wash her hands before making the call. "I think it'll be good, having Goldie back on the farm," she said, effectively sidestepping the real issue. For a moment anyway.

"That's not what I'm talking about, and you know it." Nadine slammed her hands onto her slim hips and watched Charlotte carefully.

Charlotte scrubbed her hands with an enthusiasm and attention to detail she'd never known before. "I know that she bothered you some when I first got her. But Buddy has been working with her, and Jenna assured me that she's a much better behaved dog than she was before. And if she keeps the foxes out of the henhouse. . . ." She let that last sentence trail off.

"I'm talking about Glenn Esh," Nadine said.

Charlotte shut off the water, then dried her hands on the tail end of her apron. "Oh." She feigned innocence to the misunderstanding. "I thought you were talking about the dog."

Nadine shook her head, apparently unconvinced.

Charlotte had never claimed to be an actress. She hadn't even been good in the pageants they'd done in school at Christmas and Easter. "So you have nothing against the dog, but you do have something against Glenn." It wasn't quite a question.

"I wouldn't say against," Nadine said. "I just don't feel . . . right about him coming over."

"There's something wrong with being neighborly?"

"Being good to one's neighbor has nothing to do with this." She wrinkled up her face as if trying to find the words to say what she really meant. That in itself concerned Charlotte. She had never known Nadine to struggle with words ever before. "I just don't feel like he's our kind of people."

Charlotte drew back a bit. "Our kind of people? He's Amish."

Nadine shook her head. "That's not what I mean, and I think you know it. He didn't like puzzle night, and I wasn't sure what he thought about supper. He just didn't seem to fit in."

Charlotte scoffed. "He fit in just fine. He was all about playing a game or something, but some people get too competitive and can't seem to play nicely with others so we had to work a puzzle instead. Not everybody enjoys working a puzzle as much as other folks. Nothing wrong with that. That doesn't make someone fit in or not fit in. And I'm going to marry him."

"Charlotte," Nadine started as she turned away to head for the phone shanty.

Charlotte turned back to face her mother-in-law. "*Jah*?"

"I just wonder . . ." She shifted in place. "I mean . . ." Twice in one day. This had to be some sort of record. Maybe she should call the Farmers' Almanac and let them know. Twice in one day Nadine Burkhart was at a loss for words. "I'm just concerned that you may be doing this for all the wrong reasons."

"Wrong reasons?" She frowned, not wanting to understand what Nadine was saying.

"You say you want to marry Glenn, and yet you don't really know him."

"I was just being silly." *But I will marry him.* "That's why you court," she said. "To get to know each other. And I can't get to know him if he doesn't come to supper."

Nadine's mouth twisted into a frown. She couldn't argue with that logic.

"I appreciate your concern," Charlotte started. "I really do. But I've got this. I know what I'm doing." And she was inviting him to dinner to show him just how much they did have in common, and just how wonderful it would be for the two of them to be together. And then, when Nadine got married to Amos, the good Lord willing, Charlotte would not be alone.

Chapter Eight

"Goldie!" Charlotte screeched as she bounded after the dog. Goldie had taken one look at the car and rushed toward it to greet whoever might be getting out of it. And that whoever just happened to be Glenn Esh. "Get down!" Charlotte commanded.

Glenn chuckled, but she could tell he wasn't too happy about being licked by an overgrown golden retriever puppy.

"Sorry," she said, grabbing Goldie by the collar and managing to pull her down from where her paws were braced against Glenn's stomach. "She's still a little over friendly," Charlotte explained.

Glenn brushed himself off and gave her a kind smile. Charlotte only saw it for a moment before she had to look away. When she looked back, she couldn't tell if the smile was genuine or forced, for it was gone. "When did you get a dog?" Glenn asked.

Nadine bustled from the house, carrying the leash. "I'll get her," Nadine said.

"I got her last year."

Glenn raised his eyebrows and looked where Nadine

was leading the dog away. "You didn't have her last time I was here."

"Buddy had her. He's been training her," Charlotte explained.

"Unsuccessfully, I see."

Charlotte tried not to frown. It was times like that when she saw what Nadine was talking about. How Glenn seemed a little different from most folks. Yes, Goldie was a dog. Yes, she was rambunctious, and yes, she lacked manners and training. But they were working on it, and that had to count for something. So why did he seem so down on the poor animal? But she thought she might know. Glenn Esh was used to having an orderly and clean life. He evidently had more money than most for he tended to travel around using an English driver almost everywhere he went. Fancy Amish. Wasn't that what they had originally thought? It seemed to be the case. And Charlotte was fairly certain that fancy Amish didn't have dogs that jumped up on people and tried to lick their faces before they were even introduced.

"She'll get better," Charlotte assured him. "We've been having some problems in the henhouse with foxes so we had them bring her back." She didn't add, *before her training was complete*. Which was something she wasn't certain of at all. What if this was just how Goldie was going to be? A rambunctious non-minding dog. Charlotte would rather have that than no hens in the henhouse and no eggs for breakfast. Life was a trade-off, wasn't that what they said?

"I'm glad you could come for supper." She opened the door to the house and stepped inside, Glenn right behind her.

"Me too." She turned and caught his smile. A completely genuine smile. See? Everything was going to be fine.

"I made chicken tonight," she said. She was chatting on about nothing, but somehow his smile had made her a little nervous. In a good way. "It's a new recipe."

He lifted his nose and sniffed appreciatively. "Smells good."

Charlotte smiled, all too aware that Nadine had just stepped through the front door behind them. Without Goldie, of course. "Let's hope it tastes good as well."

"Amen," Nadine muttered, then hung the leash by the door.

Charlotte ignored her, turning her complete attention to the man before her. "Would you like to sit down?" She gestured toward the sofa.

Glenn gave a small nod. Then he removed his hat, hung it by the door, and made his way over to the sofa to sit.

Nadine crossed to the fireplace and sat down in her rocking chair. For a moment, Charlotte wondered if she might pull up her knitting and begin to work on her current project once again. Instead, her mother-in-law folded her hands in her lap and looked from one of them to the other.

Charlotte sat down in the armchair next to the couch.

"So you don't let her in the house?" Glenn asked.

Charlotte turned to him. "The dog?" It took her a couple of heartbeats to figure out what he was actually talking about.

He nodded. "*Jah*. The dog."

"*Jah*, we let her in, but not when we have guests," Charlotte explained.

Glenn seemed to visibly relax. And Charlotte wondered if perhaps he was a little afraid of the dog. He hadn't seemed to be afraid when Goldie was doing her best to lick his face after he got out of the car. At that time, he'd seemed a little more disgusted than scared. But he could be afraid.

"I just hope she can keep the foxes out of the henhouse tonight," Nadine said. "We've lost eight hens this week."

"It could be worse," Charlotte said. "Paul was telling me yesterday afternoon that the fox got in his henhouse and killed all thirty of his chickens."

"Paul?" Glenn asked. "The fellow across the field?"

Charlotte nodded. "Yes. Brennaman. He's been a good neighbor." That was an understatement. He had been the best friend she had ever had, save Daniel, and he had been gone so many years now.

"That's a shame," Glenn said.

It was, Charlotte thought. Then realized that she and Glenn were talking about two different things. He was referring to Paul's chickens. She was thinking about Daniel. She had gotten over the loss. She learned to move on from his death. Just as she would learn to move on from her devastating news of this week.

With God all things are possible.

"Here, here," Glenn said. And until he spoke, Charlotte hadn't realized she'd uttered those words out loud.

"Are you okay?" Nadine asked.

Charlotte stiffened her spine and forced a smile to her lips. "Of course." She was not going to let the circumstances of her life bring her down. She had allowed herself to wallow for a couple of days, but that was over. It was time to move on. It was time for a new part of her life, and that part included getting married and enjoying her latter years with a wonderful man like Glenn Esh. It might not be her first choice. She still might need or want to have a do-over at motherhood, as the English say, but she knew as well as the next person that we didn't always get that chance. The closest she was going to come was the man sitting across from her. And she intended to make the best of it.

"Shall we go eat?" Charlotte stood. Nadine and Glenn followed suit. Together, they made their way to the dining area.

"Is Amos not coming?" Glenn asked. "I enjoyed his company last time."

"He had to work at the bakery," Nadine said.

"The bakery?" Glenn's eyebrows shot northward. "He works at the bakery?"

"Unusual, right?" Nadine said. "But that man can bake."

"Very unusual," Glenn said. He took a seat at the head of the table, where Nadine usually sat. She shot Charlotte a look. But Charlotte could only give a small shrug and head for the kitchen to bring in their supper. It took each of them, Charlotte and Nadine, three trips each to get everything on the table.

Then they sat down and said the silent prayer before beginning the meal. The chicken was very good, and Charlotte was impressed with the recipe. She would have to try more from the church auxiliary cookbook.

"Last night, at puzzle night," Nadine started, "Paul brought some savory pies that Amos had made at the bakery the day before." She looked from Glenn to Charlotte, then back to Glenn once again, no doubt waiting on his surprised response.

"Is that a fact?" Glenn said.

"You should've come," Charlotte said. "We had a good time."

Glenn took a bite of his chicken and thoughtfully chewed. "I'm sure you did."

Charlotte looked up to find Nadine staring at her, that *See what I mean?* look all over her face.

Maybe. Maybe Glenn was a little fancy. But that didn't mean they couldn't make a life together. He seemed to like her well enough, and she did like him. But more than anything, she didn't want to be alone.

Though that she wasn't admitting to anyone.

"Paul comes over a lot, I take it," Glenn said. He looked at each of them in turn, waiting for his answer.

Nadine took a sip of water and gave him a one-armed shrug. "I guess. He helps us out from time to time. He's a good neighbor."

Not exactly what she thought Glenn wanted to hear. "He's our closest neighbor," she said, wishing she had something more to say that would ease the concerns she saw in Glenn's eyes.

At least she thought it was concern. If he was starting to have some feelings for her and was thinking that the two of them might have a future together, then he needed to be comfortable with the fact that there was nothing more than friendship between her and Paul. "And he is a dear friend, to us both," Nadine said.

"I see." Glenn smiled at Charlotte, and she felt the weight slip off her heart. He understood. Paul was a dear friend. Goldie might be rambunctious, but they needed her for the hens. And if Glenn liked her as much as she liked him, then everything would work out just fine.

"Charlotte," Glenn said a few moments later. "Are you busy tomorrow night?"

Her heart gave a hard thump in her chest, and the chicken turned to sawdust in her mouth. She had been bold in asking Glenn to dinner, not once but twice, and though he had come both times and paid the driver to bring him, both times, it could've just been for food. He was a bachelor, after all. But this was different. He was going to ask her out. The plan was starting to fall into place.

God provides.

"No." She tried to say the word casually, like why in the world would she be doing something on a Friday night, but she was afraid it sounded more like the squeak of a mouse than the answer of a confident Amish woman.

"One of the members of our district is having a get-together for the mids." He smiled.

"The mids?" she asked. Her mouth was still dry, and her heart was still beating somewhere behind her tonsils.

"That's what she likes to call us middle-agers. She said it sounds nicer."

"Nicer to who?" Nadine said.

Charlotte turned and kicked her under the table, but the woman had known it was coming and moved out of the way.

She turned her full attention and a sweet smile to Glenn, completely ignoring her mother-in-law. "Mids," she said. "I like it." Which was something of a lie. She didn't care one way or another about it. It simply was.

"We tend to have a get-together once a month or so, and this month's meeting is tomorrow night. Would you like to go?"

Would she like to go? She would love nothing more.

She swallowed hard and tried not to make it noticeable, but she needed to tamp down a little bit of her excitement so she didn't gush like a young girl being asked home from her first singing.

"Just a get-together?"

"Somebody usually brings games or they'll come up with something to do. Mostly I go for the food and to see everyone. Would you like to go?" he asked again.

Charlotte looked up from her plate, once again planning to center her attention on Glenn. Instead, Nadine snagged her gaze. Her own expression was a bit unreadable, or maybe it was such a jumble of different emotions that Charlotte had trouble deciding which one was the most dominant. Concern, a little bit of happiness, some doubt even. It was starting to make her feel a little dizzy, so Charlotte turned back to Glenn. "I would love to."

"Nadine!" Charlotte called from the downstairs bathroom. "Come get this dog!" She was trying to get ready, and every time she raised her hands above her head to fix her hair, Goldie thought it was time to play. The dog danced around her, snapping playfully as she went from side to side. "Get down," Charlotte fussed, arms still above her head as she held her hair in place. She had gotten it just where she wanted it: so the gray wasn't as noticeable, tucked between the darker strands to give her a younger appearance. "Nadine!"

"Come 'ere, dog." Nadine appeared at the door and grabbed for Goldie's collar. She missed on the first try, Goldie hopping playfully out of her reach.

"I can't get ready for this party tonight with her in here." And she needed to get ready for this event. Glenn had asked her out. It was a big deal. Huge. And she needed to look her best.

Nadine swiped at Goldie's collar once again, this time catching it and gently pulling the dog toward the door. "Come on, girl," Nadine said.

Charlotte could hear the stretched and strained patience in her voice. The dog was big, beautiful, and lovable, but also a pain when over-excited. Unfortunately for them, that was most of the time.

"Anybody home?" A male voice sounded from the front of the house. For a moment, her heart sank thinking that Glenn was early, but it returned to its normal rhythm as she realized it was Paul instead.

Goldie took off running toward the front door, jerking her collar from Nadine's grasp.

"Crazy dog," she muttered following behind her.

Charlotte nudged the door shut with her foot while she smoothed her hair back with one hand and managed to get it into a bob. She looked at herself critically in the mirror, turning her head from side to side. She'd almost had it perfect when Goldie had busted into the room. Now it was merely good. But it would have to do. She didn't have time to redo it, and Paul was there. Glenn would show up at any minute. She pinned her prayer *kapp* into place and smoothed her hands down the front of her dress. There was a smudge on her apron. Of course, there was a smudge on her apron. Goldie had jumped all around her.

With a sigh, she pushed open the bathroom door and

called down the hallway. "I've got to change my apron, and I'll be down."

Nadine and Paul made noises of understanding as Charlotte made her way up the stairs and into her room. A quick apron change later, she slipped on her flat black shoes instead of her regular black lace-up shoes and made her way back downstairs. Paul was standing near the fireplace, Goldie flopped next to him with one paw over the top of his foot as she stared adoringly up at him.

"How did you do that?" Charlotte asked, with a pointed nod at the dog.

"You have to show them who's boss. She knows I'm the alpha dog. You have to be the alpha dog or she'll act all crazy."

Charlotte shook her head. "I have no idea how to be an alpha dog. I'm not a dog."

Paul laughed. "It's just a figure of speech. Show her that you're in charge, and she will fall into line. But as long as she thinks that she can do whatever she wants around you, then she will continue to do so."

"Alpha dog," Nadine said. "Got it." There was a new determined slant to her chin. Charlotte wasn't sure if she would ever be able to be an alpha dog, but maybe if Nadine could . . .

"You're all dressed up," Paul said. He gave a wide-eyed look at her shoes. No one in Wells Landing wore shoes like that, not for every day. All the women wore lace shoes, sometimes even to church. But she wasn't going to be in Cephas Ebersol's district in Wells Landing. She was going to Treager's district and out with someone who might be considered fancy Amish. So that deserved fancy shoes, didn't it?

"She's going out with Glenn," Nadine said.

Paul's expression turned purposefully blank. And Charlotte couldn't help but wonder if, like Nadine, Paul felt something was off about Glenn.

She pushed the thought away. It didn't matter what Paul thought of Glenn. Not really. She was the one who was going to be in this relationship, and she was the one who had to think about it. Not her mother-in-law, and not her best friend. She just had to hold fast and true to what she believed and everyone else would fall into line. Eventually. She hoped anyway. A car horn sounded outside.

"That must be him," Charlotte said. She went to the window and looked outside. A car waited out front but only one person was inside. She thought that Glenn would come pick her up himself, but apparently he'd just sent a car over. It seemed a little strange. She supposed she could have found a driver herself if she had known it was gonna be like this. But the car was here now.

"That's strange," Nadine said.

"Hush," Charlotte said where only Nadine could hear. "It's thoughtful."

"He could've at least come over himself and not just sent some Englisher to pick you up."

"Thoughtful," she said again this time with a little more force. "I'll see you tonight."

"See ya," Paul said. His voice was flat, toneless. And Charlotte couldn't help but wonder what he thought about this as well.

Being in a room full of people where she only knew one person was a little strange. Even stranger than having her date send a car to fetch her like she was in one of those crazy romances that Jenna had liked to read a couple of years ago.

And even then she couldn't say that she knew Glenn really well. She knew a few people's names, but it wasn't like in her own district where she knew everyone around. She wasn't even sure why they seemed so separate. Or maybe it was just this group of people. She tried to remember other people she knew in this church district. She could come up with a handful of names right off the top of her head, but none of those people were here. In fact, half the people there were Mennonites from Taylor Creek. Not that there was anything wrong with the Mennonites, or even the Mennonites from Taylor Creek. She and her family hadn't lived in the area very long, and they hadn't met everyone around. Still, she smiled, drank lemonade, and tried to appear like she belonged there.

In some ways, it made her think of her very first singing when she just turned sixteen. She was taller than all the girls and three-quarters of the boys. She wanted so badly to blend in with the walls of the barn, but she just couldn't manage. Her height alone made her stand out like a sore thumb. She felt awkward and out of place. Kind of like now. She smiled across the room at a Mennonite woman who gave her a quick nod in return. She was standing talking to a Mennonite man, an Amish man, and another Amish woman. Her face was kind and open, and Charlotte had a feeling that if she walked over, they would welcome her into their group. But she didn't know any of their names. What was the difference in standing here with her back against the wall or across the room talking to people that she didn't even know?

And where was Glenn? He had wanted her to come to this event with him and yet he was nowhere around. He had come out onto the porch to greet her when she had arrived in the car, alone, and he had taken her in the house and introduced her to the woman who owned the house and her husband. Katie and John, if she was remembering correctly. Then he had introduced her to a couple of more folks. People whose names she could not remember. And then he had disappeared. Now she stood alone, wondering if she could get the driver to come back and take her home.

No, she wanted to be there. She wanted to get to know Glenn better, get to know his life better.

If you want to change your life, you have to do things you haven't done before.

She saw that on a coffee cup in town. She hadn't known exactly what it meant until now. *Jah*, she wanted to change her life. So she was going to have to do things she hadn't done. With a smile, she pushed off the wall and walked over to where the Mennonite lady stood. "Hey," she said, thankful that her voice didn't tremble. She thought she'd gotten past all the teenage angst of her life. She supposed she had. Now she just had middle-aged angst. "I feel like I've seen you in town," Charlotte said.

The woman nodded. "I'm Sally," she said. "My sister Suzy owns the fabric store there on Main in Wells Landing."

"And you work there?"

Sally shook her head. "We're twins."

Charlotte nodded, feeling a little dumb for not realizing what Sally was trying to tell her. If Suzy and Sally were twins, then it was Suzy she had seen in the fabric store, not Sally.

Why had she thought it a good idea to move away from all of her friends and family to come to Oklahoma?

Because she thought that her family was going to stay together. It was naïve and simplistic, but she had thought that she and Nadine and Jenna would live in the one house together for always. She hadn't planned on Jenna getting married or Nadine getting married or feeling like she should get married herself. But if you want to do something different with your life, you have to do something you've never done.

Chapter Nine

"Have a good time tonight?" Glenn asked at the close of the party. They were standing next to the car that he had called. It would take her back to her side of Wells Landing.

"I did," she said, and surprisingly enough, it was true. Once she'd pushed herself off the wall and started mingling among the guests, she had found there were a lot of people in the group that she really enjoyed talking with. The lady who owned the house where the gathering had taken place was definitely fancy Amish, as she and Nadine had already supposed that Glenn himself was, but everyone else, including the Mennonites, had seemed down to earth and like good companions. They had played a couple of games and had some snacks, and then the evening came to an end.

Halfway through, Glenn had joined her and he'd stuck by her side through the remainder of the evening, apologizing for the interruption to their night. He'd had to conduct some unexpected business and had to see to that before coming back to the party. When she had asked him what sort of business, he had flipped a hand and said horses. Charlotte supposed he was like the Lapps and the Fitches and raised horses himself. It made perfect sense since he had been there at the Lapps' when they'd had church.

"Are you going to ride back with me?" Charlotte asked. Since she had ridden over by herself, she'd kind of figured she would ride home by herself. Yet the thought of riding over with Glenn and being able to talk to him, one-on-one, without anybody else around save the English driver, held massive appeal.

"I thought I would, if that's okay. Again, I apologize for not coming and getting you myself. But things happen with horses unexpectedly."

"I understand." She gave him a forgiving smile, then slid into the back seat. Glenn got into the car next to her and off they went.

Now this felt like a date, a real date. They talked about nothing and everything on the way back to her house.

When they pulled to a stop in front, Glenn got out and was around the side of the car, opening her door for her before she even reached for the handle. The surprising gesture nearly took her breath away.

"I'm glad you agreed to go with me tonight," Glenn said as he walked by her side, up the steps and onto the porch. Nadine had left a light burning in the window. It cast a small glow over the otherwise darkened porch.

Charlotte couldn't see Glenn's face all that much, but she could sense the easiness in his nature. His posture was relaxed. It made her feel comfortable and secure.

"Me too," she said.

Glenn sighed and turned toward her, taking both of her

hands into his own. "I didn't plan on doing this right now," he said.

Charlotte's stomach twisted in anticipation. Her heart beat a little faster.

"The driver is waiting," Glenn said. "But I have to tell you, Charlotte Burkhart, I'm quite smitten with you."

"*Jah*?" Her one word was small, barely a whisper, more of a breathless anticipation of things to come.

Even in the darkness, she could see Glenn's smile. It was a charming, fancy Amish smile, and she was beginning to love it with all her heart. "I might even be falling in love. I think we need to test out these waters."

"Date?" Charlotte said. "Court?"

"That's exactly what I mean. Are you up for it? To see where this might lead?"

She gave a tiny smile in return, somehow managing to keep the joy from spreading her lips all over her face. "*Jah*," she said. "I suppose I am."

"And if things keep going the way they are, would you consider getting married again?"

"To you?"

Glenn chuckled. "To me," he confirmed.

"Of course I would."

"I don't mean to rush. I don't want to rush at all," he said. "But I felt like I needed to tell you."

"I'm glad you did." It was wonderful to know that he felt the same as she. There was a future for the both of them together. And she was even more ecstatic that she wouldn't be alone for the rest of her life. If things kept on the way they had tonight, she and Glenn Esh would get married, and that would be that.

"Me too," he said. Then he squeezed her hands. "Good

night." He released her fingers and made his way back down the porch steps to the waiting car.

Charlotte stood on the porch and watched as the receding taillights disappeared at the main road. She opened the door to the house, feeling like she was walking on clouds. Nadine was standing by the fireplace, arms crossed. Goldie at her feet, for once obeying someone besides Paul.

"You can frown all you want, but you will not ruin my mood," Charlotte said.

Nadine's frown deepened. "Why would I want to ruin your mood?"

Charlotte shook her head. "Don't act like you weren't standing there listening to the whole conversation."

"And you never listened to any of mine."

Charlotte, still smiling, gave a one-shoulder shrug. "Fair enough."

"But don't you feel like you're being a tad impetuous?"

"Impetuous?" Charlotte asked.

It was Nadine's turn to shrug. "It was in today's crossword puzzle. It means—"

"I know what it means," Charlotte said. "But I don't agree. I'm not being impetuous. We didn't say we were setting a date. We just said that's what our feelings are and we'll see where it goes from here." And it was exactly what she had wanted. Why couldn't Nadine be happy for her?

"You hardly know him," Nadine said, dropping her arms to her sides.

Goldie never moved.

"That's why you date someone, to get to know them. Did you know Amos the first time he came over? No."

"How in the world are you even contemplating marrying him so soon?"

Charlotte scoffed and slipped her shoes from her feet. They were like magic slippers in that fairytale the English told. They had worked their magic tonight anyway. "I would be a fool not to marry a handsome and godly man like Glenn."

Nadine snorted, clearly unconvinced.

"I appreciate your concern," Charlotte said, hooking her shoes onto her fingers. "But it's unnecessary, and I'm going to bed now. Good night."

April slipped into May, and May into June. Charlotte and Glenn had been to a flurry of meetings with friends, dinners at home, pie at Kauffman's and many other small dates in which the two of them had begun to know each other better.

But still Nadine's attitude toward Glenn hadn't changed. The saddest part of all for Charlotte was even as she got to spend more and more time with Glenn, she was spending less and less with Paul. She did get to see him on puzzle night. Something that Glenn never came back for, but that was all right with her. They couldn't have everything in common.

"She seems to be doing much better," Paul said, watching as Goldie trailed behind Jenna. She didn't try to jump on her or run ahead of her and trip her.

"I guess you are right about that alpha dog stuff. Where do people learn things like that anyway?"

"You forget my son raises dogs."

Charlotte chuckled. "I guess I did."

"How's everything else going?" Paul asked.

"Fine," Charlotte said. That first evening, when Glenn had declared his intentions and the fact that he was falling in love with her, was part and parcel of their romance. Now he seemed determined to keep his distance from her as they got to know each other better. Not that that was a problem. It wasn't a problem at all, merely an observation.

"Good," Paul said. "Good." But he seemed distracted when he said it.

"Everything okay?" Charlotte asked.

"Sure," Paul said. "What would be wrong?"

"Can we have that snack now?" Jenna asked, walking back over, Goldie at her heels. Amos and Buddy still stood by the fence, watching the horses and shooting the breeze, as Buddy liked to say. He thought the idiom was funny. A person couldn't really shoot a breeze.

"Are you ready to eat something?" Charlotte hollered over to Buddy and Amos.

Buddy turned immediately. "*Jah*," he said.

Charlotte supposed it was an unnecessary question. Buddy was always ready to eat.

"Don't mind if I do," Amos said. Together, the two men, one young and one old, walked over to the porch where Charlotte and Paul stood. "Nadine went in to make coffee," Charlotte said.

"Coffee!" Jenna exclaimed. "Goody."

Buddy frowned and shook his head. "Jenna," he said.

Her expression immediately fell. "Oh, *jah*. Right."

Charlotte looked to Paul, who shrugged. Something was going on, and as much as Charlotte would like to ask, she didn't feel right questioning the newly married couple. It'd been a hard adjustment to allow Jenna the space that she wanted and needed to grow. It was something that Charlotte prayed about daily, but she knew God would give her the strength.

They all went into the house together and sat around the kitchen table. Nadine poured everyone a cup of coffee as Charlotte got out the cookies she'd made the day before.

She should try and put a couple back for Glenn, though he didn't seem to eat as many sweets as her family did. It was one of the things about him that she considered a little strange. Who didn't like cookies?

"So," Jenna said as everyone settled in with their afternoon snack. She stood and looked around the table. "Buddy and I have an announcement to make."

Everyone grew silent. Buddy shifted in his seat, almost more excited than Jenna. And immediately Charlotte knew what her daughter was going to say. Globs of hopelessness and despair, of worry and joy, mixed together in one big ball in her stomach as she waited for her daughter to continue.

"We're going to have a baby."

Her emotions were in more than an ordinary jumble. They were chaotic, bright, and ever-changing, kind of like the video she had seen of those northern lights in Alaska and Canada, though not as beautiful. She had thought she'd figured it all out. She thought she'd taken her desires, her dreams of having a baby and starting over, and tucked them away forever. Labeling them as something only God could provide and that no man on earth could change. She thought she'd made peace with it. Yet hearing her daughter say that she was going to have a baby had opened that box and let all of it out again.

Sometimes Charlotte felt as if she were losing her mind. One minute, she wanted a baby so bad she could hardly breathe, and the next, she was thanking God for the strength He had given her to start a new life, the life she was starting with Glenn.

And she was having a baby through Jenna. Jenna was having a baby, and Charlotte knew that she would be there to help her. She was sad that Jenna lived with the Lamberts instead of at home. Maybe if she built a *dawdi* house for them or got them a trailer like Paul had, then Jenna and Buddy could move in there and Charlotte would be able to see the baby every day. Maybe even keep the baby while Jenna went to work. Just over to the Lamberts' and since Buddy worked there as well, they could share a driver. Every day . . .

And that would get costly. Never mind that Jenna could take her baby to work with her each day.

Again and again, around and around her thoughts went until she thought she really might be going crazy.

Lord, give me strength.

"You're brooding again."

Again? Charlotte felt like she'd never stopped. Or maybe she'd had a reprieve, that little bit of light where she and Glenn were dating, getting to know one another better, that had taken her mind off her womanly troubles. But this just brought them all back.

Charlotte used a hot pad to take the cookie sheet from the oven. "You want a chocolate chip?"

"We just had snickerdoodles not an hour ago," Nadine said.

Charlotte couldn't help it. Jenna and Buddy had left, and she had nearly broken her neck trying to get to the kitchen to bake something. She supposed taking random things from the cabinets and making something that hadn't existed before was calling to her. So she had made chocolate chip cookies.

She figured Paul could eat them. They were his favorite. She knew Glenn wasn't crazy about chocolate chip. Which was why she'd made snickerdoodles yesterday. But there was nothing better than gooey chocolate chip cookies fresh from the oven.

"Ouch," she said burning her fingers as she tried to get one off the cookie sheet without using a spatula.

"Here," Nadine said. She nudged Charlotte aside and used the spatula to lift the cookie and gently lay it in her hand.

"Two please."

Nadine gave her a look but served her up another cookie.

"Two *more*."

Nadine just shook her head as she gave Charlotte the third cookie. "If you don't get this under control, you're going to be big as a house."

"I'm not sure I care at this point." There. That was the truth. She had so many other things to worry about that gaining weight from eating chocolate chip cookies was not at the top of her list. But maybe it should be.

Maybe tomorrow. Definitely not today.

"We won't ever see her anymore," Charlotte said. She licked the chocolate smudge from one of her fingers and fought back the tears that threatened.

"Of course we will," Nadine said. "Why would we not see her?"

"She's going to be so busy."

"We're all busy. We all manage to get over here for puzzle night, now don't we?"

"Except for Glenn," Charlotte said.

"Paul seems to make it." Nadine seemed to be on this Paul campaign lately, trying to make Charlotte see what a handsome and godly man he was as well. But Nadine didn't understand the nature of their relationship. They were friends. Charlotte wasn't sure she understood it herself sometimes.

"Paul lives a stone's throw away."

Nadine shrugged then scooped up her own cookie. "You've got to get this under control before *I* get big as a house," she said.

"I don't think Amos would care one way or the other."

"Of course not," Nadine said. "He's not that kind of man."

Charlotte finished the third cookie and reached for another. "You think Glenn is?"

Ridiculous question. Why would Glenn care what she weighed? She was a good cook and she would be a good wife to him. Things like size didn't matter, at least not for most. And no one that she had ever known. But Glenn was different . . .

"Fancy Amish," Nadine said, as if pulling the words straight from her thoughts.

"Hush," Charlotte said.

Nadine gave a careless shrug. "He is."

"I know."

But they'd been having such a good time these last

couple of months. It had been a little rocky at first, but she could chalk some of that up to nerves. She had been in a new situation and a little unsure of herself. Now, their relationship was completely different, somewhat comfortable, easy. Though Glenn hadn't said one word about his feelings since that first night that he had declared he was falling in love with her.

Yet despite all their differences, they managed just fine.

Well, she thought they had anyway. Since he hadn't said anything about his feelings or how they had grown, she could only assume that they were getting along just fine. Not that she was complaining. Two months wasn't long for an Amish courtship. It wasn't like he should be telling her every day of his love for her. But she knew then, just as she had known from the beginning, that she and Glenn were supposed to be together. It was God's plan, and He would carry it through.

"Is it serious?" Nadine asked. "You and Glenn?"

Charlotte smiled despite her churning, doubting thoughts. "Of course. I told you. We're going to get married. I just know it."

"I suppose you will," Nadine said. "That's what Amos said too."

Amos and Nadine were getting married. This was the proof of it right here. She had been waiting for Nadine to finally admit that she and Amos were getting married. Now it was coming. "Do you have a date?" The question had a choked sound, as if it had to be squeezed through a throat too narrow to adequately produce sound. She supposed in that moment that was just the case. Her throat had tightened until she could barely breathe.

Nadine waved a hand as if it were of no consequence. "Nah."

Charlotte grabbed another cookie and nibbled at the edges when she wanted to stuff the whole thing into her mouth and chomp away. "You would tell me though, right?" she asked.

"I would tell you." Nadine shot her a quick, gentle smile. It was meant to be reassuring, but somehow it only made her feel lonely.

She had to use a cold spoon to get rid of the dark bags under her eyes the following day. If Nadine noticed them before Charlotte attended to them, she didn't mention them. For that, Charlotte was grateful. Her attitude made her feel ungrateful and petty. And she had spent the night crying and praying, telling the Lord how grateful she was that Jenna was going to have a baby and how grateful she was that she herself had had a good life. It hadn't been perfect, but whose was? And she was grateful. She was blessed. Even if there were things she still felt were lacking.

Charlotte had just finished the breakfast dishes when a knock sounded at the door.

"Charlotte?" Paul. "Nadine?"

"In here," she called in return. She started to dry her hands on the edge of her apron, then grabbed up a dish towel instead. No need to look completely disheveled when her friend saw her. She had taken care of most of the puffiness and discoloration under her eyes caused from yesterday's tears; there was no need to draw even

more attention to her sad state by dirtying up her apron
first thing.

"Hey," he said, stopping in the doorway that led to the
kitchen.

"Good morning," she returned. "Would you like some
coffee?"

"Love some." He moved toward the pot as if he was
about to pour it himself.

Charlotte waved him away. "I'll get it. Go ahead and
sit down."

With a quick nod, he made his way to the table and
settled down into the seat she had come to view as his.
Now, that was strange. But whenever he came, he always
sat in the same place. Just as she and Nadine did. Jenna sat
at the end and the place he occupied was his alone. She
tried to remember where Buddy sat when all five of them
were here, but she pushed the thought away before she
spilled the coffee worrying about things that didn't
matter. It was Sunday, there was no church, and her good
friend had come calling.

"Where's Nadine?" he asked, then murmured a quick
danki as she placed his mug in front of him.

"She's in the barn." They took turns with the work so
neither one got tired of the same old chores. Today, the
house was Charlotte's responsibility and Nadine had the
barn. Tomorrow, they would switch.

Paul nodded, slower this time than before, his gaze
sweeping over her face, seemingly inspecting each wrinkle
and line. She had taken care of most of the ravages her
crying jag had caused to her face, but Paul was astute.
He noticed more than most, and she knew it was only a
matter of time before he asked her what was wrong.

She only hoped that she could be strong and answer him truthfully. Or at least without sobbing like a child. She hadn't been this weepy since the first time she had been pregnant. Maybe it was the changing hormones of menopause causing her crazy tears.

"I wasn't expecting you today," Charlotte said.

He shrugged and took a sip of his coffee. "I thought I might come work with Goldie for you a bit."

She nodded and smiled. "That would be wonderful. She's being a little bit better, but I want her to stop nipping at the chickens."

A chuckle escaped Paul, but he quickly sobered. "I'm sorry. It's just that you brought her back because there was a fox getting in your henhouse and now she's after the chickens?"

Charlotte shot him a look, but all in good fun. "She's not really after the chickens. She just likes to nip at their tail feathers and hear them squawk."

"I never heard of such a thing."

"She's one of a kind," Charlotte drawled.

Paul laughed again.

"I was hoping that one of them would turn around and peck her hard on the nose. I figured that would cure her, but so far the hens are too scared to react. They just squawk and run away."

"Which I'm sure Goldie thinks is great fun."

"Hilarious."

Paul took another sip of coffee. "I'll see what I can do about that today."

She smiled. "I would really appreciate it. She seems to respond so much better to you."

"Alpha dog," he explained.

"So you say." She sipped her own coffee as a moment settled between them. She couldn't say it was comfortable. Nor was it particularly uncomfortable. It simply was. This moment. They looked at each other, connected by their gazes and nothing more, save the love for an ornery pup with more energy than sense.

Then she looked away, out the window, and the moment was broken.

"Are you okay today?" he asked.

She knew it. She had known he was going to ask. She was just glad he didn't mention all the reasons why he had asked.

She swallowed hard. "*Jah*," she lied, though only then realizing that since Paul had come over, it wasn't as much of a lie as she had felt earlier. "I'm fine."

Chapter Ten

"Alpha dog," Charlotte said, giving a nod to Paul.

He returned it, encouragingly.

Charlotte led Goldie into the side yard, where the chickens were happily pecking, looking for ticks and bugs, and the little rocks they needed for digestion.

"Whoa," Paul said.

Charlotte stopped just at the edge of the yard. "Sit."

Goldie whined and pulled on her collar, trying to get to the chickens.

"Tell her again," Paul said. "Firmer this time. Like you mean it."

"Sit."

"Charlotte, really." He sighed. "Is that how you talked to Jenna when you found out that she had been swimming in Millers' pond with Buddy?"

"Sit," Charlotte said sternly.

Goldie looked up at her, but Charlotte kept her gaze front like Paul had instructed her earlier. He had said that eye contact would be important, but only after she had established dominance. And that she wouldn't relent when she looked into those big brown eyes of Goldie's.

The dog whined.

"Sit now," Charlotte barked.

Without further complaint, Goldie eased down onto her haunches, unhappy, but not fighting with her mistress.

"I did it!" Charlotte released Goldie's collar and clapped her hands, proud of herself for helping to train the pup.

Goldie immediately sprang forward, snipping at the chickens as she loped through the yard.

Paul laughed and shook his head. "You can't let go," he said. "You have to be the alpha dog for more than a few seconds." He whistled, a shrill sound made by inserting his thumb and his forefinger into his mouth.

Goldie stopped chasing the chickens and cantered back to his side.

"You have got to teach me how to do that," Charlotte said, impressed with the skill.

"Of course," Paul said. "But let's get this other down first."

They practiced again and again until Goldie could stand next to Charlotte without her hand on her collar and manage not to run after the chickens. The desire was still there and Paul told Charlotte that she would have to work on this with her every day. Until Goldie gave up the hope that there would be the opportunity to chase the chickens.

Paul slipped Goldie one of the treats he had put in his pocket before they had come out to the yard to work with the dog.

"Want some lemonade?" Charlotte asked. Dog training was not the easiest and it was definitely thirsty work.

Especially on such a bright summer day. The sun was shining, the sky blue, and the temperature in the mid-nineties. Soon, they would be in the throes of the blistering heat that was an Oklahoma summer. There was a reason people said, "Hotter than the Fourth of July." Whoever had coined that phrase had definitely been to the Sooner State in the summer months.

"That sounds like a fine idea."

They started toward the front porch, Goldie leading the way, tongue lolling out the side of her mouth as she headed toward the bucket of water sitting next to the steps.

Paul was already on the porch, and Charlotte had one foot on the first step when she heard it. The rattle of a buggy. She turned to see who might be coming down the drive. She wasn't expecting anyone. Nadine and Amos had gone fishing first thing, stating they wouldn't be back until supper. Jenna and Buddy had come over the day before and were supposed to go to his parents' house today to spend time with them and tell them the wonderful news about the baby.

But it wasn't Jenna and Buddy coming down the drive, or even Nadine and Amos coming home early. But Glenn Esh.

At least, it looked like Glenn.

Charlotte squinted against the bright sun, raising one hand to shade her eyes. *Jah.* That was him.

She should be happy to see him, this man whom she would certainly one day marry, but she couldn't say that happiness was the first emotion to come to her. No, first was something of a tired feeling. That feeling a person got when they had to be at the top of their behavior. She didn't feel that way around Paul. With her neighbor, she could relax and be herself, but with Glenn, she always felt as if she was one mistake away from being judged as lacking.

She pushed the thought away. Well, she tried to anyway. Surely she only felt that way because of the first party that they had attended together. She had been uncomfortable then, and it had put her on edge. Soon enough, she knew that would disappear altogether.

"I guess I'll take a rain check," Paul said. His voice sounded slightly defeated. Or maybe he was just tired.

She stepped to one side so he could come back down the porch steps and into the yard.

Glenn pulled his buggy to a stop; then he gave a jaunty wave and hopped to the ground.

"See ya later," Paul said as Glenn hobbled his horse and made his way toward them.

Before Charlotte could say one word, Paul turned and started across the yard to the field he traversed to get home.

"I'm sorry," Glenn said. "I didn't know you had company."

Charlotte tamped down the annoyance she felt. She hadn't wanted Paul to leave. Yet she understood how it must feel a little awkward to him to be there when she and Glenn were basically courting. But she hadn't gotten to tell Paul bye. Or to thank him for coming over. Offer him the rest of the chocolate chip cookies to take home. Or even give him a glass of water or the promised lemonade for his help in training Goldie.

"It's all right," she said, even though it wasn't. "Paul came over to help me with Goldie."

Glenn looked over to where the dog was now lying on the porch asleep. "Whatever he did, it worked." He chuckled when he said it, but somehow those words annoyed Charlotte as well. Or maybe this was just another one of those hormone things. She hadn't felt this way when Paul was there, maybe because he was helping her with Goldie and not just criticizing the dog.

Then again, she still wondered if Glenn had something against dogs in general.

"Would you like some lemonade?" she asked, leading the way onto the porch and up to the front door. Goldie didn't move as Glenn tromped up the steps behind her.

"That would be nice, thank you," Glenn said.

She motioned toward the swing that sat at one end of the porch. "Have a seat, if you like. I'll get us the lemonade and cookies."

Glenn nodded. "*Danki.*"

Charlotte bustled into the house and straight to the kitchen. She stopped only long enough to wash her hands before pouring glasses of lemonade and gathering up some cookies for them to share. There were a couple of snickerdoodles left in the container. She should grab them for Glenn, but some mean-spirited imp that lived inside her started grabbing the chocolate chip cookies instead.

Surely a man couldn't not like dogs and not like chocolate chip cookies. She must've read this all wrong.

Charlotte placed everything on a tray and carried it out onto the porch.

Glenn stood as he saw her push through the screen door. "Do you need some help?"

"I've got it," she said. She set the tray on the boxy table that was closest to the swing and sat down next to Glenn. She handed him a glass of lemonade and took one for herself, gulping down half of it in a single drink.

"Wow," Glenn said. "You worked up a thirst."

She nodded and resisted the urge to wipe her hand against the back of her mouth in satisfaction. She probably should have gotten a glass of water first. She and Paul had been out in the yard so long working with Goldie that she was most likely a little dehydrated. "Dog training is thirsty work."

"I would say so. But well worth it."

Charlotte pressed her lips together but didn't reply. She couldn't tell from his tone if he was teasing her or if he was somewhat serious. But one thing was certain, she didn't need him telling her that the puppy she had picked out was more than a handful. Goldie had ripped dresses, torn-up flowers, moved flowerbeds, and a host of other things as proof all her own.

At least Paul's helping you do something about it.

"*Jah.* Well, it's going nicely." Glenn hadn't asked, though she felt obliged to make sure he knew.

She sucked in a deep breath. This whole conversation was making her way more irritated than it should. Another one of those hormonal things? How was she to know? She had never gone through menopause before.

Alpha dog.

Paul shook his head at himself as he trudged across the field. He could almost feel Glenn's eyes on him as he walked away. And he resented that stare. He had been harping and harping on Charlotte about being the alpha dog in her relationship with Goldie, and yet he was allowing himself to be pushed out of Charlotte's life by the likes of Glenn Esh.

Okay, that wasn't fair. Glenn seemed to be an okay fellow, decent enough. But he seemed a little too slick for Paul's taste. A little too fancy. The Bible told them to be humble, not to be proud. And yet he felt Glenn was excessively prideful.

Or maybe he just didn't like the man because Glenn liked Charlotte and she liked him.

If he was being completely honest, that was the long and the short of it.

He should have done something sooner. He should have told Charlotte how he felt months ago, but he hadn't known then that it would be so urgent that he did. He'd thought he had time to woo her, make her see him in the same light that she had once viewed Daniel. Just as he viewed her as he had once viewed Marie. Older now. Wiser now. But still filled with such supreme love.

And now this.

"Everything all right?" Obie called from the doorway of the barn.

Paul sighed and tried to pull himself together. He had hoped he could make it all the way to his trailer before someone saw him. That way, he wouldn't have to explain. Anything. But mostly his disgust with himself over his own behavior. He was upset with Glenn for interrupting his afternoon. He was upset with Glenn for getting there before him. He was upset with Charlotte for caring about Glenn when Paul had been there all along. But he supposed that was more his fault than hers. But more than anything, he was upset with himself for keeping his feelings hidden from her until it was too late.

He switched his angle and headed toward his son. "Everything's fine," he called.

Obie squinted at him, the look almost a frown. "That didn't sound fine."

"It's fine," Paul said again. This time, his voice was even rougher than before.

"If you care about her," Obie said. "You should just tell her."

Paul stopped. He blew a hard breath out his nose and propped his hands on his hips. Obie had it all figured out. He made it sound so simple. Just go to her and tell her how you feel. It sounded easy enough that anyone could do it. "But what if that person you are telling is already in love with someone else?"

"I guess I need to remind you that Clara Rose thought she was in love with Thomas Lapp for a long time."

"No, you don't." Paul knew the story. Clara Rose had thought herself in love with Thomas Lapp until Obie had told her that he loved her himself, that their friendship had grown into something more. And yet she had still almost married Thomas Lapp out of pure obligation.

"As far as I know, they haven't announced a wedding date," Obie said.

His son was trying to tell him that it wasn't too late. As far as Obie was concerned, it wasn't too late until they exchanged vows.

"No," Paul said, trying to put everything into proper perspective. "I don't think they have." He and Charlotte were good enough friends; he trusted her to tell him if something big like that was going on in her life.

It was true that when it came to second marriages, the couples kept more to themselves. The weddings weren't as large, and such a big deal wasn't made at every turn. But she would still tell him if Glenn had proposed.

"The way I see it," Obie said, "you still got plenty of time."

Maybe he did. Thomas Lapp releasing Clara Rose from her obligation to him on their very wedding day was a unique situation and circumstance, to be certain. Not to say that it couldn't happen again. It was just unlikely. But as long as Glenn hadn't proposed to Charlotte—and as long as Charlotte hadn't accepted—there was still hope for Paul.

He gave his son a quick nod of thanks; then, with a smile on his face, he turned and made his way to his trailer.

He was a good man, Glenn Esh, Charlotte thought as she sat on the porch swing next to him. This thought superseded the fact that he didn't like chocolate chip cookies. And even when he seemed not to care for her dog. He was a good man in his heart. Godly. Kind.

"It's strange when a spouse dies," Glenn started.

Charlotte turned in her seat to get a better look at him. Her legs were longer than his so she tucked them up under so he could be the one to push the swing. As crazy as it seemed, she didn't want to remind him that she was taller than he was. Some men had a problem with that sort of thing. "I know what you mean."

He glanced at her quickly, then clasped her hand into his own. "I know you do. When Joanne died, our youngest was fifteen. A girl needs her mom, *jah*, but she was old enough to cook and clean. I was grieving. I just didn't see the need to remarry."

Charlotte closed her eyes and briefly absorbed the warmth of his hand covering hers. It was the first time that she could remember him touching her since the night he'd told her that he was falling in love with her.

Her heart gave a hard pound in her chest. Excitement? Anxiety? She wasn't sure which. But something was changing. Like the atmospheric pressure right before a storm. She could feel it, almost smell it, but she didn't know if the change was going to be good or bad. "I understand," she said, opening her eyes.

But he was staring straight ahead. "The house is always too quiet," he said. "But you get used to it after a while."

"The hardest part for me was Jenna. When she got hurt, everything changed." Everything had changed. Charlotte had dedicated her life to Jenna, caring for her, making sure she was happy and as healthy as possible. Some might say that she had been a tad overprotective. But who wouldn't have been given the same situation? She had been so wrapped up with her daughter, her life, her dedication to God, that there hadn't been room for anything or anyone else. Especially not a man who would want and need things from her. Clean clothes, hot meals. She would be expected—no, it would be her job even— to care for her husband. And she didn't feel that she could do that and care for her daughter as well.

"I just never imagined my house without her." He shook

his head. And stared down at their hands clasped together between them on the swing. It was almost as if he hadn't realized he had reached for her hand at all. "I expected to sit on the porch swing and watch the sun go down, read the Bible with her, and spend time together. You know, that quiet time without any interruptions."

"*Jah*," Charlotte whispered. She had expected the same thing. Except she hadn't had children who could help. She'd had a child who'd needed her more than anything else. And she had devoted her life to Jenna.

"I still want that," Glenn said quietly.

Charlotte's breath grew shallow, her mouth dry, and her heart seemed to stutter in her chest.

"The only way I can have that," he said, "is if I have a wife."

She tried to swallow, unable to say anything as she waited for him to continue.

"We get along just fine," he said. "These last couple of months are proof of that, *jah*?"

"*Jah—jah*," she stuttered, realizing when he looked at her that he expected an answer.

"Comfortable," he was saying.

Charlotte nodded.

"And I like it. It's just the way I wanted it."

"Me too," she barely managed. She sent a small prayer of thanks heavenward, grateful that she could even get the words out.

"I think it's time," he said. Then he chuckled, still staring out over the hill toward Aaron Yoder's house. "I'm making a mess of this."

Charlotte's heart softened. Glenn had always been so

smooth, so well put together; to see him flustered was little charming.

"What I mean to say," he continued when she didn't speak, "is that we should get married, don't you agree?" He turned to look at her then, and she felt as if God had granted all of her hopes and dreams in that one fell swoop.

"*Jah*," she said. "Of course we should."

Charlotte was sitting on the couch when she heard Amos's buggy pull up outside. It was a little before supper and though she had expected her mother-in-law to be home a little later, she was glad she was early.

Charlotte was ecstatic. A great weight had been lifted from her shoulders. They had all found love and happiness in Wells Landing. Of course, she would only admit it to herself that she wasn't crazy, crazy in love with Glenn Esh. Not like she had been with Daniel, but who got to love like that twice? She had done her duty. She had raised Jenna, allowed her to grow into a wonderful young woman. Jenna had found love and was married, soon to have a baby of her own. Now was the time for Charlotte to pick up her own life. And that life was going to be with Glenn. Charlotte Burkhart would no longer be alone.

The doorknob rattled; then Nadine managed to get it open. She stepped into the house, her expression like a thundercloud as she slammed the door behind her. "That man!"

Charlotte watched as Nadine growled under her breath.

"Of all the crazy ideas."

Nadine flounced into the house and flopped down in the rocking chair closest to the fireplace.

"Have a good time?" Charlotte asked.

Nadine shot her a look that would have wilted fresh-cut flowers. "It would have been better if someone wasn't so worried that I'm a better fisherman than they are."

"Are you?" Charlotte asked.

Nadine crossed her arms and harrumphed. "I guess it's all in how you look at it. I catch more fish than he does. Mine might not be as big as his, but I catch three to his one. You tell me?"

"Does it matter?" Charlotte asked.

Nadine turned to look at her, some of the anger falling away. "What's got you in such good spirits?"

"Am I?" Charlotte asked.

Nadine rolled her eyes. "I'm really not in the mood, but yes, you are."

"Glenn proposed." Somehow, she managed to get the two words out without squealing, without squirming in her seat, and without acting like a schoolgirl.

"What was that again?" Nadine waited, stiff as a board as she waited for Charlotte to continue, to repeat the good news.

At least Charlotte thought it was good news. "Glenn proposed tonight." It was getting easier to say the words, the more accustomed she got to the idea. It was just what she had hoped for.

Nadine was on her feet in a moment. "And I suppose you said yes."

From her tone, Charlotte gathered that Nadine wasn't that happy with the idea. Or maybe she was just in a bad mood.

"Of course I did."

"Well, that is a mistake." Nadine fairly spat the words at her, then stormed upstairs. A few moments later, Charlotte heard her bedroom door slam.

"She's just upset with Amos," Charlotte said to herself. *Jah,* that was it. She was upset with Amos for whatever fishing disaster they had experienced. And Charlotte was certain hearing that she was remarrying was something of a shock. After all, Charlotte had been married to Nadine's own son not so very long ago.

That had to be it. It wasn't that Nadine wasn't happy for her; she was just not used to the idea that Charlotte was starting over after Daniel's death. Maybe if she had remarried before now. Maybe Nadine had accepted the idea that Charlotte would never remarry.

Well, that wasn't the case. She was marrying Glenn Esh, and they were going to live happily ever after, as the English say. And the sooner Nadine accepted that fact, the better off they would all be.

"I'm sorry," Nadine said the following morning. "I shouldn't have said that to you last night."

Charlotte smiled a little to herself and mentally patted herself on the back for her understanding and deductions. Nadine might even be a little jealous. It was no matter; any contention that rose between them, they always managed to put aside.

"It's okay," Charlotte said. "I understand."

Nadine turned her head to one side as if studying her, kind of like Goldie did when Charlotte said her name.

Except Nadine's ears didn't flop quite like Goldie's did. Okay, not at all, but the look was the same, inquisitive and questioning.

"Do you?" Nadine asked.

Charlotte poured herself a cup of coffee, then got one for Nadine as well. She placed it on the table in front of her mother-in-law and took the seat across from her. "Of course I do."

"He's just not right for you," Nadine said.

Charlotte stirred a teaspoon of sugar into her coffee and clinked the spoon on the side of the mug before setting it to one side. "Is that really it?"

"You think he is?" Nadine asked. Her voice was gentle and caring, and Charlotte knew that the concern was genuine. She might be a little on the grumpy side, but her mother-in-law was nothing if not loving.

"Of course. He's godly and handsome, and he seems to have himself together, monetarily speaking. He would make a good husband."

Nadine nodded. "*Jah*," she said. "But would he make a *good husband*?"

For some unknown reason, Charlotte's stomach fell to the floor, but she managed to keep her expression neutral. "Of course. What kind of question is that?"

"An honest one," Nadine said. "I wouldn't feel right if I didn't tell you, but I don't think he's the man for you."

Of course she didn't. But Nadine had found her soulmate, maybe even twice in one lifetime. Charlotte couldn't count herself that lucky. Couldn't even consider it. It would be disrespectful, arrogant toward God, to expect Him to provide so much for one person. And what she had with Glenn was plenty. Enough. For all the days to the end of her life. What more could she ask for than that?

"Love," Nadine said as if she had read Charlotte's thoughts.

"Glenn cares for me," Charlotte said. "And I care for him." Surely that would be enough.

"Charlotte!" Nadine called. "Come get this dog."

Charlotte bustled from the kitchen, dish towel in one hand, mixing spoon in the other. "What's wrong?"

It had only been a couple of days since Paul had come over and taught Charlotte how to install herself as the alpha dog in the relationship. Goldie had done so well since then. But tonight was July Fourth. And the noise coming in from outside was loud and unpredictable. Most places in town wouldn't allow for the lighting of fireworks so folks came out to the country and shot them off in random places.

It always worried Charlotte, times like this when they hadn't had a lot of rain and the grass was already beginning to grow brittle. Paul had come over earlier in the day and used the water hose to soak down the roof on the off chance that a stray spark might find it. He had assured her that the chances of that were slim, but he'd wanted to allay any fears that she might have.

"I guess all these firecrackers," Nadine said. Goldie stood at the front door, her front paws braced upon the wood and barked.

"I've never seen her like this," Charlotte said. "Gimme a minute."

She bustled back into the kitchen, set down the spoon

and the towel, then grabbed a treat and headed back out to help Nadine.

"Sit," she commanded.

Goldie didn't even turn, just barked once more, loudly at the door.

"I don't hear any firecrackers right now," Charlotte said.

"You've heard them though. They've been going off like gunfire all night."

"*Jah,* but not right now." And still Goldie acted as if monsters were at the door.

"That's my point," Nadine said.

Charlotte stepped forward and grabbed ahold of Goldie's collar. She tugged the reluctant dog away from the door. With one hand, she held the collar, and with the other, she forced Goldie's butt to the ground. But the dog was unwilling. She barked again, not once taking her eyes from the door.

"What's wrong with you?" Of course Goldie didn't answer but squirmed in place as if she couldn't sit there for a moment longer. She started to rise onto her feet.

"Sit." The command was firm and strong, perhaps the most alpha-dog command she had ever given.

Nadine shook her head as if perplexed with the whole situation. "There were a lot more fireworks earlier, and she wasn't acting like this then."

It was true. Fireworks had been going off all evening, even before it got completely dark, but Goldie hadn't been acting up so.

"You don't think . . . ?" Charlotte didn't finish the thought. She didn't have to. Nadine knew exactly what she was talking about.

Unfortunately there were people who thought that harassing the Amish was great sport. Usually it was young English boys with nothing better to do with their time. Nadine and Charlotte hadn't had a big problem with this since they had been in Wells Landing, but Charlotte knew it was bound to happen.

And she would rather it be some teenage prank instead of the alternative, which was possibly a robber.

Charlotte pushed the thought from her head. Just because the dog was barking didn't mean trouble was brewing. Something was happening, but it wouldn't do to call whatever it was trouble before they knew the truth.

"Here." Charlotte motioned Nadine over. "Take her collar."

Nadine did as instructed with a frown on her face. "What are you going to do?"

"I'm going to go see what it is."

Nadine opened her mouth to protest, but Charlotte interrupted before she could utter one sound. "It's okay."

They needed to trust God that it was okay. And that was just what she was going to do.

Charlotte approached the door. She took a deep breath, smoothed her hands down the front of her apron as if about to greet a visitor she wanted to impress. Then, exhaling her air, she threw open the door.

Of course there was nothing on the porch, just empty darkness.

Behind her, she heard Goldie whine. At least her barks had stopped.

"Maybe whoever it is went into the barn," Nadine said.

Or maybe they had run. With any luck, her opening

the door had scared them away. Especially if they were pranksters out for a harmlessness joke.

One could only hope.

Charlotte stepped onto the porch. It didn't seem as dark as usual out there, maybe because the sky was still lit up with fireworks. It practically surrounded them, even though the sound hadn't quite reached them yet.

"Do you see anything?" Nadine asked.

"Nothing," Charlotte replied.

"Ouch."

Charlotte turned back to Nadine just as Goldie pushed past her out onto the porch.

"Sorry," Nadine said, shaking her hand as if her fingers were stinging. "I couldn't hold her any longer."

Charlotte gave her mother-in-law an understanding smile. "I get it."

But she wasn't sure if they would be able to catch Goldie in the dark. Not as wound up as she had been all evening. With any luck, she might head over to Paul's since that was her original home. But Charlotte wasn't counting on it. The dog was too hyper tonight, for certain.

Then, behind her, Goldie barked three barks in rapid succession. The sound was so unexpected, Charlotte nearly jumped out of her skin, but the next sound nearly did her in. For Goldie's barks were followed by the terrified cries of a baby.

Chapter Eleven

"I'll be." Nadine had moved to stand in the doorway.

Goldie, proud of herself for alerting her mistress to what had to be the issue that had been causing her such distress tonight, moved back closer to Charlotte, nudging her head under Charlotte's hand as if needing a pat on the head for a job well done.

Charlotte stood immobilized for a long while. Well, it seemed like a long while. And it seemed like a heartbeat. Then she rushed toward the infant carrier sitting just under the front window. The swing at the end of the porch moved erratically, as if whoever had been there had dropped the baby on the porch and pushed past it with rapid fear. Charlotte supposed they had jumped over the side of the porch railing to get away. Yet she wasn't as concerned about that. She was concerned with the baby.

Finally, she had unrooted her feet from the porch planks and made her way over.

"It really is a baby." Nadine's voice was full of awe. Charlotte wasn't so sure herself until she actually clasped her hands around the handle of the baby carrier and found it to be solid. Real. She lifted it as the baby continued to cry, Goldie trying to lick the baby's toes. Charlotte carried it into the house. Her hands were shaking so that she thought she might drop it. She carted it to the couch and set it on the cushions as quickly as she dared. Then she collapsed down next to it, a bit in shock.

"Pick her up," Nadine said.

Charlotte roused herself from the stupor. "I'm going to." But she was glad Nadine had jumpstarted her thoughts and actions. Of all the things that she would've expected to find on the porch, an infant girl—if the color of the blankets and tiny pink sleeper she was wearing was any indication—might possibly be at the very bottom of that list.

Yet the solid weight of the infant was real. Her warmth, her cries, and her sweet baby smell. Charlotte did her best not to inhale too deeply; then again, there was nothing sweeter smelling than a baby.

She cuddled the child close to her, gently easing her head down onto her shoulder as she made shushing noises and patted her gently on the back.

The cries stopped until they became nothing more than shuddering hiccups.

"She's sucking her thumb," Nadine said. "A baby."

Goldie dropped to her haunches at Charlotte's feet. She placed one paw on Charlotte's knee but otherwise made no move to get to the baby. She simply sat and watched as Charlotte soothed the infant.

A baby. Where had she come from? Who had left her there?

Charlotte rocked the baby from side to side as Nadine stood and went back to the door. They had left it wide open in their surprise.

Nadine took the flashlight from the table next to the door and turned it on before stepping out onto the porch once again.

"Hello?" she called as she disappeared from Charlotte's sight.

Surely this wasn't a part of some joke. Surely whoever had left this child here would be back for her. Perhaps they had frightened whoever it was when they had opened the door. Or perhaps Goldie's barking had accomplished that and the frightened mother—or father—had run away. But who would leave a child and not come back?

No one. That much she knew for certain. Especially not a child as sweet and lovable as this one.

The baby had nestled into the crook of Charlotte's shoulder. Her steady, even breathing told Charlotte that she was asleep. She couldn't see her, but she could hear the sharp little smacks as she continued to suck her thumb. The thought brought a smile to Charlotte's lips. Nothing sweeter in the whole wide world.

"I don't see anyone out there," Nadine said, coming back into the house. She shut the door behind her, turned off the flashlight, and placed it back in its original spot by the door.

"I think if someone was still out there that Goldie would be carrying on, don't you?"

"I suppose." Nadine sat down in her rocking chair, watching Charlotte with the baby.

It felt so natural, sitting there holding the child. What was the saying? Like riding a bike. Not that she had ever ridden a bike. Not even during her running around. But she knew it meant something hard to forget. And that's what holding a baby was like for her. So natural, nothing she would forget. Like instinct.

"She's a pretty little thing," Nadine said.

"Honestly, I didn't get a good look at her face," Charlotte replied. She had picked the baby up and held her close, not bothering to register any more than the color she wore and that she looked to be about two months or so. She was still tiny and small, but she had the filled-out look that didn't exist in most newborns.

Charlotte eased back into the sofa cushions, doing her best to get into a more comfortable position without disturbing the child.

"What do we do now?" Nadine asked.

"Do?" Charlotte turned her attention once again from the top of the baby's head to her mother-in-law. Charlotte couldn't keep her eyes off the child for more than a second or two, even though all she could see was the thatch of clean-smelling brown hair that held a rusty tint in the living room light.

"Yes, do." Charlotte nodded toward the baby. "She belongs to someone. It's not like we can just keep her."

The thought hadn't occurred to Charlotte. She hadn't thought beyond the moment they were in. Holding the baby, soothing her while she slept, and just absorbing all that she represented. A new life, a beginning, a fresh start. "No," she finally murmured. "I don't suppose we can."

A moment passed as they both thought through the events of the night. Charlotte supposed that was what Nadine was thinking about since those thoughts completely dominated her own mind. There had been firecrackers, a barking dog, and now a baby.

"Do we call the police?" Nadine asked.

Charlotte figured it was the most logical thing to do, but . . . "You shouldn't be out walking in the dark. Not on a holiday."

That was true enough, but it also gave Charlotte a little more time with the baby. That's all she wanted. Just a little more time to hold and cuddle her. "Besides, what if the mother comes back and the police are here? She could get in trouble. I wouldn't want that for anyone. Not if she was just scared off by Goldie."

Nadine's mouth twisted into something akin to a thoughtful frown. "What was she doing on our porch?"

"I don't know."

"And were you ever scared so badly that you left your baby behind?"

"No." And she had nothing more to add to that. She had never been in the situation, but she couldn't imagine anything making her leave her child behind. Not for any reason. Which only left one answer to the puzzle—the mother had meant to leave her on Nadine and Charlotte's porch. She had left the baby on purpose.

But that couldn't be.

It was too fantastical to even imagine.

So she wasn't going to. "Let's give it some more time," Charlotte said. "If the mother comes back, I don't want her to be in trouble with the police because we were too jumpy."

Nadine nodded, but Charlotte got the feeling that she wasn't happy about it.

"Hand me that blanket," Charlotte said, nodding toward the thin cotton blanket in the carrier.

Nadine didn't hesitate. She stood and grabbed the soft

pink cloth. But as she picked it up and handed it to Charlotte, a long white envelope fell to the floor.

"What's that?" Charlotte asked.

"It's an envelope," Nadine replied as she bent to scoop it up.

Charlotte shot her a look. "I can see that. What does it have inside?"

Nadine settled back into the rocking chair. As Charlotte lay the blanket over the child, Nadine opened the envelope and took out a single sheet of paper.

"This is Amber. She is my daughter. Yours now. Please take care of her. I can't do it any longer. Feed her, love her. I know you will. Thank you." Nadine turned the paper over to see if any more was written on the back.

"That's it?" Charlotte asked. She couldn't get her hopes up. Who just gave their baby away? But it seemed as if this mother had. It also seemed as if she wanted Charlotte and Nadine to have the child. It wasn't as if their house sat right on the road. Whoever had left the babe on their porch had meant to leave her there. That much was obvious to Charlotte.

And there was one other thing.

"That's all." Nadine folded the paper to rights and stuffed it back into the envelope. She tossed it onto the couch next to Charlotte, then stood. She made her way over to the door before Charlotte realized what she was about.

"Where are you going?" she asked even though she knew.

Nadine picked up the flashlight. "To the phone shanty to call the police."

"No!" The one word, spoken so loudly, disturbed the

baby. Amber. "No," Charlotte repeated quietly this time. "You don't need to get out in the dark."

Nadine stopped, flashlight in hand, fingers already reaching for the doorknob. "Charlotte."

Charlotte shook her head. "The mother left her here with us because she knew we would take care of her. What if she comes back?"

"She's not coming back." Nadine frowned. "The letter says so. 'Yours now.'"

"*Jah*," she admitted. "It did say that. But she could change her mind. And you know how the police will be. Where are they going to take her at a time like this?"

She could almost see Nadine's resolve melting right before her eyes.

"They'll cart her on into Pryor and put her into the system."

"I don't even know what that means," Nadine said.

"Me either," Charlotte admitted. "But it doesn't sound good, whatever it is."

"Charlotte."

"Not when she can stay here. Just for tonight." She was loath to let the child go. It seemed as if God had planned this start to finish. Glenn had proposed, and now Charlotte had this baby in her arms. Everything that she had been wanting and praying for. A man to spend her time with, to grow old with, and a child for a second chance she so desperately needed to move past this time in her life. It was all right there before her.

Nadine put down the flashlight and sighed. "Just for tonight."

Charlotte smiled. "Just for tonight."

* * *

Charlotte smiled into the darkness. It was a miracle. A dream come true. God's plan in action. How could it be anything else?

She looked over to where the baby, Amber, peacefully slept next to the bed. Charlotte had wanted to put her on the mattress next to her but had managed to refrain. She was already so attached to the baby. Mostly because she believed, truly in her heart of hearts, that God wanted her to have this baby. Why else would He have made it so Amber would be on her porch tonight? It all made sense as far as she could see, but until she could convince Nadine of the truth, then she needed to be careful with her heart. And that of little Amber as well.

She wasn't sure what sort of name Amber was. She had heard it before, but it sounded so English. Once it was determined that the baby would be hers and hers alone—well, and Glenn's too—then she would come up with a nickname. Maybe Amby or Amy. She knew men named Amos who went by Amy. Why not an Amber?

The problem with keeping the baby overnight became clear just a few short minutes after the decision had been made. Amber stirred against Charlotte's chest as a foul smell filled the room.

"She needs to be changed," Nadine pointed out unnecessarily.

And the problem was, what could she change her into?

Charlotte took the squalling baby into the kitchen and managed with one hand to find the softest dish towel they had. If she was remembering correctly, they were old diapers picked up from somewhere or another. They made great dusting rags for delicate furniture. And in this case, flipped right back to their original duty with no extra effort.

She found a couple of large safety pins in the junk drawer. One wet wash rag later and the deed was done. She should have gone upstairs and gotten some talcum powder from the bathroom, but she would next time. And she was certain there would be a next time, if she could convince Nadine not to call the police.

"Look what I found." Nadine set the plastic grocery sack on the table where the baby had been just moments before.

"What is it?"

"A present from Amber's mother." Nadine unloaded the sack. Two diapers and a bottle, along with a pacifier, which Amber already had shown she didn't need. It had been obvious from the start that she preferred her own thumb.

"That's wonderful." And it would get them through the night. She picked up the bottle. It was still cool to the touch. Cool enough that she didn't hesitate to give it to Amber when she reached for it.

Thankfully, it had been one of the refillable kinds of bottles so she would put more milk in it in the morning. Then, after that, she and Nadine would go into town and get the baby everything she needed to stay healthy and happy right there with them.

Charlotte smiled into the night and thanked God for answering her prayers and blessing her with the one thing that only a few hours ago had seemed like an impossibility. A child of her own.

* * *

The following morning, Charlotte awoke to the sounds of Amber crying. She had slept through the night, all the way until 4 AM. It was a little early for Charlotte, but such a lengthy night of sleep was a blessing to be sure.

She pulled herself out of bed and unstrapped the baby from the carrier. "We need to get you a better place to sleep," she murmured to the child as she cradled her close. Maybe there was something in the attic, but she doubted it. The barn had been filled with junk when they had moved into the house, but she didn't remember seeing anything in the attic. Still, there was a chance. And she would look the first chance she got.

"There, there," she soothed, taking Amber over to the bed for a quick diaper change. There was no need to check. All babies woke up wet. But they would need to get more diapers, and soon, if they wanted to keep her happy. One of the biggest surprises that she'd had when Jenna was a baby was that they went through a lot of diapers. And quickly too.

Once Charlotte had Amber in a clean diaper, she rested her against her shoulder. Then she grabbed the carrier and toted it and the child downstairs. The baby had to be hungry. That was just part of it. Like they woke up wet, babies also woke up hungry. But the bottle that she had given her last night was gone and it was the only one she had.

Charlotte placed the carrier on the table and bounced Amber in place to distract her from her unhappy, hungry state while she looked for something for her to eat. It was too soon to feed her any real foods, even soft, pureed ones. She opened the fridge, hoping to find some solution inside. And then she spotted it. The goat's milk she had gotten from Helen Ebersol, the bishop's wife. Helen had told them that goat's milk was better for a person than cow's milk, but Charlotte had no idea how true that statement was. She only knew that Amber needed something to eat, and in that moment, it seemed like the logical choice.

With one hand, Charlotte took the goat's milk from the fridge, got out a pan, and managed to turn on the stove, all the while bouncing the baby on one arm. There were some things a person never forgot. She blew kisses into the crook of Amber's chubby neck and made the baby laugh as they waited for the milk to heat. Then she placed her into the carrier so she could get the bottle cleaned and ready. She should have gotten up last night and cleaned it, but she had been too in love to think beyond the moment they were in.

God had provided.

And He had said that He would.

And my God will meet all your needs according to his glorious riches in Christ Jesus.

Philippians, she thought it was. Though she couldn't remember chapter and verse. She would look it up later. She needed to commit it to memory, for God had surely provided for her, all that she needed. And glorious riches were an understatement.

Then again, who needed riches when she had a sweet and loving little baby to care for. Not her, that was certain.

* * *

"Are you sure you don't mind going to the store for me?" Charlotte asked sometime later.

Nadine had given her a look that was half reprimand, half resignation, but Charlotte was holding firm. They couldn't just call the police. Nadine might not believe that the mother of the child had left Amber with them on purpose, but she couldn't deny the fact that Charlotte could take better care of her than 'the system' would take care of her.

"I guess not." It was as good of an answer as Charlotte could hope for.

"And what are you going to tell anyone that you run into?"

"That we're buying this stuff in preparation for Jenna's baby."

Charlotte smiled. "That's right."

Nadine looked down at the list she held in her hand. "There are quite a few items on here."

"Babies need a lot of things," Charlotte replied serenely.

"Are you sure about this?"

"Positive," she said with a nod. "And let me get you some money."

Amber still cradled next to her, Charlotte stood and reached for the coffee can perched on the top shelf over the sink. "Mad money," Charlotte explained, then took out a handful of bills. "Use this."

Nadine looked down at it as if the money were about to come to life and slither away. "If you're certain," Nadine said.

Charlotte followed her to the door. "I've never been more certain of anything in my life."

* * *

After Nadine had left to go to town, Charlotte put Amber in the carrier. Then, with Goldie on her heels, she made her way across the field to Paul's house.

She marveled at the chance that the child had been dropped on her doorstep and not his. How easy it would have been for Amber to have been left at any other house, for that matter. The musings just further solidified Charlotte's growing beliefs. God wanted her to have this baby. He had made it so.

She had spent a great deal of time last night thinking about the baby and where she might have come from. She felt a little like Bithiah, the pharaoh's daughter who had pulled Moses and his basket from the reeds and claimed him as her own. Bithiah had felt that the gods had given her a child. In a sense, they had. Just like God had made sure that Amber had ended up in a household that would love and cherish her.

Charlotte figured that the mother of the child was an English teenager. She was most likely unmarried and had no way to care for herself or the baby. Charlotte believed her to be English because of the name she had given the infant. Amber was not something an Amish woman of any age would think about naming a child. So it stood to reason. And sometime during the night, Charlotte had come to like the name. Amber. Wasn't that like a precious stone that was made when tree sap fossilized? She wasn't sure where that information had come from, but it was there all the same. Amber came from nothing. Just like she had appeared on Charlotte's doorstep.

The best she could figure, the child's mother needed

her to care for Amber, and that's just what she planned to do.

Nadine might not like it much, but who were they to argue with the plans of God? And she knew in her heart Amber coming to her was nothing short of God's perfect plan.

"Whatcha got there?" Obie was the first to spy her. He was winding up a length of rope next to the barn when she came over the small hill where their house sat. The trailer was a little behind the main house, but still visible from where she was.

"A baby." The words were a happy rush from her lips.

Obie stopped what he was doing. "A baby?" He tilted his head to one side as if that might help him better understand what she was saying.

"*Jah*. That's right." She stopped right there in the middle of the yard, breathless. Not from the exertion of toting the baby all the way across the field between their houses, but pure elated excitement.

She placed the carrier seat gently on the ground near her feet. Goldie sat obediently next to the baby, guardian of the new life they had been afforded.

"Charlotte?" Paul came around the side of the house, somehow alerted to her presence.

"Hi, Paul," she said, still out of air. "Come see."

The closer he got to her, the slower he began to walk, as if this was some sort of trick and something ugly was going to jump out of the baby car seat to scare him.

He peered over the edge of the gingham fabric cover. "It is," he breathed. "Where . . . ?" he started. "Whose . . . ?"

"I don't know. There was a note. Her name is Amber,

and her mother left her for us to care for. Isn't it amazing?" Wasn't God amazing? Wonderous!

"What in the world?" Clara Rose exclaimed, coming down the porch steps to join them.

"Someone left a baby on Charlotte's doorstep," Obie said, rope still hanging loose in his hands.

"Just now?" She looked back over toward Charlotte's house as if maybe she could catch sight of the person who had given her their baby.

"Last night. Goldie was going crazy, barking and carrying on. When we went out onto the porch to see what was going on, we found her."

"Did you call the police?" Clara Rose asked.

Charlotte shook her head. She was not going to be ashamed of the decision they had made. This was an act of God as surely as a woman giving birth. And God had planned this for her.

"You need to," Clara Rose said. "Someone could be looking for her."

"We checked the paper this morning. No one said anything about a missing baby. Plus there was a note from the mother telling us her name and that she wanted us to care for the baby."

Clara Rose bit her lip. Then her voice lowered as if she were talking to a small child. Charlotte was not at all happy about the tone. "You don't know if the person who wrote that letter was really this child's mother. What if she took the child and left her with you so she wouldn't get caught?"

Charlotte raised up to her considerable height. "Why must this younger generation be so suspicious?" She looked from Paul to Obie to see if either one of them had the answer. Neither man spoke. "Why would she steal a baby and then give it away? That doesn't make any sense."

"Leaving your baby on a stranger's doorstep doesn't make any sense either." Clara Rose laid a protective hand over her stomach.

It was a sure sign that she was with child. And Charlotte could understand her concern. There were people in the world who couldn't have children and there were people who cherished their children. These were the ones who couldn't understand the desperation this young mother must have felt when she had jumped over the porch railing and run away so she wouldn't get caught. How terrible that must have been for her!

"She wanted me to have the baby, so she left her on my porch. It doesn't get any simpler than that."

Everyone was looking at her as if she had lost her mind. These were good people, kind and godly. Their strange perusal of her made her wonder if perhaps she was a little wonky in the head.

No. She stiffened her back, straightened her shoulders. This had nothing to do with them. This was between her and God. "I told Nadine that we shouldn't call the police. What if the mother comes back and wants her baby? What then? She'll never get her baby back if we give her over to the police."

"Maybe she shouldn't have the baby if she abandons it with strangers." Clara Rose sniffed, but Charlotte could see the doubt beginning to form in the shadows of her eyes.

"You don't mean that," Charlotte gently chided.

She shook her head. "But I worry for this child."

"There's no need to worry," Charlotte said. "God has seen to her. He brought her to me, and I intend to take care of her."

"Forever?" Obie said, a small frown settling between his dark brows.

"Why not?" She shrugged, unable to keep the smile of pure pleasure from her face. God was good. And this just proved it.

Chapter Twelve

Paul looked from the tiny baby in the carrier to Charlotte's elated face. He couldn't figure out which one of them was the prettiest. In the end, he decided that it was a tie. Charlotte happy was about the most beautiful thing he could imagine. She might have been satisfied up until now, living her life as best she knew how, but she hadn't been happy. Truly, deeply happy.

And this precious creature that someone had left on her doorstep was making her happy, delighted.

She looked very contented as well, this baby. "What's her name?" he asked, all too aware that Clara Rose and Obie were staring at him as if he'd gone a little off in the head.

He wasn't sure what to make of the situation. Charlotte had been given something that seemed to be elevating her life. How could he say that was a bad thing? Plus, she had a point. If they called the police, they would turn the baby over to Child Protective Services. Paul didn't know much, but every day there seemed to be some story in the paper about someone who was in 'the system' and had been failed by it. He wasn't even sure what made up 'the system.' But he knew what leaving the baby with Charlotte would mean.

"Where's Nadine?" he asked. "What does she think about all this?"

"She's gone to town to get some things for the baby. Diapers and such."

"And what does she say?" Clara Rose asked.

"She was hesitant at first, but she knows that putting the baby in some kind of English foster care would be a bad thing."

"But it is an English baby," Obie argued.

"Of course," she said. "What Amish woman would abandon her child? However just because she's English doesn't mean that she can't learn our ways."

Obie pressed his lips together. He looked like he wanted to say more, but he didn't.

"Why don't we go inside?" Paul suggested.

Charlotte shook her head. "Everyone just wants to talk me out of keeping Amber, but that's not going to happen. I won't give her up. Not without a fight. Or good reason."

He could understand that. Her faithfulness and tenacity were just two of the things that he loved about Charlotte.

"I'm sorry," Clara Rose said. "I have no right to tell you one way or the other. It's just . . ." She trailed off.

"It's hard," Charlotte said, filling in the blank.

"*Jah*." Clara Rose and Obie both nodded at the same time.

"I've been praying lately for a purpose. For something to happen in my life. Something big." She gestured toward the pink and white carrier where the baby rested, rosy and healthy. "This is what God saw fit to bring me. Who am I to argue with that?"

And there was no arguing with Charlotte. Paul couldn't think of one good reason to involve the police in the matter, other than it was the right thing to do. But by whose standards? That was something he couldn't figure out.

Part of him knew that he should convince her to call the police. He wasn't sure about the law regarding such happenings. It wasn't every day a baby was left on a stranger's doorstep. And he wasn't sure about 'the system' that everyone talked about. The only thing he was sure about was the love and care that Charlotte would give the child.

After she had said all her prayers for something big and for God to help her, to give her something to make her happy, how could she not?

What had Bithiah done when she found Moses? She had named him and called him her own. Of course, it had eventually brought down the kingdom.

He pushed that thought aside. Charlotte might be able to turn loose of the baby in a day or so. But she wasn't ready right then. And until she was ready, he knew that little Amber would be well cared for. And that was something he couldn't say about all the children in the world. And surely there was something to be said for that.

Nadine returned a couple of hours later with everything, plus a little more than was on her list.

"I thought she could use this," Nadine said, holding up a set of footie pajamas with little yellow ducks wearing rain boots and carrying umbrellas as they splashed in soft blue puddles. It was sweet and whimsical and completely unlike Nadine.

"That's considerate of you," Charlotte said with a smile.

Nadine sank down into the kitchen chair opposite Charlotte as they watched Amber sleeping in the baby carrier. "She needs a better place to sleep."

Charlotte nodded. "I thought I would look up in the attic and see if the previous owners left anything up there."

Nadine nodded. It was a possibility. Considering how much they had left in the barn. When Nadine and Charlotte had cleaned it out last year, they had wondered if the people were hoarders. If they were, and if there was a cradle or crib in the attic, that would surely be in their favor.

But they found no baby items when they looked a short time later.

"She can sleep there for now," Charlotte said. Babies slept in car carriers all the time. And she could nap on Charlotte's bed with pillows around to keep her from rolling off onto the floor.

But Nadine didn't say what Charlotte knew she was thinking. That maybe this was a sign as well. Yet it couldn't be. Why would God bring Amber to Charlotte just so she could be taken away?

There had to be more to it all.

"I wonder what Jenna is going to say."

Charlotte nearly made herself dizzy whipping her head

around to look at Nadine. "Why would she say anything?" She cradled Amber close, unwilling to put the baby down for long. She might view her as a gift from God, and she might get to keep her for now, but there was a time coming when she knew that the baby would have to go to the proper channels. However that wasn't something she wanted to think about right then.

Nadine gave a casual shrug. At least, Charlotte thought it was meant to be casual. In reality, it came out sort of stiff and jerky. "Tonight is puzzle night."

Charlotte had been so wrapped up in Amber and everything going on. And who could blame her? It wasn't like she had a baby left on her doorstep every day. She had been so engrossed that she had completely forgotten that today was Wednesday and tonight was puzzle night.

There was no way to cancel, even if she wanted to. And she didn't. Just because she had Amber didn't mean that everything had to stop. The thought was ridiculous.

"I'm sure she'll be thrilled." After all, what was there not to be thrilled about?

Nadine pressed her lips together, but she didn't have to say the words for Charlotte to know what she was thinking. This couldn't last for long. Yet what was the harm in her enjoying it while it did?

"She's just so beautiful," Jenna said. It had been an hour since everyone had arrived at Charlotte and Nadine's to work on the puzzle, and not much puzzle working had been done. At least, not by the ladies. Priscilla, Jenna, Charlotte, and Nadine were all a little too enamored of the baby girl to worry too much about puzzles. And that left Amos, Paul, Emmanuel, and Buddy to work on the puzzle alone. Which meant they sat around the table, the puzzle board out in front of them, while they talked about things like fishing, farming, and camels. Standard stuff.

"She is, isn't she?" Charlotte said. Surely that wasn't prideful. It wasn't as if she'd had anything to do at all with the baby girl's looks.

"Are you going to keep her?" Jenna asked.

"I wish I could," Charlotte said. Oh, how she wished she could. Yet it just didn't seem possible. Not forever anyway. "I feel like her *mamm* will come back for her."

"That's what you keep telling yourself," Nadine said.

Charlotte couldn't quite figure out what her mother-in-law thought about the whole thing. She went around frowning and chastising Charlotte in one breath, then buying duck-covered footie pajamas and cooing to the child the next. She supposed Nadine wanted to be reasonable about it, but when faced with the cuteness of Amber, all reason crumbled.

"And it's true," Charlotte said. "She could come back at any time. And I would feel just horrible if I gave her baby to the police and she had intended to come back for her all along."

"And that's what you keep telling yourself too."

Charlotte frowned. But didn't let Nadine's almost truth sour her own attitude. "I just want what's best for this little girl and right now I can't see how turning her over to the police would be what's best for her."

"And you checked the papers to see if anybody is missing a baby?" Priscilla asked.

They had already covered this once before, but it seemed like the most popular question that kept cropping up.

"*Jah*, we checked the papers. And I will check them again in the morning. And I'll check them every morning until this baby's *mamm* comes back. Because I do believe she'll come back."

Priscilla looked down at the baby cooing in Jenna's lap. "I don't know about her, but I would find it awfully hard to leave something like her behind."

Which was exactly why Charlotte herself was having such a hard time. That and she really, truly wanted to believe that God had brought this baby to her. Even as she really and truly believed she would not get to keep her. The idea held more of an appeal to her. In a heartbeat, she would accept this gift that God had given her and raise the child as if she were her own. But she knew that wasn't to be.

Somehow, deep inside, she knew that as much as she wanted to believe this baby was hers and had been meant for her, Amber belonged to someone else. But in the meantime, she was going to take care of the little one as if she were her own.

Thursday morning dawned early again for Charlotte and Amber. The baby woke up at four-thirty as she had been doing the past two days. Charlotte dragged herself out of bed and made the baby a bottle, then sat down in the rocking chair to feed her.

She had forgotten just how much work babies could

be. Maybe that's why the good Lord gave them to people when they were younger. She didn't remember Jenna being this much work, even as the happy, healthy baby that she had been.

But it was joyous work. Her arms ached from holding the baby. The muscles were unaccustomed to handling such weight on a regular basis. Her legs ached from getting up and down on the floor with the baby, and she was tired. Amber was a good sleeper, but she still woke in the middle of the night needing something to eat. Babies' stomachs just weren't big enough to hold enough food to carry them through the night, so her waking was to be expected. It was just that Charlotte's forty-three-year-old body wasn't accustomed to such trial. But it was a good tired, she told herself as she gently rocked Amber that morning. A child needed to know that she was loved. Charlotte had always believed that was the main thing. And it was the primary reason why she didn't want to turn Amber over to the authorities.

As far as she could tell, little Amber was at least two months old. She hadn't gotten any teeth yet, though her neck was strong and her eyes bright and attentive. Charlotte also knew that someone else had been taking care of the baby before now. And Amber could know on some level that she had been left in another's care. How would Amber feel if Charlotte turned her over to someone else so soon? She felt certain it would traumatize the infant.

Or was she just kidding herself? Was this just a way for her to justify keeping the baby for a while longer?

Lord, please help me through this. Please give me wisdom, and strength, and energy, she jokingly added. Though it really wasn't much of a joke. The good Lord brought this baby to her, and surely He could afford her a little more energy to see this through.

Strength, energy, wisdom. Amen. Those were the three things she needed most, and she knew that God would provide. And she would just have to tough it out until He did.

"Have you been down here all morning?"

Charlotte jerked awake, not realizing until she heard Nadine speak that she had been asleep at all. "What time is it?"

"Just after six."

Charlotte looked from the sleeping baby to Nadine, then back to the clock on the wall. Just after six. Time to get up. Her knees popped and her back protested as she stood. She must've made some sort of noise for Nadine turned to look at her, concern on her face. "Are you okay?"

Charlotte nodded, though she didn't feel as if she could take even one single step. "Of course I am."

Nadine shook her head. "You have to do something about that fib telling, daughter." She crossed the living room, hands outstretched. "Give me that baby. Then go splash some water on your face. Maybe do a stretching exercise or two."

Gratefully, Charlotte handed the baby over; then, slowly gathering speed, she made her way to the downstairs bathroom. Just a small break, then she would be back on Amber duty.

When she emerged from the bathroom ten minutes later, her hair was back in a ponytail and covered with a bandanna. Her face was washed, her teeth cleaned, and her bladder empty. It was a good way to start the day.

She just wished she had more energy. That would make everything perfect.

She made her way to the kitchen, where Nadine was whistling under her breath as she cooked sausages and pancakes while Amber chewed on a teething biscuit that her mother-in-law had brought home the day before.

"What are you going to do about tonight?" Nadine asked as she stirred the meat around in the pan and expertly flipped over the pancake so it would cook on the other side.

"What about tonight?" Charlotte blinked trying to remember exactly what day it was. Last night had been puzzle night. That made it Wednesday. So today was Thursday. Tonight, Thursday night. And—

"I'm supposed to go out with Glenn," she reminded herself.

Nadine nodded. "You're not going to take Amber to something like that, are you?"

Something like that was a party in Glenn's district, but since all of his friends were about their age, no one brought children. Their children were either old enough to be married or to watch the other kids who weren't. And certainly no one brought an infant.

But even more than that . . .

"Glenn doesn't know," Charlotte said in whisper. She hadn't seen him in a couple of days, not since before the Fourth of July, when Amber had been left on her doorstep.

Nadine scooped the sausages from the pan and laid them on a paper towel to drain. "What are you going to do?"

What was she going to do? She looked back over to where Amber, continued to gnaw on the little biscuit in her hands. "I guess when he gets here tonight, I'll just explain to him that there's been a change of plans." That sounded perfectly logical. It wasn't like she wanted to leave the baby with Nadine. She wasn't about to ask. She had taken this responsibility on herself, and she would see it through. And surely Glenn would understand. He was kind and godly, an understanding man, after all. It might be a little bit of a surprise to him, but he would become accustomed to the idea. And it was only a couple of weeks. After that, Charlotte knew that she would be unable to pretend that the mother was coming back for Amber. Then she would have to turn the baby over to the authorities. But maybe—just maybe—if no one claimed the baby, she might be in line to adopt Amber for herself.

The idea came to her during the night, one of those times when she was about half asleep and still caring for the baby. She already had a connection established with Amber. Surely she had shown her willingness to care for the child. So maybe when the child was up to be fostered or even adopted, Charlotte would be first in line. With any luck, Glenn would be thrilled as well. After all, they were getting married. Though they hadn't set a date yet. it would be soon; Charlotte just knew it.

"It's all going to work out," Charlotte said with a firm nod. Positive thinking. That was what it came down to now. The more positive she was, the more positive things would turn out, and that was just what she planned on doing.

* * *

"I guess I just forgot how many diapers babies go through," Charlotte said sometime after lunch. The bag of diapers that Nadine had bought the day before was almost gone. They might have enough to make it through the evening but surely not through the following morning.

Nadine sighed and grabbed her purse. "I guess I need to go into town and get some more." Her mouth still held that sour twist, but it disappeared entirely when she turned her gaze to Amber. Nothing like a baby to bring out the good feelings in everyone.

"I would really appreciate it."

Nadine nodded. "I know that."

Nadine left, and Charlotte glanced at the clock on the mantel. It was off to one side these days, the picture that Nadine had painted on a date with Amos still taking center stage over the fireplace. Charlotte didn't mind. It'd been her idea to place the painting there, and she still liked it very much.

Twelve-forty-five. One o'clock was a good time for a nap, she thought. She looked down to where Amber sat in her car carrier, rattling a set of plastic keys and kicking her legs as if trying to fend off multiple intruders. Happily fend off multiple intruders. She didn't look as if she was anywhere near ready to take a nap.

Jenna had been a model child, but Charlotte had heard about children who would get more excited the more tired they got and she wondered if perhaps Amber was one of these children.

Charlotte was tired. Plum worn out. And she could use a tiny break herself.

She scooped Amber from the carrier and took her over to the couch. They could lie down together. Perhaps even

Charlotte's heartbeat would soothe the child to sleep. Charlotte herself might not actually get any sleep, but at least she could rest and not worry about the baby being too alert at a time when she should be taking a nap.

Charlotte propped the two of them up on pillows and wrapped her arms around the baby, and gently patted her on the back. How good it felt to hold her. How wonderful she smelled. How easy that warm weight nestled under her chin. That was the last thought she had before she drifted off to sleep.

"Charlotte?"

She jerked awake, instinctively wrapping her arms around Amber, but unable to determine what was happening. She had no idea of the time. And it took her a moment to figure out where she even was. She was at home. She was holding Amber. She was sleeping. Now Paul was standing over her.

"Paul," she said, trying to push herself into a seated position with one arm while she held tight to Amber with the other. Paul may have startled her awake, but the baby was sleeping soundly, mouth moving as she dreamed. "What are you doing here?"

He reached down and gently plucked the sleeping baby from her chest and cradled her close. "I just came to check on you."

Remarkably, Amber stayed asleep. Charlotte tried not to notice how natural Paul looked holding the baby. Or how handsome. Was there anything more precious than a man holding a baby? Not that she could think of.

She pushed herself upright and tried to wipe the cobwebs of sleep from her brain. "Okay."

"How are you?" he asked as he eased down into the couch next to her. He made no move to hand Amber back to her. And though Charlotte loved holding the baby herself, her second-favorite thing was watching Paul hold her.

Charlotte smiled and wrinkled her nose. "It's an adjustment is all." But it wouldn't last forever. She didn't have to remind Paul. He knew as well as she that the baby would have to go to someone in authority, and soon. Just not yet. *Please, God. Not yet.*

"I brought you some things." He nodded toward the side of the chair, where two paper grocery sacks, both full of miscellaneous baby goods, sat along with an independently standing mobile to be used for floor play.

"*Danki.* That's so kind," Charlotte said.

"Don't thank me," Paul said. "Clara Rose sent it over. I just brought it."

"But it's still very kind," Charlotte said.

"I think she wants the toy back, but the rest, she didn't say."

"I'll take care of all of it and send it back to her as soon as . . ." She didn't finish the rest. As soon as she could deny it no longer and had to take Amber to Child Protective Services.

"I just want to give the mom time," Charlotte said.

Paul nodded. "You don't have to convince me. I understand."

It was one of the things that she loved about him. Just one of the many things that made him her best friend. Paul always understood.

"Do you think I'm making a mistake?" Charlotte asked. She didn't have to elaborate as to what her mistake might be. Paul knew.

He took a deep breath and shook his head. "I think you have to do what you have to do, Charlotte." He paused for a moment as if gathering his words. "Who knows what's right and what's wrong in this situation?"

That was exactly what she had been thinking. How could the situation be right at all when the mother had left her child? Could it be that God wanted Charlotte to have this baby, this beautiful creature so perfect and tiny? Who was to say? How was she to know?

I just want to give her time to come back. I just want to give her time to realize what she might've done. I just don't want to be hasty. But she said none of those things to Paul. She didn't have to.

"When the time comes," Paul started, "I'll get us a driver and we'll go into town together."

"You'll go with me?" She hadn't thought that far into the future. She hadn't thought about going alone or going with somebody. She hadn't thought past just accepting that she knew she had to go.

"Of course I will." Paul smiled. "What are friends for?"

Chapter Thirteen

"He's here," Nadine said, glancing out the front window. She dropped her crocheting into the basket next to the rocking chair and stood. She cast one last look at Charlotte, then started from the room.

Charlotte stood as well. "Where are you going?" She patted Amber on the back, trying to burp the baby before Glenn knocked on the door. She wasn't sure that this new formula was sitting quite right with Amber. Charlotte wondered if the birth mom had been through something similar before determining that she couldn't take care of the baby. Or maybe Amber had been on a different formula entirely. Charlotte had no idea. She didn't have much experience with English baby formulas and, according to Nadine, there were about two thousand different kinds.

"I thought you might want some privacy." Nadine nodded as if trying to convince Charlotte as well.

"That's not necessary," Charlotte said. But she and Nadine both knew she was only trying to make excuses.

She was only trying to have a buffer between her and Glenn.

"I think I'll just go upstairs and read." Nadine was halfway to the second floor before Charlotte even took her next breath.

She needed to remain positive. For some reason, she had gotten it into her head that Glenn wasn't going to be happy about her keeping Amber for a while. Why wouldn't he be? It wasn't like it was a forever sort of thing. Just the thought made her heart beat high in her chest. She wanted it to be forever. And maybe it would be, given a chance. But she wasn't sure what God had in store for her. And Glenn had confessed his love. He had asked her to marry him—wasn't that part of the wedding vows? Children or no children? Or maybe just good times and bad. But didn't they both go together, almost the same thing?

Amber finally let out a burp as Glenn knocked on the door. Charlotte felt something warm and wet down her back. The baby had spit up.

No time for that now.

She crossed the room and opened the door, a bright smile on her face.

Glenn stood on the opposite side of the threshold. His smile froze, then fell from his face. "Whose baby?"

Charlotte continued to smile as she stepped back and allowed Glenn to enter the house. "It's kind of a long story." She handed him a burp rag, then turned her back to him. "Can you get that?"

She couldn't see his expression since she wasn't facing him, but she could hear the strain in his voice. "Get what?"

"The spit-up. I'm pretty sure she spit up on my back just before you knocked. Can you get it off for me?" There was a moment of thick silence; then she felt the towel and the pressure from his hand on her shoulder.

"There." His voice was flat.

Charlotte turned around.

Glenn held out the burp rag as if it were contaminated with a deadly substance.

Charlotte took it from him. "*Danki.*"

He gave a quick nod and then strode even quicker to the kitchen. She heard the water running for a moment before he returned smelling of the hand soap she kept by the sink. "Whose baby?" he said again.

Charlotte gave an uneasy chuckle. "It's kind of a long story," she said.

"You already said that."

"Come sit down and I'll tell you."

He warily eyed her, then made his way into the living room. He sat down on the couch and looked around.

For the first time today, Charlotte saw the room with fresh eyes. It looked like the baby department at Walmart had exploded. She'd had the baby for two days and yet there seemed to be baby things on every available surface. Diapers, wipes, burp rags, bottles, toys, blankets, diapers.

She eased down into the rocking chair and turned Amber around to face their guest.

"Glenn, this is Amber."

He frowned. "Are you babysitting?" He stopped. "I mean, you knew we were going somewhere tonight."

She gave him another soft, encouraging smile. "I'm not babysitting. Someone left her here the other day."

He shook his head. "Left her here? You mean came by and asked you to keep her for a couple of days?"

She shook her head, and beside her chair, Goldie thumped her tail against the floor in support. "Tuesday evening. The fireworks were going off and Goldie was going crazy."

"There's a surprise," Glenn said dryly.

Charlotte chose to ignore that. "When we finally went out onto the porch to see what all the commotion was all about, there was Amber."

He stared at her for a full minute before managing to find his words. "And she was just there? Nothing else?"

"There was a bag of things and she was in the carrier. Oh, and there was a note from her mother telling us to take care of her and that she was ours now."

Glenn shook his head "You can't keep her." He stood as if agitated and flopped back down again. "It's not like she's a puppy."

Charlotte's back stiffened. "I know that. But we talked it through and we're going to keep her for two weeks. You know, see if the mother comes back. I figure that within two weeks if the mother doesn't change her mind, she's not going to. I don't want to take Amber to the police and then have a confused young mother not be able to get her back."

"How do you know the mother's young? Did you see her?"

"No," Charlotte said. "We didn't *see* anything. But I figured the mom is young and English, probably not married, and most likely confused. A baby is a big responsibility." And Charlotte couldn't imagine that anyone, even young and confused, could walk away from this sweet one for long.

"You should take her to the police right now. I'll get us the car, and we can take her in immediately."

Charlotte shook her head. "I'm not going to."

"Charlotte," Glenn started, his voice sterner than she had ever heard it before. "You can't keep her."

"Then consider me to be babysitting. This is Amber, and I'm babysitting for her mother."

"I believe there are laws against this, Charlotte."

The thought that she was breaking the law made Charlotte's stomach clench. But even worse than being unlawful was the thought that Amber's mother could return to find her baby gone.

She knew that there were people—English people—who would probably think that anyone who could walk away from the child deserved to have it turned over to Child Protective Services and to most likely never see it again. Charlotte was not among them.

"I thought we could stay in tonight," Charlotte said, trying to change the subject. "We could maybe play cards or work on the puzzle. I think we may have a board game or two left from when Jenna was younger."

Amber picked that moment to decide that the formula Charlotte had fed her was not agreeable. The warm spit-up trickled down the fingers she had wrapped around the child's middle.

Glenn looked horrified. "She's throwing up again," he said.

"I think it's the formula. We've got to figure out something." She stood and propped Amber on her hip while she grabbed up a new burp cloth and tried to clean herself.

But now, in addition to having dribble all down her back, she had it all down her front as well. A new dress, a clean dress, was in order.

"*Jah*, you do," Glenn said. The words were stern, but his voice was gentle and Charlotte knew he meant well.

"I'll just go change," she said, starting for the stairs.

"*Jah*," Glenn said. "I think I should go now."

Charlotte stopped halfway to the staircase. "You don't have to go. I thought we were going to stay in tonight."

He didn't say the words, but she could see it in his expression. *I thought we were going out.* "I think you got your hands full," he said instead. He was out the door before she could utter one word of farewell. But it was no matter. Just as he shut the door behind him, Amber released the rest of her supper all down the front of Charlotte's dress.

It took two more trips to town on Friday to get a formula that Amber could keep down. Charlotte also discovered early on Saturday morning that if she premixed the formula and kept it in the refrigerator until it was time for Amber to eat, she seemed to tolerate it better. It was only by chance that she had discovered this, and she thanked God once again for such small miracles.

"Are you ready to go?" Paul asked bright and early Saturday morning. The sun was just barely up in the sky, but everyone knew that it was the best time to hit garage sales.

Charlotte cast a quick look at Nadine.

Her mother-in-law held Amber in one arm and waved them away with the other. "Just don't go overboard," she warned them. She didn't have to remind Charlotte that Amber would probably be there for only another week at most, but Charlotte hoped that if the baby's mother returned, she could gift the items to the young mother. Maybe that would take some of the stress off her, to have plenty of goods to help take care of the infant.

Every morning, they had looked in the paper to see if anyone had reported a missing baby. No one had. More than anything, Charlotte knew that if Amber had been stolen, someone would report the crime. If that was the case, she'd have no choice but to take the baby in to Child Protective Services. But there were no missing babies in the Wells Landing area. Surely, if something that big happened in Tulsa, they would hear about it as well. But there was nothing in the Tulsa paper either. Nadine had picked up one yesterday during one of her formula runs into town. No missing babies was just proof to Charlotte that she was doing the right thing by keeping the baby. At least for a little while longer. Which meant she would need a few more things to get them through.

"We'll only be gone a little while." By eight, eight-thirty at the latest, most of the good stuff was gone.

"I see you have your trailer, Paul Brennaman," Nadine said. Her tone was a hair away from accusing, but Charlotte didn't comment.

"By nine for sure," Charlotte said and followed Paul to the door.

She wasn't about to explain it to Nadine. But Paul had the trailer in case they found something big for the baby, like a crib. But only if they could get a good deal on it. Charlotte didn't need Nadine reminding her that, one way or another, the baby would be gone in ten days or fewer.

Charlotte was all too aware, even as she prayed for a way to keep the child.

How could she not? she thought as she climbed onto the tractor with Paul. She had prayed for such a miracle and, lo and behold, it had happened. There had to be something to that. Had to be.

Wasn't that what faith was all about? Believing against the odds?

She had believed. She had prayed. And God had delivered. But she still had some work to do. She didn't know how she knew. She just did.

"A crib?" Nadine screeched when Charlotte got home a few hours later.

Charlotte nodded. "It's lovely, *jah*?" It was a beautiful crib, cherrywood, dark and shiny. The mattress was new and the couple was even selling the sheets. In fact, the house had been a treasure trove for Charlotte and Paul.

The couple who lived at their second stop of the day had four children of their own, but in the typical English way, they planned for no more. Thus, they were selling all their baby goods. They had toys, clothes, and other essential pieces like the crib and a matching changing table.

Charlotte had known that it was presumptuous of her, but she'd had to have the items. How could God know that she was truly dedicated to caring for the child, if she didn't show Him? Buying the items would make her ready, and when God's final plan fell into place, Charlotte would be prepared.

She ended up spending nearly two hundred dollars at the one house and swore Paul to secrecy. It was her own money that she had saved from taking in sewing and such. When she and Nadine had moved down to Wells Landing, they had sold their individual houses in Yoder and split the cost of the new house. She still had that money saved, but this was different.

"Of course," Charlotte laughed as if she bought second-hand cribs every week. "She needs a place to sleep."

Nadine shook her head but didn't say anything more as Paul unloaded all their finds. Charlotte knew that she had spent too much on something that might not happen, but again, wasn't that faith? And she had nothing if she didn't have faith.

"How was she while I was gone?" Charlotte asked. She bustled into the kitchen and washed her hands, then reached for the baby.

"The trick worked with the formula. She didn't spit up once."

Charlotte smiled and kissed the spot where Amber's chubby neck met her chubby shoulder. "That's my girl."

Heavens how she had missed her!

How was that possible? She had barely been gone three hours, but it felt as if she had been gone a lifetime. What was going to happen when she had to turn the baby over to someone else?

She buried her nose in the sweet-smelling crook there and inhaled. She told herself that she would be okay turning the baby over to her mother. That was the main reason why she wanted to wait and see if the mother came back for her. But she wasn't sure how she would feel when—*if*—the time came when she had to turn her over to the state. She wasn't allowing herself to think about such matters.

Because she had faith. And faith would see her through. It had come to her last night that if God truly wanted her to have the baby, He would see it through. And that meant not turning her over to the state. Didn't it?

"That's everything," Paul said, dropping the last box by the door.

Charlotte smiled at him. "*Danki*," she said. He really was a true friend. "Come back for supper?" Charlotte invited.

"I thought Glenn was coming over," Nadine reminded her.

"That's right. But that doesn't mean that Paul can't come too."

Nadine frowned as Paul shook his head. "That's okay," he said. "Some other time maybe."

Charlotte nodded. "Some other time," she returned, but she wished more than anything he was going to be there that evening and she couldn't for the life of her figure out why.

"I don't understand," Glenn said as he sat at the table, his meal practically untouched before him.

"There's nothing not to understand," Charlotte said.

"Except for maybe that," Amos quipped.

Nadine sent him a look that clearly said, *Keep quiet!*

Amos ducked his head over his plate, but Charlotte had the suspicion it was only to hide his grin.

For some reason, Amos thought Glenn's problem with Amber was funny, but to Charlotte it was as serious as it could be.

She and Glenn were supposed to get married. He had

asked her. She had accepted. Who had known then that they would be having to jump the hurdle that now faced them?

"A baby." Glenn shook his head as if it was the most bizarre thing that he had ever heard of.

And that was what Charlotte couldn't understand. He had five children of his own!

"I told you," Charlotte said. "Nadine and I agreed on two weeks, then I'll contact the authorities." She had grown to hate that word. But she had faith. Faith to over-come.

The verse from Isaiah was never far from her thoughts. *So do not fear, for I am with you; do not be dismayed, for I am your God.*

"I just thought . . ." Glenn shook his head.

He needed time. That was all. It had been a shock to her and it was something that she had been praying for. It had to be an even bigger shock to him. And an adjustment period would surely be necessary. That was all.

"This looks like a little more than two weeks." He gestured toward the many new items that had been added to the growing pile of Amber's things. What had started out to be just a carrier and a bag of diapers had turned into a regular nursery of gadgets. The crib and changing table were up in Charlotte's room, but everything else—toys, playpen, swing, and stacks of clothes and blankets that still needed a good washing—were stacked all around, waiting for their turn.

She didn't want to admit it, but it did. It looked like way more than two weeks. And there went that faith thing again. Surely Glenn would come to realize what a blessing having Amber around would be. Or maybe he would just realize how important it was to Charlotte. Either way, she knew he would change his mind about the baby. After all, who could argue with God's plan?

"I just want to make sure she's got everything she needs," Charlotte said.

"I'd say she does," Nadine quipped.

Charlotte shot her a glare.

Glenn sighed and looked over to the laughing baby.

That's it, baby girl, she thought. *Keep turning on the charm*. It was almost guaranteed that he would be wrapped around the baby's finger before the end of the week.

Glenn smiled.

Charlotte hid her satisfied grin. There was a reason God had made babies lovable and cute. To melt the hearts of men like Glenn Esh. Skeptical men.

He reached out a finger and Amber took hold of it. She gurgled and laughed, then tried to pull his finger into her mouth.

With a slightly horrified look, Glenn pulled away and wiped his hand on his pants. At least that was what it looked like he was doing, but surely Charlotte had seen the gesture for something other than what it truly was.

He stood. "Let's go for a walk."

Charlotte shook her head. "I can't go for a walk."

"Why not?" He gestured toward the front window. "It's a beautiful day."

That part was true. The sky was an impossible shade of blue, and the sun was shining. Beautiful. And hot.

"It's almost a hundred degrees out there," she protested. "I can't take Amber out in that."

"Then leave her here," he said hopefully.

Charlotte stood as well, hoping that if she did her

rising irritation would stretch itself thin enough that it wouldn't come out in her next words. "I'm not going to do that."

"We'll watch her," Amos offered. "Ow."

Charlotte could only assume that Nadine had kicked him under the table for his offer, but she wasn't sure if it had more to do with them watching the baby or Glenn being a jerk.

"It will be fine," Glenn said.

Charlotte shook her head. Thankfully, Amos and Nadine remained quiet. "It won't be. Her mom abandoned her. I'm not going to have her think that I'm abandoning her too."

Glenn frowned. "You won't be abandoning her."

"She doesn't know that. All she knows is that she needs someone, and right now that someone is me. If I go out walking around with you, she won't know what's going to happen next." She shook her head. "No. It's not a good idea at all." It wasn't a good idea, and she wasn't backing down on her decision. This was a precious child they were talking about.

Glenn stared at her for what seemed like five full minutes, but it couldn't have been more than one. He took a deep breath as if he was about to say something, maybe protest more, but in the end, he exhaled and gave her a quick nod. "Fine," he said. And he made his way to the door. He pulled his hat off the peg next to it.

"Are you leaving?" Charlotte asked.

"*Jah*," he said. "I got some things I need to get done. I just forgot about them until now. And with tomorrow being Sunday . . ."

Charlotte nodded, though she had a feeling he wasn't telling her the complete truth.

Lord, open his eyes and make him see the blessing before us. Thank you. Amen.

"Be safe driving home."

"Are you going to be at church tomorrow?" Nadine asked.

Glenn's gaze flicked toward Amber, then back to the group of adults as he placed his hat on his head. "I'm staying in my district tomorrow. We're supposed to have a visitor."

He didn't elaborate, and Charlotte didn't ask. It was obvious that he didn't want to attend church with them. And that was his prerogative. He just needed some time, time to get used to the idea of Amber, and only the good Lord could help Charlotte with that. The only problem was He had less than ten days to melt Glenn's frozen heart and open him to the possibility that lie ahead. But with God, she knew, all things were possible. After all, look what He had accomplished in much less time than that!

"Well, that went well," Amos said.

"You're terrible, you know that?" Nadine said.

"What?" he asked. "I didn't do anything."

Charlotte turned from the door back to her mother-in-law and Amos. "No, it's fine. He's shocked. That's all. He just needs a little more time. And I'm going to honor him with that."

"Don't get me wrong," Nadine said. "She's a great baby. But she doesn't belong to us, and I can't help but feel that keeping her here for any amount of time could be a mistake."

Charlotte stiffened her back and sat down at her

sewing machine. She'd been working on a dress for Amber for church the next day when Glenn had come by, and now she needed to finish it or it would never be ready in time for the service tomorrow. "Love and care are never mistakes."

She didn't know much about English law, at least not when it came to people leaving babies on doorsteps. This felt more like the baby had been left just for her. And if she hadn't been, Charlotte still wanted to give her mother time to come back for her.

"We agreed to two weeks," Charlotte said.

Nadine nodded.

"By my math, that means I have nine days left." Nine days to convince everyone around her that Amber staying was just part of God's plan for them all.

Chapter Fourteen

By the morning, Charlotte's confidence was beginning to wane. And she couldn't blame it on a sleepless night. For the first time since she had brought Amber into the house on that fateful Fourth of July, the baby had slept for more than four hours at a time. They had worked out her spitting-up problem, and food was staying down. She seemed, for all intents and purposes, to be happy and healthy.

"I'm just not sure I should go," Charlotte said to Nadine over breakfast.

Amber was sitting in the car seat at one end of the table, Charlotte having already fed her while Nadine made biscuits and gravy.

"To church?" Nadine asked.

"*Jah*," Charlotte said. "Most new mothers don't bring newborn babies to church."

Nadine shot her a look but didn't have to say a word.

"I know I'm not her mother. And I know she's not a newborn. But . . ."

"You're worried about what everybody's going to say."

Charlotte threw up her hands in despair. "Wouldn't you be?"

"The people who are going to talk about this are going to find out about it eventually. She's been here for almost a week, and I've been going to town and buying diapers like they're fixing to stop making them."

"And I appreciate that," Charlotte said. "More than you'll ever know."

"I do it as much for her as for you," Nadine said. "She's a cutie. And she can't fend for herself. But there are people—"

"Don't say it," Charlotte interjected. "We agreed." And that two-week agreement kept getting brought up between them time and time again.

"Fine," Nadine said. "I won't say it. But you can't duck out from church because someone left a baby on your doorstep."

Charlotte sighed and stirred her last bite of biscuit around in what remained of her cooling gravy. "I guess you're right."

Nadine smiled in that self-satisfied way she had. "I know. And there's also the fact that you sewed her the cutest little dress."

That she had. She had missed making tiny little clothes for tiny little people. In fact, she had missed everything about being a mother, something she'd never thought she would say.

Probably just the hormones talking.

"The dress is cute," Charlotte said.

"And you're going to put that cute little baby in the cute dress and everybody can ask tons of questions and you're going to answer them and then, come next week, if her mother doesn't show up . . ."

"I know. I know," Charlotte said. She stood and scraped the last bite of her food into the trash, something she had never done in her entire life. But she just couldn't seem to eat any more today. *Jah*, she was that nervous.

"Now, about the dishes," Nadine said. She stood and started gathering up the jelly and applesauce from the table and putting all the things back into the icebox.

"You've been doing the dishes a lot lately," Charlotte said.

"I don't mind," Nadine said. "And I'm sure you'll find a way to make it up to me."

"I can make you some pumpkin bread," Charlotte suggested.

Nadine shook her head. "Please, no," she said. "My waistline can't handle any more desserts."

As she had known she would be, Charlotte was the talk at church. They had arrived a little bit late. Not for the service itself, but for all the visiting and talking that went on beforehand. They got in there just in time to take the baby carrier from the carriage and walk into the front door of the Widow Kate's house.

Charlotte could feel all eyes on her as she hefted Amber and her car seat through the living room and toward the back of the house, where the Widow Kate's bonus room sat, ready for the congregation.

She did her best to keep her eyes forward and her chin up, as if she came to church with a baby every Sunday.

"There she is," Jenna said, smiling and waggling her fingers at Amber. She held Nancy in her lap, bouncing the toddler to keep her occupied. "See the baby?" she cooed.

"Baby," Nancy said, and Jenna took her chubby little hands between her own and clapped. "Good job." But nothing more could be said as the church service began.

It was very hard to concentrate on the words that Strawberry Dan spoke to them. It would have been better if she could have blamed her inattention on Amber or needing to care for her, but the child seemed to take to an Amish church service as if she had been born to it. She fell asleep during the first song and remained that way for the balance of the service.

Charlotte tried to pay attention, she really did, but every time a father stood to take an infant from his wife in order to give her a break during the service, her concentration was broken. When it came to pass that she knew that she was going to get to keep Amber, would Glenn do the same thing?

Of course he would, because by then he would be accustomed to the idea of having a baby in the house. And yet . . .

Just as she had known would happen, the minute that church was released she was flocked by women. Half of the district wanted to know exactly how she had come to be in possession of a baby while the other half stood to one side of the yard and talked about her.

There was a part of her that wished she knew what they were saying and another part of her that wished she knew why women were so mean to each other. In the end, she waved it off. This was God's plan for her, and there was no man—or woman—on earth who could say otherwise.

"It's a miracle," she heard one woman say. And she knew that to be true.

"You aren't just going to keep her."

Charlotte turned as Eileen Brennaman came up. Charlotte might have only lived in Wells Landing for a year or so, but she had heard about the problems Eileen Brennaman had in trying to conceive a child. She had even tried adoption, and it hadn't worked. Now, someone had dropped a baby off on Charlotte's doorstep when she just as easily could have left the baby with Eileen.

Then Eileen would be in the same position that Charlotte was in.

Except Eileen had wanted a baby far longer than Charlotte, and Eileen had never had the blessing of a child of her own.

A flush of guilt flowed through Charlotte's face; then she shook her head and pushed the thoughts away. She couldn't question God's plan.

"I thought it best to keep her for a little while." Charlotte gave a wavering smile. "Just a couple of weeks. I want the mom to have time to come back for her, if she changes her mind."

Eileen pressed her lips together but gave an understanding nod. It was perhaps among the hardest of life's disappointments to deal with: the loss of a child and the inability to have children. Menopause. And she certainly couldn't tell Eileen that she had prayed because Charlotte knew without asking that Eileen had done the same. Yet

Charlotte's prayers had been answered with a child while Eileen's prayers had seemingly gone unnoticed.

God give you peace, she prayed. *Amen.*

"Then what are you going to do?" someone asked.

"Then I'll take her to Child Protective Services." *Unless God intervenes first*, she silently finished. She hated to even think about taking sweet little Amber to Child Protective Services, even if she knew it was the supposed "right" thing to do. The right thing, as far as she was concerned, would be to honor the wishes of the mother and allow the child to remain with her. Why, that girl, the mother, could have been watching Charlotte and Nadine, and maybe even Jenna, for a while. She might have known in her heart that she wanted Charlotte to have little Amber. She might have planned it from the time she got pregnant until that very moment.

Charlotte reined in her thoughts. She admitted to getting on her own internal soapbox, but it was so easy when her thoughts reflected and backed up her desires. She knew that the government took care of things like abandoned children, but it wouldn't be quite the same.

But the Lord takes care of those who take care of themselves. It might not be in the Bible, but it was about as true as anything she knew.

After several coos and *oohs* and *aahs* over Amber and how cute she was, it was time to go home.

Charlotte felt as if a great weight had been lifted from her shoulders when she climbed on to the buggy and started for home. She had made it. Absolutely made it until the end of the service.

"I wish Glenn had been here today," Charlotte said.

Nadine just gave a grunt and a nod.

"I know you don't approve," Charlotte said, as she kept her eyes on the road ahead. It was mostly unnecessary; their horse knew the way home. He could probably walk it in the dark with blindfolds on, but the road gave Charlotte something to look at other than Nadine's disapproving expression.

"It's not about approving or disapproving," Nadine said. "It's about—"

"About what?" Charlotte asked when Nadine abruptly stopped speaking.

Nadine shook her head, pressed her lips together. "I shouldn't say."

"I don't know what's stopping you now."

"Do you realize that you sound almost crazy?"

Charlotte let out a bark of laughter. "Crazy? I sound crazy?"

"You said you thought God wanted you to have this baby and that's why she was left on your doorstep."

"You don't believe in God's plan?"

Nadine paused long enough that Charlotte wondered if she was trying to get her words together or she was even going to speak at all. Finally she said, "How do you know this is God's plan?"

"Of course it's God's plan." It was something they had been taught from a very early age, all about God's will for the world, the circumstances around them. Everything from the color of their eyes to where they lived, God had a hand in.

"What if it's just a plan of a young, scared girl?"

It was one thing they agreed on, that Amber's mother must be a young English girl, maybe without any support from her family, confused and alone. Why else would she have left the baby on a stranger's doorstep?

Or maybe they weren't strangers. Maybe they had seen the girl in the grocery store or the post office. They could have run into her countless times before and never even realized they were destined to meet like this.

"How do you know that her plan isn't part of God's plan?"

Nadine threw up her hands and resignation. "I cannot."

"Why are you even saying these things?"

Nadine shook her head. "I suppose until you understand. I don't think the mom is coming back for that baby, and I don't think you're going to be ready to hand her over to Child Protective Services in a week. I'm even worried what they're going to say when you tell them that you've had the baby for two weeks. Did you know you could go to jail for that?"

Charlotte laughed in an incredulous way, even as her stomach fell. Jail? She hadn't thought about jail. "I'm babysitting." She stiffened her shoulders as if daring Nadine to contradict her. "Can you go to jail for babysitting?"

"So you're going to Child Protective Services to tell them that you were babysitting for a friend and that she never came back for her baby? What are you going to tell them your friend's name is?"

Charlotte released her breath in an exasperated growl. "I don't know. I just know that I have a purpose in this and it's been so very long since I had a purpose." There. She admitted it. Jenna was all grown up, Goldie was behaving, Nadine was getting married. Charlotte was left out in the cold. Thank heavens for Paul. Without him, she didn't know what she would've done.

And Glenn too, she hastily added.

But for the life of her, she couldn't figure out why Glenn and Nadine seemed so opposed to her caring for Amber.

As if realizing she was the topic of conversation, Amber let out a cry from the back.

Charlotte glanced over her shoulder, then handed the reins to Nadine. "Hold this. I think she needs her bottle."

"I can't drive from the side. The horse won't know what to do."

Charlotte grabbed the bottle from the diaper bag. "Just give me a minute."

"In a minute, I will run off the road." Nadine reached for the bottle that Charlotte held. "Give it to me."

Reluctantly, Charlotte gave Nadine the bottle and took back the reins to the horse. She wasn't sure they were quite in danger of running off the road, and she surely couldn't take that chance. Not with such precious cargo in the back seat.

Nadine turned in her seat to better feed the baby in the back. She didn't take her out of the carrier seat, just held the bottle while they rode along.

"I'm not against her," Nadine said. Her voice had taken on a whimsical quality. "I really am concerned for you, Charlotte."

"I'm fine," Charlotte said.

"I hope so. I know you've been having a tough time of it lately."

Tough time was right, but it was time to change all that. She had so many blessings, and that's what she needed to concentrate on. She needed to focus on the good things in her life. God had given her a chance to take care of this baby for even a short time, and who knew what He had in store for later. God had brought Glenn into her life and he had proposed, and now she was going to get married and she wouldn't be alone in her final days. It was another huge blessing that she tried to remind herself of daily. She still had Paul as the most wonderful best friend any person could ask for, male or female. And she had a wonderful family. A grandbaby on the way. More blessings than she could count. Not even counting the fact that her dog had finally started minding.

"I'm not going to say it's going to be a breeze if I have to take her to Child Protective Services," Charlotte started.

"*When* you take her into Child Protective Services," Nadine corrected.

Charlotte rolled her eyes at her mother-in-law. "But if that's God's plan, then that's what I have to do."

"It's not going to be easy."

Charlotte sighed. "Whoever said God's plan had to be easy?"

They checked the paper every day to see if someone had reported a missing child. To both her dismay and her elation, no one had. And with each day that passed, Charlotte fell a little more in love with Amber. And with each day that passed, she became a little more questioning of God's plan. She had thought at first that this was about the mom being able to change her mind and come back for the baby. And still Charlotte hoped against hope that

A NEW LOVE FOR CHARLOTTE 201

it was somehow the answer to her prayer of wanting a baby of her own.

But as Tuesday blended to Wednesday and somehow Wednesday became Tuesday of the following week, Charlotte knew that her time was at an end.

"It's been two weeks," Nadine said just after she finished the breakfast dishes. Her voice wasn't triumphant or even self-satisfied. Instead, she sounded sad, a little wounded, as if maybe she had been hoping this would turn out differently as well.

"I know." Charlotte finished changing Amber and buttoned up her little romper. She picked her up and cuddled her close, loving the solid warm weight, padded diaper butt, and the sweet essence that was innocent baby.

"I don't suppose Glenn will go with you."

Charlotte closed her eyes and held the baby close. So much love in such a tiny little creature. And then only for a short time. God sure knew what He was doing when He had made babies babies.

"I didn't ask him," she finally answered. And the truth of the matter was Glenn was perhaps the last person she wanted to go to Child Protective Services with. He had been waiting for this moment, waiting for the time when she would have to give the baby to someone of authority, as he liked to say. They were going to be married in a few months. And she didn't want to see triumph on his face as she handed the baby over to whoever was in charge of such things at Child Protective Services. She was afraid that would take their relationship to a place beyond repair.

"Amos and I can go with you."

"I think it's something I should do by myself." But that wasn't the exact truth. She didn't want to do it alone, but she didn't want anyone to witness her sadness when she handed the child over.

Not that she would admit it, but maybe it had been a mistake to keep the baby for two weeks. She had grown so terribly attached to her.

Even Goldie loved the sweet baby. And now she had to give her to strangers and Amber would go into the system. The mere thought of that, even though Charlotte didn't understand exactly what it meant, broke her heart in two separate pieces.

"You want me to drive? We can take the trailer and the two of you can ride in the back."

Charlotte shook her head. "I called Bruce Brown yesterday."

Nadine's eyes widened in surprise. "You did?"

"He's the best driver in these parts, *jah*?"

"That's what I hear," Nadine said.

"I asked him if he could accommodate a baby on the drive, and he said yes. He'll probably be here in about another hour."

"You want me to get her bag ready?" Nadine offered.

"That would be really sweet if you did," Charlotte said. Right now, she just wanted to sit and hold the baby close, listen to her heartbeat, pray that she knew someone cared. It just seemed brutal to hand her to someone who had no stake in the game. Was that how Amber's mom had felt when she had run off the porch and left the baby behind?

No, Charlotte would rather imagine that she'd been watching them from afar and chosen hers, out of any house in the area, as the best place to leave her precious child. It was little more than a fantasy, but it made her feel better.

"I won't just take you in and drop you off," Charlotte vowed, hoping on some level the baby understood, maybe instinctively, what she was trying to tell her. "I can't do that to you. I'll be by to check on you. I may not get to see you. I'll be honest, little one, I don't know what they'll do with you once I walk away. But do try to be good for whoever takes care of you."

Charlotte blinked back her tears. She wasn't going to cry. She couldn't cry now. She hadn't even left the house. If she started crying now, how would she be when she actually got to the offices?

She swallowed hard and continued. "I don't know much about 'the system' everyone talks about, and it doesn't sound good, but God will watch after you. If this was in His plan for you, I know He'll watch after you."

She kissed the top of her head and then inhaled that sweet baby scent.

She wouldn't believe this was a cruel joke played on her by a loving God. Though, at that moment, it felt a little like that. He had delivered her a baby after all her prayers, and now she had to turn around and give it back. Not even back. She would feel much better if she was actually giving the baby to her biological mother, but she was handing her over to a stranger, in an office, and she had no idea what would become of the child after that. Amber might be only two or three months old, but Charlotte wanted to be able to tell her what would happen.

Or maybe she just wanted to know for herself.

A knock sounded on the door just as Nadine came back down the staircase carrying the full diaper bag.

"Who could that be?" she asked.

The door opened. Paul Brennaman stood on the other side. "Anybody home?"

"Hi, Paul," Charlotte said, proud, or at least satisfied, that her voice didn't sound choked.

"I just came by to check on you today."

He had remembered.

"Are you going to drive the buggy into town?" he asked.

Charlotte shook her head, then laid her cheek against Amber's downy, rusty-colored hair. "A driver is coming."

She opened her eyes in time to see Paul turn toward Nadine. "I suppose Glenn is coming?"

Nadine frowned, then waved a hand as if wiping away his words. "Nope."

Paul's forehead crimped in confusion. "So you're going with her?"

"She said she wanted to do this by herself."

Paul made his way over to the couch and sat down next to Charlotte. "You can't go by yourself."

"I can. And I will. Bruce knows what's going on."

"Bruce Brown?" Paul asked. "The driver?"

"*Jah*," Charlotte said.

"He's a good driver. He's a good man. But you need a friend there."

She wasn't strong enough to argue with that. She wasn't strong enough to be a friend to someone while handing over this child who had come to mean so much to her.

"I'll go." Paul's words were emphatic.

"I told her Amos and I could go with her."

Charlotte shook her head. "I think I should do this alone."

To her surprise, Paul reached out and covered her hand where it lay on Amber's back. "No one should do anything alone when they have a good friend who is willing to do it with them."

"I don't know that I can do it." And that was the honest truth. She didn't know she could be there and give this baby up all the while knowing that someone was there watching her, someone that she cared about.

"I'll be there to help you be strong," Paul said. "I know I haven't spent as much time with her as you have, but I hate to see Amber go. Together we can do it. Two is always better than one."

Two was better than one. That was why she was marrying Glenn.

"That's true," Nadine said. She dropped the diaper bag into the armchair next to the couch and took up her place in the rocking chair. "Where would we be without our friends to help us through?"

Charlotte had no idea. And she never wanted to find out. But the biggest surprise of all was that Nadine, the mother of her late husband, had just lately become one of her best friends. She shouldn't be surprised at all. She should just call it what it was—all part of God's plan.

Chapter Fifteen

"This is it." Bruce Brown pulled the car to a stop in front of the square brick building.

Child Protective Services. It didn't look like much. Certainly not a place where she wanted to leave this baby whom she had come to love more than her next breath. Certainly not a place important enough to hold such business. Only the official seal of Mayes County, Oklahoma, positioned at one side of the door, gave it any official look at all.

"Thank you," Charlotte said. She held the folded bills she had already prepared over the back of the front seat toward Bruce. She couldn't look at Paul. She was afraid she would completely break if she did.

Bruce turned in his seat and pushed the bills back toward her. "Not this time."

Charlotte wanted to protest but couldn't. Not right now, anyway. His kindness was almost more than she could take on top of the stress of giving this baby to strangers. So she swallowed hard, gave a stiff nod, then fumbled with the car door trying to get out.

Paul had his door open in a heartbeat. "Here, let me."

He got out and walked around the car as Bruce said, "Just call me when you're ready, and I'll come get you." His voice was quiet and solemn. He knew as well as they did that when he came back, he would be faced with a more solemn time than he was right then. Without a doubt.

Thankfully, Paul managed to get her door open. Charlotte smiled in his direction, but still couldn't meet his gaze. She handed him the diaper bag, then got out and unhooked Amber's car seat.

"We'll call you," she said. Somehow she managed to get words around the lump in her throat. Suddenly she remembered a poster she had seen in town. The picture had been of snowcapped mountains, the words about love and freedom. If you love something, set it free, and if it comes back to you, it was meant to be yours. Something like that. She loved Amber and she was having to set her free. And aside from burying her husband and suffering through lost pregnancies, this was by far the hardest thing she had ever done.

Rain began to fall softly as Bruce Brown pulled away from the curb. Charlotte looked at the square building once more, took a deep breath, and started toward the glass doors in front. The sky was gray and spitting rain, a perfect reflection of her mood.

Paul didn't say a word. He just held the door open for her and they stepped inside.

Glass-enclosed cubicles sat on either side of her. In front of them was the desk in the shape of a half circle. A blond woman sat behind it, a headset plugged in the one ear. A testament to how many phone calls she took in a day, Charlotte supposed. They approached the desk, and she held up one finger as if to let them know she would be with them in a moment. That was the bad thing about this headset, Charlotte thought. You never knew when a person was really on the phone or just waiting for you to talk to them.

As they waited for her to finish the call, Charlotte went over in her head what she was going to say. She should start with her name, of course. Maybe something like, *Hello, my name is Charlotte Burkhart. And I have a baby here that someone left on my doorstep.* It sounded okay enough, she supposed, but somehow it didn't encapsulate all that she wanted to say. She wanted to explain it to the receptionist—Betty, according to her nameplate, which was pinned to her raspberry-colored shirt. Charlotte wanted to tell her how much she loved Amber, how good of a baby she was, and everything else that she had learned in the last two weeks. And that really wasn't all the truth either. She wanted to fall on her hands and knees and beg them to let her take Amber back home. To pretend as if she had never been there. But Paul's presence gave her strength. She would see this through. It was the right thing to do. Right? Yes. It had to be the right thing. If it wasn't, or if she didn't believe it was, then she wouldn't be able to sleep when she got home tonight.

"How may I help you?" Betty asked.

Charlotte took a deep, shuddering breath, the words she had formed suddenly deserting her. "I'm Charlotte," she said.

The woman waited for her to continue.

Paul shifted next to her.

Charlotte didn't seem to be able to say any more. What were the words she needed?

She sucked in another breath and tried again. "My name is Charlotte Burkhart, and someone left a baby on my porch."

Betty drew back in surprise, her blue eyes widening. "Oh, my. One moment please." She punched a button on the phone as Charlotte's heart begin to pound. "Julie? Yes, I have a lady here who has a baby she said was left on her porch. I don't know when. Yes. That's right. Okay."

"Ms. Briggs will be out here in just a moment to talk with you." She motioned toward the line of chairs in front of glass cubicle. "You may have a seat while you wait."

"*Danki*," Charlotte said. Then she shook her head. "Thank you." She started toward the chairs, but only made two steps in that direction before a woman appeared down the hallway to the left of the circular desk. "Hi," the dark-haired woman said. "I'm Julie Briggs. I hear you have a baby."

Charlotte turned around and nodded. "Someone left her on my porch." Just saying the words sounded ridiculous. Who would leave a baby on the porch? And she wondered if the woman believed her at all. Julie Briggs's eyes went wide, much like Betty's had, then she motioned for Paul and Charlotte to follow her back down the hallway where the line of glass cubicles continued.

"Follow me."

Charlotte felt Betty's gaze on them as they walked past, but she could do this. She knew she could. Only because she had to. Only because Paul was with her.

"Have a seat," Ms. Briggs said as she ducked into a cubicle that seemed a little bigger than the rest. She sat behind her desk and waited for Paul and Charlotte to get situated.

"And this is the child?"

"*Jah*," Charlotte said.

Ms. Briggs nodded. "And this was last night?" She turned toward her computer and started typing.

"Fourth of July," Charlotte said.

Ms. Briggs stopped typing. She turned to look at Charlotte. "That was two weeks ago."

"I know," Charlotte said.

Ms. Briggs didn't seem to know how to respond. "You kept the child for two weeks? Without contacting us?"

Charlotte nodded. "I wanted to give the mother time to come back. In case she changed her mind."

Ms. Briggs seemed to think about that. Paul simply sat next to Charlotte, lending her strength in his quiet presence. How she wished she could scoot her chair a little closer to his, close enough that maybe she could feel his warmth and gain even more courage from him. More courage than she was already getting. This was harder than she had thought.

Lord, I trust in You. I believe in You. I know You want what's best for me. I know You want what's best for Amber. Amen.

"Normally people bring the child in immediately," Ms. Briggs said.

Charlotte nodded. "I understand. But I have a note." She reached into her purse and pulled out the envelope they had found in the carrier with Amber. She handed it across the desk to the woman. "As you can see, she left me with permission to care for the baby."

Ms. Briggs took up a pair of reading glasses from her

desk and perched them on the end of her nose as she looked over the note that Amber's mother had left. "I see," she said. She scanned the page one more time, then let it fall to her desk. "It would need to be a legal document," she said. "And the signature is not legible. We don't even know who Amber's mother is. Or if it was even her mother who left her on the porch."

Charlotte nodded. "I understand. I only want what's best for the baby."

Ms. Briggs nodded, and Charlotte tried hard not to dislike the woman. She was only doing her job, yet Charlotte felt that her job was simply to take Amber from her.

"May I see the child?"

Charlotte wondered what would happen if she told Ms. Briggs no. Instead, she stood and hoisted the carrier onto her own seat. With trembling fingers, she unhooked the giggling baby and, for a moment, held her close. She wondered if this might be the last time she ever held her.

She pushed the thought away. She trusted in the Lord.

I will trust, and not be afraid: for the Lord Jehovah is my strength.

That wasn't all of the verse and she couldn't remember what book or chapter, but it was enough. She would have courage. She would have strength, because she trusted in the Lord.

Charlotte did her best not to cuddle Amber close to her one last time, even if she wanted to bury her nose in that soft crook where her neck met her shoulder. She wanted to kiss the soft spot just behind her ear and smell the sweet baby smell that she had missed so much. She wanted to inhale the memory so she could hold it forever, but was this the memory she wanted to remember?

Handing her over to Ms. Julie Briggs at Child Protective Services?

What if she never gave her back?

I will trust in the Lord.

"She's a good baby," Charlotte said. She was proud that at least her voice didn't sound strained, or choked, and she didn't sound near tears. But this was important. She had done what she was supposed to do. She was bringing the baby to the authorities. Surely they would let her keep Amber until they found her a proper home? Yet why couldn't Charlotte's home be the proper home? That was what she wanted to know. God had left this baby for her. Surely they could see that as well.

"She seems healthy," Ms. Briggs said. "And well taken care of." She ran a hand down the pale pink dress the baby now wore. "Did you make the dress for her?"

Charlotte returned to her seat and nodded. "I did."

"That was very kind of you."

"I need to know," Charlotte said. "May I keep her?" The sentence sounded ridiculous. Why shouldn't she keep her? The mother had left her, Amber, for Charlotte to keep. What gave the county or the state or whoever the right to give her to someone else? It just didn't make any sense. Which had to mean that God was on her side.

Ms. Briggs gave her a pained smile. "That's not up to me. If you have registered as a foster parent, then I will do what I can to get her placed in your home, but these sort of things . . ." She shook her head. "It's not up to me."

She cradled the baby in one arm, then buzzed someone on her intercom phone. "Susan, I have an infant for examination."

Charlotte sat in shock. "You're going to keep her now?"

Paul reached out and patted her arm, but she hardly noticed. "I thought I would have—"

She stopped as Ms. Briggs sadly shook her head. "These matters are out of my hands. But if you fill out the foster paperwork and the documentation, we'll do what we can about getting her placed with you."

"But—" Charlotte said. She was interrupted as the door behind them opened and a woman, most likely Susan, stepped inside. She wore creased brown slacks and a gold-colored sweater with short sleeves. Her auburn hair was flipped off her neck, and she smiled politely at both Paul and Charlotte. Then she took the baby from Ms. Briggs and disappeared back out the door. It seemed to happen so fast that Charlotte didn't have time to breathe before it was all over.

It was all over.

Amber was gone.

"I need to get some more information from you," Ms. Briggs said. But Charlotte could barely understand the words over the buzzing that had started in her ears. Amber was gone.

Paul cleared his throat. "What do you need to know?"

"Last name?" Ms. Briggs said.

"Burkhart," Paul supplied.

"Address?"

Paul scooted a little forward in his chair, most likely to answer Ms. Briggs's question, but Charlotte managed to pull herself together in time to give the woman her address.

She asked other questions, things that Charlotte had never even thought about. If the baby had had bruises when she found her. Had she been left in the cold? *How could it have been cold?* Charlotte thought. It was July.

Ms. Briggs also wanted to know if the baby had been left with food, that sort of thing. There seemed to be a million questions, but the one Ms. Briggs kept asking in various ways was why it had taken her two weeks to bring the baby in.

She couldn't very well say, *I wanted to keep her for myself. I thought God had left her for me.* Not if she wanted to have the woman even consider giving the baby back.

But Charlotte was really beginning to think that, no matter what she said, she wasn't getting Amber back. She had a feeling that she could fill out all the foster paperwork they had in this office and the next one over and she still wouldn't have that baby.

"What happens to her now?" Charlotte asked.

"She'll get registered into the system. That's why it's very important for you to fill out the paperwork if you would like to foster her until we find her a permanent home."

"If I foster her, can I be on the list to be her permanent home?" As she spoke, tears started to form in her eyes and slid down her cheeks. Charlotte let them fall, unashamedly. Ms. Briggs looked from her to Paul and back again. "Anything is possible."

Empty.

She felt empty. Beyond empty if there was such a thing. She felt as if she had lost her arm or leg; something precious had been torn away from her. In reality, she supposed it had.

Paul had helped her fill out the foster care paperwork, and Ms. Briggs promised to have it pushed through the system as quickly as possible. There was that phrase again, *the system*. It was like it didn't exist beyond anything of this world. Kind of like when people said *they*. As in *they say* . . .

Paul called Bruce Brown to come back around and get them, and he arrived within five or ten minutes. The woman behind the desk kept her head down and refused to look at either Charlotte or Paul as they waited in the hard-backed chairs provided in the little narrow hallway that led to her desk.

Empty and alone.

Paul helped Charlotte into the car, and they silently drove back to Charlotte's house.

Once again, Bruce refused any payment for his services, and Charlotte understood why he was a favorite driver among the Amish. He was as kind and caring as a man could be.

Charlotte and Paul got out of the back seat. Nadine met them on the porch.

"Where's Amber?" She looked around as if they might be hiding her someplace. Then she watched as Bruce turned his car around and, with a small wave, made his way back down the driveway toward the road. "Where . . ."

Paul shook his head.

Charlotte was thankful for his quiet answer. She had cried all the way home, silent tears of loss. This was supposed to turn out differently. She had trusted God;

she had trusted the system. It seemed they both had let her down.

"Are they going to allow you to foster her?" Nadine asked.

Once again, Charlotte couldn't speak. Or maybe it was that she was reluctant to. She was afraid that once she started talking, she might end up screaming, and if that happened, she wasn't sure she would be able to stop.

Why was this happening? Hadn't she trusted God? Hadn't she done the right thing? Why was doing what was right coming back on her? Why did it hurt so much? Why hadn't it turned out in her favor? Why? Why? Why?

"We filled out the paperwork," Paul said as they filed back into the house. "But the lady who helped us said that babies were usually placed quickly, and it'll take at least a week to get Charlotte's paperwork in order and that was if she put a rush on it."

Nadine collapsed onto the sofa as if her legs weren't strong enough to hold her any longer. "So she's just . . . gone?"

Charlotte felt as if someone had ripped out her heart, leaving a big, gaping hole where it had been. "She's gone," she finally managed. And nothing would ever be the same again.

"Be sure you keep an eye on her," Paul said to Nadine a few minutes later.

Charlotte had gone to the kitchen, and Paul suspected she was in there finding something to bake, leaving he and Nadine in the living room to work out the rest of it.

"She seems to be taking it quite well," Nadine said. "Better than I thought, anyway."

Paul nodded. "That's what has me worried. I feel like she's bottling things up." She might be crying or she might have tears in her eyes on her cheeks, but she wasn't expressing her full emotion. That had him concerned.

"I'll watch her."

Paul stood "I'm just across the hill if you need anything." He needed to get home. He had a little bit of work to do, but he also needed a little time to work through all this himself. He would miss that little munchkin. He had gotten used to having her around.

"I suppose I should go call the Lamberts to let them know that puzzle night is cancelled." Nadine stood as well.

He had forgotten it was Wednesday.

"Don't you dare." Charlotte stood at the doorway leading to the kitchen. Paul wasn't sure how much of their conversation she had overheard, but she had definitely heard the last part. "We will not be canceling puzzle night."

"Charlotte," Paul and Nadine said at the same time.

They turned to look at each other. Paul nodded in Nadine's direction, allowing her the lead.

"We really need to cancel puzzle night," Nadine started. "I think you need rest."

Charlotte shook her head. "There will be no resting. It is puzzle night and that is the night I get to spend time with my daughter, and I will spend it with her working the puzzle of her choice. Right now I'm baking scones for us to have, and I would appreciate if the two of you did not make plans for me behind my back."

"I'm sorry," Paul said. "We're just concerned about you."

Charlotte gave a stern nod. "Accepted. And I appreciate your concern. But it is not necessary. I have faith. God got me into this mess, and God's going to get me out of it."

One way or another. Paul heard the words, but she didn't say them. But that was Charlotte. She was thankful, she was true, and she was strong. And he was glad she had faith. That would see her through.

"And I will see you at six o'clock." She pinned Paul with another look.

He nodded, then grabbed his hat from inside the door. "See you then," he said, then made his way out of the house down the porch steps.

He walked stiff-legged back across the field, feeling as if someone was watching him. Most probably Nadine, looking out the window after him, wondering how she was going to handle the afternoon by herself. In all truth, he felt like he couldn't get away from the house fast enough. He supposed he just needed his own time to sort through the events. Charlotte had been so happy to have that baby, to be able to care for her. And he had been happy that Charlotte was happy. Now he still couldn't help but believe that eventually she would lose this small bit of control she had over her emotions. The dam would break, and it would all come spilling out. He just hoped they were all ready for that when it happened.

"How'd it go?" Clara Rose asked as he started across the yard.

He stopped and turned toward his daughter-in-law. "Is Obie in there?"

She shook her head. "He went over to Elam's. I take it not so good."

Paul sighed and started toward the porch. "Can I bother you for a cup of coffee?"

Clara Rose opened the door and motioned Paul to come inside. "Anytime," she said. "You know that."

He took Paul Daniel from her as he stepped into the house. It didn't compare, but he couldn't help but think how he would feel if someone came and got the child. He would be beyond heartbroken. Devastated. It had to be some measure of how Charlotte felt in that moment, though she acted as though all was fine.

He sat at the kitchen table, the toddler balanced on one knee, as Clara Rose poured them both a cup of coffee. "Would you like a snack? Some cookies maybe?"

He shook his head. "Charlotte likes to bake when she's agitated. I figure there'll be more than plenty for puzzle night tonight."

Clara Rose slid into her seat, her eyebrows raised, mouth slightly open. "You're still having puzzle night?"

"She said we had to have it. That she wanted to spend time with Jenna."

Clara Rose took a drink of her coffee. "I can understand that."

"She also said that God got her into this mess and He would see her through it."

"I can see that too." Clara Rose nodded.

"But I lost her though," Paul said. He had been hoping against hope that something would happen between her and Glenn, something big enough that she would forget about the other man and see Paul for more than just a friend.

"How so?"

Of all his family, only Clara Rose and Obie knew that he was in love with Charlotte. Now especially, he planned to keep it that way. "When we were filling out the paperwork for her to foster the baby, they asked if I was her husband. In fact, they called me Mr. Burkhart. I had to correct them. But when I did, I could tell that the worker didn't like that answer. Well, she didn't like it when Charlotte told her that she wasn't married. Then Charlotte said she was engaged."

"To Glenn," Clara Rose said.

"Who else?" Paul asked with a shrug.

"And you think this means you lost her?"

"What else could it mean? She even gave them his name and contact information. I guess they check that sort of thing. I suppose they feel there are enough English single-parent homes that they didn't want to create an Amish one." He bounced Paul Daniel on his knee as he shook his head. He felt the need, the urge, to move and just keep moving. As if he could outrun the truth. But there it was, staring him straight in the face.

"So you think Glenn will marry her so she can get the baby? I don't understand," she said. "If they were going to get married anyway . . ."

Paul set the toddler on the floor and stood, unable to remain in one place for any longer. "That's just it. I was hoping they wouldn't get married."

"That sounds like exactly what's going to happen unless you say something to her. Are you?"

"Am I what?"

"Are you going to say something to her? How is she supposed to know how you feel if you don't tell her?"

"What if I tell her and she laughs at me?" He shook his head, unable to handle the immature feelings he was having. He couldn't stand that rejection. He supposed he would rather lose her to Glenn and keep her as a friend than lose her altogether. The biggest problem of all was he didn't think he could win her in the end.

Chapter Sixteen

"I was just getting used to having a baby sister," Jenna said with a frown over their puzzle that evening.

"You'll have enough on your plate when your own baby comes," Charlotte said. "Besides, I'm not sure this is over yet." She said the words as if she wasn't certain of it, but she was certain. It was not over yet. She had put her faith in the Lord. She had put her trust in God, and she knew He would see her through.

Unfortunately, God had to work through Child Protective Services. Charlotte had filled out all the paperwork; she had done everything she was supposed to do. She had taken care of the baby, and taken care of her well. She was engaged to be married and would provide a loving, stable home for a child who had been left for her. It was only a matter of time.

It had taken her a while to gather her thoughts and get everything in line to see the big picture of what was happening around her. A little while, a lot of prayer, and a couple of batches of cookies, but she knew that Amber was to be hers. She knew that she and Amber and Glenn would be a family, loving and caring and leaning on each other through good times and bad. She knew. But she couldn't let her knowledge or her faith make her appear arrogant. So she added words like *maybe*, *I suppose*, and *soon*.

"I'm glad to see you taking it so well," Nadine said.

"Just don't take it so well that we can't get a coconut cake this week," Amos said.

Nadine bumped his elbow with her hip. "Behave yourself, Amos Fisher."

She frowned at the man, but Charlotte smiled. That was what they needed, a little levity to the situation. Things had gotten way too serious today, and she knew that seriousness would not solve their problem. Only prayer, positive thoughts, and belief in the Lord.

"I might can see my way to baking you one later this week," Charlotte said. "But I gave you the recipe."

He nodded and fitted up a link of three pieces into the main puzzle. It just about completed the Dutch plate in the picture. "That you did, and as good of a baker as I am, mine just doesn't come out the same as yours."

"Did you use fresh coconut?" Charlotte asked.

"As fresh as I can find," Amos said.

Charlotte shook her head. "I mean fresh coconut like 'cracked it open yourself and shaved it from the husk.'"

"That I did not do."

Charlotte gave him a satisfied nod. "Well, there you go then. It just depends on what lengths you are willing to go to make it the best cake ever."

"I suppose so," he said.

Just like with anything in life, Charlotte was willing to go as far as it took to get the things that she wanted, the things that she needed in this world. Amber was one of those things. And she was willing to go as far as she had to in order to make it happen.

Charlotte kept herself busy. She wanted to sit at the window and watch for Child Protective Services to bring Amber to her. She checked the phone shanty three times a day, but otherwise made herself stay at the house. She needed to do her work, all the things she normally did, including playing with Goldie and reorganizing the tack room in the barn. But four days had passed and no one had come.

Now it was Sunday morning, church Sunday. And she would have to go to church without the baby.

Truth be told, she had thought she would have Amber back by now. She had done nothing but take care of that child, and she had taken care of her well. She had brought her back with clothes, formula, and all the things they needed to take care of her, but she hadn't told them that they needed to premix her bottle so she wouldn't spit up. She had thought about calling Ms. Briggs at the Child Protective Services offices and telling her that the bottles needed to be made in advance, but she'd feared it might make her look a little too zealous and that could work against her. So she had remained at home, remained positive, and waited for Amber to come back to her.

Now it was Sunday and she had to go to church and face all the members of their district without the baby she had proudly shown everyone the church Sunday before.

She was still trusting in the Lord. He would see her through.

That didn't make it easy though. She arrived at church

with her head held high, but it was more than difficult to smile and tell everyone that she had taken the baby to Child Protective Services—as was expected of her—and that she didn't know how she was doing. Or where she was. Or who had her now. Charlotte only knew that Amber was "in the system."

But she had to believe that the Lord would bring her back. Each day, it became a little more difficult. And today was the hardest by far. It was one thing to hold the hope at home alone, or with friends, and quite another to do so with everyone in the district around her.

She knew they were talking about her when she wasn't around. The thought shouldn't have bothered her, but it did. The Amish were always talking about their neighbor. They cared about each other and they couldn't spread the word of someone's trials if they weren't spoken of, but she wanted to stand up and tell everyone that she had faith, she had hope, and that Amber would be brought back to her. Even if she had started to wonder if that was the truth.

She had believed it one hundred percent on Wednesday evening. Now, her faith was beginning to wane. And that was something she wouldn't admit, not to anyone but herself.

Maybe that was why she was so determined to make everyone know that she had faith. Unwavering faith.

"That was a brave thing you did," Maddie Kauffman said, sidling up to Charlotte where she stood at the edge of the yard at Titus and Abbie's. It was their turn to host church, and the meal afterwards usually turned into a show of camels.

Thankfully, Jenna hadn't gotten in the pen with the

large animals since she had found out that she was having a baby, but Charlotte still worried about her being around such beasts day in and day out.

"What's that?" Charlotte said.

"Turning that baby in."

Brave. She could hardly call what she did brave. She did what anyone would have done. And now she had to be patient and wait for her reward. Wait for the good Lord to return Amber to her.

She shrugged, unable to give any part of her thoughts as an answer.

"They could have said all sorts of things, that maybe you hurt the baby. Or didn't care for her properly."

The thought sent Charlotte's stomach plummeting. "I would never."

"Well, I know that and you know that, but they don't know that. And you know how the English can be."

The English had never been anything other than good to Charlotte. The Amish in Yoder had a wonderful relationship with the Englishers who lived there too. It was the same in Wells Landing, as far as she could see.

Still, the thought had her worried. Perhaps she wouldn't get a chance to foster Amber. Perhaps they would think that living without electricity wouldn't be good for the baby. In the summertime, it was hot and there was nothing to do about it but open the windows and pray for a breeze. In the winter, they could at least build a fire and put on extra clothing. What if whoever was in charge of placing Amber was prejudiced against the Amish? There were those out there who felt the Amish were backward and unclean. And she supposed some were, but it certainly

didn't describe her household. But if they already had
their minds made up . . .

"I see Nadine," Charlotte said, without responding to
Maddie. She was only trying to stir things up. And it had
worked. She had certainly stirred up Charlotte. "Excuse
me." She brushed past the other woman and went in
search of her mother-in-law.

She found her with Amos, talking about the best place
there was to fish.

"I'm ready to go now," Charlotte said.

"Amos and I are heading over to Taylor Creek for a bit."

"In your buggy?" Charlotte said.

Amos shrugged. "It's not that far. I want to show Nadine
a new fishing site I've been hearing about."

"Isn't it too hot to go fishing?"

Amos shot her a look that clearly said that wasn't possible.

But she didn't want to go home alone. And if they went
over to Taylor Creek, that's exactly what would happen.
She would be alone. With her thoughts. And right now,
that seemed like a disaster waiting to happen.

But what choice did she have?

"I'll see you when you get home," she grumbled and
turned away to get her buggy.

This had nothing to do with jealousy, she thought as
she drove home. This was purely survival. And she wished,
so wished, that Nadine was right beside her in that moment.
Charlotte supposed she could drive on over to Glenn's
and visit, but it was a goodly way over to his house and
he hadn't come to their church service. In fact, he'd been
more aloof than ever since she had taken Amber in to
Child Protective Services. She wasn't sure why that was

exactly. He had never seemed very keen on the idea of Amber staying with Charlotte, but she had figured he would come around soon enough. It seemed now that Amber wasn't around, he should be even closer to her. But right now, that wasn't the case.

Maybe she could go home and try out a new recipe. She had found a cookbook with a bunch of chocolate desserts in it at the last garage sale she had gone to. Maybe she could make two or three. She wondered how much cocoa she had as she pulled down the drive.

Glenn's buggy sat directly in front of the house.

It was as if she had called him with her thoughts. But she was glad to see him. And she supposed she could make one of the recipes in that cookbook to try with him this afternoon. The best part of all, she didn't have to be alone.

"Fancy seeing you here," she said as she hopped down from the buggy. Charlotte unhooked the horse and took her over to the barn. She gave the mare a scoop full of oats and promised her a good brushing later.

"I didn't get up in time to drive over for the service today," he said. "Woke up with a headache."

Charlotte made a sympathetic face. "That's too bad. I hope you're better now."

He nodded and gave her that slick Glenn smile. "*Jah*, of course."

Charlotte hooked one arm over her shoulder and started for the front door. "Come on inside. I'll see if I can rustle us up something to snack on."

She walked into the house, for the first time realizing that it still very much looked like a baby lived there. She hadn't taken all of the things with her to Child Protective Services, and honestly she hadn't known exactly what Amber would need. Plus she had held some sort of hope that Amber would be coming back to the house with her. As it was, there was no baby, but there was a baby swing, stacks of diapers, tiny clothes, and all sorts of toys in the living room. There was a line of bottles in the kitchen and baby furniture upstairs in her room. All just waiting for the time when she got Amber back again. And that was exactly what she wanted. Faith was not believing anything to the contrary.

But she looked at the room now from Glenn's eyes. She supposed, to him, it looked a little messy, a little unkempt, seeing as how Amber was with another family until Charlotte could get put through the foster system.

Well, that was too bad. She would be back soon enough and that was something Glenn needed to accept, especially if he and Charlotte were going to get married. As far as she knew, the wedding was still on.

"I have some brownies from yesterday," Charlotte said as she buzzed into the kitchen, Glenn trailing behind.

She turned as he made a face. "Brownies?" His voice sounded uncertain.

"*Jah.*" She nodded, then waited for him to continue. Everyone knew that brownies were the ultimate dessert, so why did he seem so unsure?

"I'm not a big fan of chocolate," he finally admitted.

Charlotte couldn't help the drop in her jaw. Thankfully she didn't have to use her hand to put her chin back in place. "What does that mean 'not a big fan'?"

"I don't like it," he said with a shrug.

How in the world could anyone not like chocolate? The idea was unfathomable and just another of the differences between the two of them. As far as Charlotte was concerned, chocolate was a gift from God. Proof that He loved them.

Well, no matter. It was just food, right?

"Would you like some coffee?"

Glenn nodded and slid into place at the table. He waited as Charlotte puttered around, getting the coffee ready and heating water on the stove.

She poured them each a cup of coffee, then sat in the chair opposite him.

"*Danki*," he said.

She gave him a nod. Then she took a sip of her coffee and sighed. "It sure is quiet without her here," she said.

Glenn looked around as if trying to figure out if they were missing someone. It wasn't like they needed to be chaperoned. They were engaged, after all. "Nadine," he said with a nod. "Where is she?"

Charlotte bit back another sigh. "Not Nadine. Amber."

Glenn nodded, traced a line on the table that only he could see. "*Jah*, Amber."

"And to answer your question, Nadine and Amos went to Taylor Creek to look at a new fishing hole. I'm not sure exactly what that means."

Glenn gave a small chuckle. "Neither do I, really. Those two really do love fishing."

"I'm glad they have that in common," Charlotte said. It was good to have things in common with the person you loved. She and Daniel had had a great many things in common, and then they had had Jenna, which had brought them even closer together. If Jenna had had her accident before Daniel had died, Charlotte felt that would have brought them even closer to one another.

And she had things in common with Glenn. Like . . . something. She had to have something in common with Glenn or they wouldn't have agreed to marry. Maybe they didn't have much in common, she and Glenn. But everyone said that opposites attract. Maybe that old adage was really true.

"I suppose," Glenn said. "There's a get-together next week."

"In your district?" she asked.

"Over at Chris Mast's house."

Charlotte thought back and tried to place Chris from the last get-together she had been to. "Is he a Mennonite?"

Glenn nodded. "A good fellow. He and his wife are going to host a game night for everyone."

Game nights always sounded like great fun, but unfortunately Glenn's idea of a game night and Charlotte's weren't exactly the same idea.

Opposites.

And when a couple was opposite, they just had to try a bit harder. This get-together would be her turn at trying harder and enjoying a game night set up by his friends. That was what people did when they were in love, right?

"Sounds like fun," she lied. Well, it wasn't a complete lie, more of a stretched untruth. It did sound fun, just not the way they would execute it. But she so wanted to spend time with Glenn. She needed to spend time with another, doing something to keep herself busy until Amber came back.

Lord, please let Amber come back. Amen.

"It's on Thursday."

She nodded in agreement. It would've been better had the get-together been tomorrow night or Tuesday or maybe even one get-together every night of the week. She desperately needed to stay busy.

"I thought we might announce our intentions to everyone," he said.

His words took Charlotte by surprise. "Intentions?" she asked.

He nodded. "*Jah*. Of course."

"A-about getting married?" she stuttered.

"*Jah*." He chuckled. "You wanted to keep it a big secret?"

"*Jah*. Well, no. I mean, I don't have feelings one way or the other, but most couples keep a second marriage a little bit of a secret until closer to time."

"Maybe, but I like to do things a little differently. Besides, why shouldn't we tell everyone that we're getting married this fall?"

This fall? Her heart gushed with emotion. She wasn't going to be lonely or left behind. She might be left heartbroken if Amber didn't come back to her, but at least she wouldn't be alone. Or lonely. At least she would have Glenn there to comfort her.

"That would be wonderful," she said. Her face flushed with heat, and she figured she was the color of an overripe plum. But it didn't matter. She and Glenn were getting married in the fall. They were telling his friends come Thursday, and hopefully no later than Friday she would have some word on her foster parent status. Until then, she would continue to pray for Amber, her safety and her health. And to say thanks to God for all the blessings He had allowed her.

"You're in a good mood," Paul said sometime late Monday afternoon. He hadn't been able to spend any time with Charlotte on Sunday. He had come over the hill, spotted Glenn's buggy, then disappeared back the way he had come.

Paul wanted to spend time with Charlotte, but not with Glenn around. He supposed he was a glutton for punishment, but he didn't like the reminder of her relationship with the other man. The problem was Paul couldn't very well ignore it with the man in the same room. So he had bided his time until today, when he knew he could come over and visit without anyone else there to bother.

Charlotte smiled. "I am. *Jah.*"

She was in a wonderful mood.

"Did I miss a visit from Child Protective Services?" he asked.

"No." Then she looked from one side of the empty yard to the other. Empty except for Goldie, who was sniffing around the tree either tracking a squirrel or looking for a good place to pee. "Glenn asked me to marry him."

Paul frowned and did his best to hide his pain at the words. "I thought he had already asked you."

"Well, *jah*," Charlotte stuttered. "I mean we set a date."

Paul's heart withered right there in his chest. Now it was real. With a date. How could he deny that it was truly going to happen when they had set a date? He supposed he should have learned from his son and Clara Rose that it wasn't over until it was over, but he knew. This was it. He had well and truly lost Charlotte to another man. "When?" he croaked. He was still glad that the word sounded like a word and not the strangled cry it felt like as it bubbled up inside him.

"This fall." She smiled as if the world were hers on a silver platter.

"When?" he asked again.

"Sometime." She gave a negligent shrug.

"So you didn't set an actual date?" Paul asked.

"Well, no," Charlotte said. "But we decided on this fall."

"And that's what has you in such a good mood?" He wasn't sure he would ever understand women.

She smiled again. "*Jah*. See, Nadine and Amos are getting married in the fall. I think, anyway, so I won't be here all by myself for long if at all. And if everything goes well with Amber and the fostering, then I should have her back before long."

And all her dreams would come true.

But something she'd said bothered him. He couldn't figure out exactly what it was, and he didn't take the time to examine it while he was spending time with her. It was July, and if she and Glenn were going to get married in the fall, then Paul only had a few more months to spend time with her as friends until that would have to end. He was certain Glenn wouldn't want his wife hanging around with another man. Paul knew he surely wouldn't allow such a thing. But until then, until they said their vows, he swore to spend as much time with her as possible.

Somehow, Charlotte made it through the week without losing her elevated mood. She had to work at it, to keep her spirits up. She had to remind herself every day, sometimes more than once, that she had faith in God. Even more, she had faith in God's plan for her. And Amber. And Glenn.

She had read and reread every scripture she could find on faith.

Philippians 4:19 *And my God will meet all your needs according to his glorious riches in Christ Jesus.*

Psalm 107:9 *For he satisfies the longing soul, and the hungry soul he fills with good things.*

1 Corinthians 10:13 *God is faithful, and he will not let you be tempted beyond your ability.*

Jeremiah 17:7 *Blessed is the man who trusts in the Lord.*

Psalm 28:7 *The Lord is my strength and my shield; my heart trusts Him and He helps me.*

Proverbs 29:25 *The fear of man lays a snare, but whoever trusts in the Lord is safe.*

Psalm 56:4 *In God I will praise his word, in God I have put my trust; I will not fear what flesh can do unto me.*

Psalm 91:2 *I will say of the Lord, He is my refuge and my fortress: my God; in Him will I trust.*

She even wrote them down in a notebook with a few others. Each morning, she sat at the kitchen table, under Nadine's carefully watchful gaze, and wrote them again.

She had to keep her faith. That was the only way. She had said it before and she would say it again: God had brought her here and He would see her through. And the only solution she could see was that Amber was coming back to her. Soon, she hoped.

She had thought she would see the baby before now. It had been almost two weeks.

Ms. Briggs had said that it would be at least a week before they heard anything, but Charlotte had called every day this week with no answers. She had talked to Ms. Briggs on Monday and Tuesday. Just normal conversation of *I'll check into it* and *As far as I know, Amber is doing just fine.* Then Ms. Briggs told her not to worry. She would let her know when the time came. And she would call Charlotte back then.

Charlotte took that to mean that Ms. Briggs didn't have time to talk to her about it every day. Yet on Wednesday she found herself back in the phone shanty, just to check on things. But Ms. Briggs didn't answer her phone. Charlotte left a message, stating all the pertinent facts—as if Ms. Briggs didn't know them already—and said she was calling to check on Amber.

This morning when she called, Charlotte didn't leave a message. When the recording clicked on, she simply hung up. She didn't want to be a bother, but she needed things to go back to the way they needed to be. Amber at home, with her, and not "in the system."

Psalm 27:14 *Wait on the Lord: be of good courage,
and he shall strengthen thine heart: wait, I say,
on the Lord.*

She needed to put that one in her notebook too. But
waiting was so hard. And worrying was inevitable.

Chapter Seventeen

"Game night was cancelled," Glenn said a few hours later when he came to her house. Once again, he had hired a driver and Charlotte had to wonder what Bishop Treager thought about his excessive use of cars. Or maybe Treager didn't think it was excessive. It was obvious that Glenn didn't. And if Charlotte was telling the truth, she preferred riding in a car to chugging along on a tractor. Buggies were great for Sunday, which as far as she was concerned was the perfect time to slow down and let God's word catch up to you. But it was nice to sit in the back seat with Glenn, side by side, and not have to holler over the engine in order to be heard. Or worry about driving and traffic and all the other things that came with travel.

"Do we have any new plans for the evening?"

"My daughter has invited us to eat supper with her family."

"Oh." Family dinner. She wasn't quite prepared for that, but she had made a special dress for tonight so at least she looked her best.

Strange, but she and Glenn had plans to marry and she had never met his children.

She supposed it was time, to be certain.

"That sounds nice," she said truthfully. It would be nice to meet his daughter. She just wished she had been better prepared, mentally, for the encounter. But it was one daughter. Charlotte could handle that.

"Betsy decided that all the children should meet you," he said a bit sheepishly.

"All of them?" He had five children. All were married, and all but one had children of their own. That was a lot of Eshes to meet in one night.

"I was going to tell you, but I was afraid you'd start making excuses."

She turned on the seat to face him. "Why would I make excuses?"

"It's been a hard couple of weeks."

"It has," she agreed. "So why would you think it a good idea to ambush me with family?"

He held up both hands. "I can see now that I was wrong. Do you want to go back home?"

She did. Then she thought of his daughter. Even though she had never met her, Charlotte knew that Betsy had probably been cooking all day long and cleaning all week and doing everything to make a nice supper for her father and the woman he planned to marry. Charlotte might be a little overwhelmed by the idea, but she couldn't disappoint the woman that way. It seemed unnaturally cruel. Charlotte Burkhart might be a lot of things, but none of them was cruel.

"It's fine," she said finally, maybe even a bit primly. Not much of the drive to Glenn's house was left. It might be an even shorter time till they got to his daughter's. She needed to get herself together.

People could spout off as much as they wanted about not caring what other people thought, but she did. And she could admit it. What other people thought was important to her. She wanted his children to like her as much as she wanted to like them. If she and Glenn were to be married—and they were—she wanted a loving and peaceful household for them all.

Isaiah said *So do not fear, for I am with you; do not be dismayed, for I am your God.* She had been reading her Bible a lot lately, and the verse had just popped into her head. Chapter forty-one, she believed it was. Perhaps she should add it to her notebook. But it certainly fit there as well.

She would not be fearful. She would not be dismayed. She would face his family, show them who she was and how much she cared for Glenn. God would see them through the rest.

Faith.

That was all she needed. A little bit of faith.

Of course, the Lord would see her through, but Glenn was right there by her side as she met all his children. And all their children. Five adult children. Twelve grandchildren and more to come, or so it would seem.

And they welcomed her into their midst as if she had been born to be a part of their family.

Betsy was kind and caring, as was her sister, Joy. Glenn's sons, Isaac, Johnathan, and Ben were as handsome as their father, and their wives were as gracious as the rest of the Esh clan.

Charlotte felt embraced and enveloped into the fold, if not even a bit overwhelmed.

About the middle of the evening, she stopped trying to remember everyone's names. She had the adults down, including the wives, Meredith, Amanda, and Leah and the husbands, Jacob and Samuel.

The children were another matter altogether. They didn't stand still long enough for her to pin them down into her mind and commit their name to her memory. She did recall Katie Ann and Joshie, but only because they were infants. Who their parents were was another matter entirely. It didn't help that the kids took care of one another's children without a second thought about it. Someone was always holding Joshie, the youngest, who looked to be about the same age as Amber, and it was never the same person. Glenn himself held him through most of the supper, and the sight made Charlotte smile. It warmed her heart to see him so caring and loving with this baby. With all his grandchildren really. He hugged them and allowed them to climb on him and pull at his beard as he tweaked their noses and tried to tickle them before they ran away.

And suddenly she realized why he had been so stand-offish with Amber. He was afraid to fall in love with her and then have to let her go. It all made sense now.

She could only admit it to herself, but she had been worried that he hadn't wanted children to be a part of their lives. Watching him with the tribe of Eshes, Glicks, and Detweilers that surrounded them, she knew that it was a protection effort on his part. And once she got

Amber permanently—and she fully intended to have Amber for her very own and forever—Glenn would be able to turn loose and love her in the same manner he loved the children that now surrounded him.

"That's a pretty big smile you got there." Joy Glick eased down onto the couch next to Charlotte. The move was slow and calculated. Joy was largely round with a baby on the way. Any day, if the look of her was any indication, but all the women assured Charlotte that Joy had at least three more weeks to go. "You must be thinking about something fantastic."

"As a matter of fact, I was."

Joy waited patiently for her to continue.

"My Amber."

She frowned, but only a slight one, more confused than anything. "I thought your daughter's name was Jenna."

So it was true, Glenn had been telling them about her since before this evening. She hadn't been entirely certain everyone was telling the truth about that, but if Joy knew Jenna's name . . .

"It is. But I—" How to explain this one? "I found a baby. Her name is Amber."

Joy pulled away, to better look at her, Charlotte was sure. Joy folded one hand across her bulging stomach and stared wide-eyed at Charlotte. "Found it?"

"Well, someone left her on my porch."

Joy blinked again, then recovered enough to call her sister and one of the others over. "Betsy, Amanda." She waved for them to join them. "Say it again," she commanded Charlotte when the two women were close enough to hear.

"Someone left a baby on my porch."

Betsy sat down as if her legs had grown weak. "I heard about that," she whispered. "That was you?"

Charlotte nodded, feeling like something of a celebrity as Amanda went to find Meredith and Leah to share the news with them. In a matter of moments, all five girls were hanging on her every word, wanting to know all the details about Amber and her stay with Charlotte and Nadine.

"You had heard that someone had found a baby, but Glenn didn't tell you that it was me who found her?"

Betsy shook her head. "Not a word."

"And she stayed with you for two weeks?" Leah asked. "However did you give her up?"

"It was hard," Charlotte admitted. "But I have faith in the Lord. He'll return her to me."

Amanda's eyes grew wide. "You're going to get her back?"

Charlotte nodded. "Of course. I applied to foster her, but I hope to adopt her after that. They couldn't make any promises, but the lady at Child Protective Services told me that, since I was getting married and could provide the child with a stable home, I would be at the top of the list."

"Even though you're Amish?" Leah asked.

"I don't think they were concerned with that." Charlotte hid her own doubts. She knew that there were laws against religious discrimination, but she also knew that the English could manipulate things until they came out the way they wanted them to. Especially when it came to children.

"Does Dat know?" Joy asked. She looked over to where her father sat, talking with his sons.

Did he? As remarkable as it seemed, Charlotte had never talked to him directly about the adoption. She had just sort of assumed that he knew. He did know how much Amber had meant to her—still meant to her—but had they talked about what would happen after Charlotte was cleared for fostering through Child Protective Services? She just couldn't remember. It was such a part of her, loving and adopting Amber, that she couldn't imagine not having talked to Glenn about it. But it was so hard since he lived in a completely different church district. Wells Landing might not be very big, but it was when a person had to travel by buggy or tractor.

Paul knew. Of that she was certain. Surely, if Paul knew, Glenn did as well. But perhaps she should talk to Glenn about it on the way home. When they were alone and riding in the back of the driver's car. She could talk to him then and make sure he understood her plans for adopting Amber.

But that time never came. When nine o'clock ticked over on the clock, a honk sounded outside.

"That's your ride." Glenn turned to her with a smile.

"You're not going with me?"

He shook his head.

He had ridden over to pick her up, but he was sending her home alone. Which meant no time in the car to talk. And she certainly didn't have time to right then. As soon as Glenn announced that she was going home, all ten of the grandchildren had to give her a hug. Only Katie Ann and Joshie were left out of that ritual. Each of the sons had to shake her hand and tell her that they were glad to meet her. Then after a sweet hug from all the daughters, including a very bulky one from Joy, Glenn walked her out onto the porch.

"I hope you had a good time," he said.

"I did. Your family is gracious and loving," she replied. And it was the truth. She had loved them all, and she would be happy to join them as part of the family.

"I'm sure they're all watching," Glenn said, his smile never wavering.

Charlotte gave a light laugh. "I'm sure you're right about that."

"So I'll see you Sunday?" he asked.

"Of course."

Charlotte, Nadine, and Amos were heading to Glenn's district for the church service. It would be good to go visit. She needed to get used to their ways. She and Glenn hadn't talked about where they would live after they married, but since he had stopped looking for a house, she'd figured they would move into his.

"And Monday," he added as if he could see her disappointment that he wasn't driving home with her. But it was unnecessary really. Just a time-eater for him.

"Bowling," Charlotte replied. She had almost forgotten. But with any luck she would be able to talk to him more about Amber and her plans to adopt the infant. The baby had been abandoned by so many. She wasn't going to add her name to that list. Not if she could help it.

He handed her the folded-up bills to pay the driver. She thought momentarily about refusing, but she accepted the money. Then she gave him a small smile and headed down the porch steps and to the waiting car.

* * *

"Someone's here." Nadine skipped down the stairs and rounded the corner for the kitchen, just as Charlotte walked out to the living room.

"Who is it?" Charlotte asked.

"Someone in a blue car," Nadine answered.

Charlotte tossed the dish towel over one shoulder with a small frown and started for the door. "It's not Glenn?" Not that she was expecting him. But she didn't know anyone who had a blue car. Come to think of it, she really didn't know anyone who had a car other than the people who drove for the Amish.

"If he's out there, I didn't see him," Nadine said. "Just a woman in one of those English suits. You know, like the women wear."

Charlotte supposed she did. She thought they were called business suits, but she wasn't sure what that had to do with anything at all. "She must be lost." Why else would anybody be coming down the drive on a Friday morning?

A knock sounded at the door. Charlotte turned to Nadine. Whoever it was, if they were indeed lost, they had surely figured that out by now.

Nadine gave another small shrug. "Maybe they need directions."

"Maybe," Charlotte said and opened the door. It was in that moment they heard the cries. Screams, really. A baby. Had to be. And a very unhappy one at that.

"Can I help you?" Charlotte asked, for a moment wondering why, if the woman was lost, she felt it necessary to drag her screaming child from the car to come to the door to ask for directions. Then her gaze fell to the infant in the car seat at the woman's feet. "Amber," she breathed.

Though for a moment she hadn't quite recognized her. She looked thinner than she remembered, as if she had lost weight in the two weeks since Charlotte had last seen her. And she was more unhappy now than she had been the first night when Goldie had barked in her face and scared her half to death.

"Ms. Burkhart?" the lady in the navy-blue suit asked. "Charlotte Burkhart?"

"That's me," Charlotte said and stepped back to allow the woman to enter. She might not know who she was, but the woman knew Amber and that was enough for her. But she couldn't stand hearing the baby cry like that. The woman hooked one arm through the car seat's carrier handle and hoisted Amber into the house.

"I'm Sandra Cummings, Mayes County DHS."

The woman sat Amber still in the carrier on the floor just inside the door and reached into her handbag to retrieve some papers. Most probably to prove who she was. But she seemed to be having a hard time locating the paper she needed. In fact, she seemed a little frazzled, and Charlotte had a hunch that Amber had been crying the entire way out to their house.

For a moment, Charlotte felt a wave of panic blaze through her. Why had Ms. Cummings brought Amber all the way out here? They had never come for a house visit, and they had never even called her since she had dropped Amber off at the office over two weeks ago. Maybe this was like what Maddie Kauffman was talking about and they were going to accuse her of some heinous crime against the child. The thought had her stomach clenching and her knees threatening to not hold her up.

"For pity's sake," Nadine said. "Pick her up."

Leave it to Nadine to be the voice of wisdom. Somehow, it solidified Charlotte's knees and eased the tension in her belly as she moved to unhook the baby from the carrier seat. She stopped before actually carrying through the action. "May I?" she asked the woman, who was still digging through her large black handbag.

Sandra Cummings smoothed her hair back from her face and nodded as she continued to dig through her bag. "It's in here somewhere."

"What is?" Nadine asked as Charlotte unhooked the latches holding Amber in the car seat and released the baby from the contraption.

How she had missed her! More than she had even known until that moment.

"My papers," Ms. Cummings said. "I must have left them in the car." She turned back toward the door, her intent to fetch them clear, though Charlotte barely heard her over Amber's cries.

"Do you have a bottle for her?" Charlotte didn't know why she thought the child needed to be fed. Instinct, maybe? This sounded like her hungry cry, and she did look terribly thin. Or had Charlotte just forgotten exactly what she looked like as it had been so long?

The woman bustled back, her frazzled state obvious as she dropped the diaper bag on the coffee table. "In there somewhere." Then she headed back out the door. Charlotte gently shushed Amber and tried to get her to stop crying while she fished in the bag with one hand, trying to fetch the bottle.

"I'll get it," Nadine said with a small frown toward the door. She dug in the bag, rifling around as Charlotte did her best to calm the baby. She rubbed her back and gently bounced her from side to side, but her cries were still near deafening. And they broke her heart. She had taken the baby to Child Protective Services in good faith. She had given them a happy, gurgling baby, chubby and . . . happy. This was not the child she turned over to them. It seemed like an eternity, but could have only been a few seconds, before Nadine found the bottle. She tested the milk inside and headed over to Charlotte.

"It's okay?" she asked, and Nadine gave a nod. Then Charlotte cradled the baby in her arms and held the bottle for her.

Amber stopped crying immediately, tears staining her cheeks and drowning her beautiful blue eyes. But those eyes were now centered on Charlotte. In a look that she could only describe as accusing.

"It's okay now, baby girl," Charlotte said. And she hoped that was the truth. "I've got you now." And she wasn't sure if she could let her go. What had happened in these last two weeks?

"Oh, thank heavens," Sandra Cummings said, bustling back inside the house, neither knocking nor waiting for a second invitation to enter.

"Did you find your papers?" Nadine asked.

Ms. Cummings sighed and held them up. "But I'm more excited that she's not crying any longer." She closed her eyes and took a deep breath as if relishing the almost deafening quiet that came in the aftermath of those terrible cries.

"What happened to her?" Charlotte asked. But she didn't take her gaze from the baby's.

"And she's eating," Ms. Cummings said. She moved toward the couch opposite of where Charlotte sat with the baby. "May I sit?"

Charlotte nodded as Nadine said, "*Jah.*"

"I feel like we're going about this all backwards," Ms. Cummings said. "I told you who I am. I work for DHS. And I've come to ask you to foster Amber, officially known as Amber Doe, here in your home."

"Praise be," Nadine said, her arms raised to heaven.

"Yes," Charlotte said.

Ms. Cummings nodded. "That's good. That's good." She opened the folder of papers that she had come back into the house with and checked something off on the first page. "There are a few steps we have to go through. Your acceptance is the first, of course, and we thank you for that. I have been told to make sure you understand that this is a temporary situation."

Charlotte popped the bottle out of Amber's mouth with a resounding smack, then turned her that she could rub her back and release any air that the baby might've swallowed while feeding. She had eaten so fast she was probably going to have a bellyache no matter what Charlotte did at this point. "I understand," Charlotte said. Though she knew this was temporary, this was God. This was her holding her fate. This was everything she'd been dreaming of.

"Very good," Ms. Cummings said. "Now, I have to inspect the home."

"It seems like you would have done that a while back," Nadine said. Normally Charlotte would've shushed her, but she was too busy absorbing all the warmth and love from Amber. She was so very, very glad to have the baby back.

"Normally that's how it would've happened, but it seems that Miss Doe here has been classified as failure to thrive."

That got Charlotte's attention. She snapped her gaze toward the other woman. "She was not failing to thrive when she was here," she said. At once, she wanted to remember everything that Maddie Kauffman had told her after church, and in the same moment, she wanted to forget it all as quickly as possible.

"No, no," Ms. Cummings said. "She was doing very well here, and she seemed very happy when you brought her into Child Protective Services. But since she has been in the care of the system, she has been struggling."

Amber let out a lusty burp.

Nadine chuckled. "That didn't sound like a struggle to me."

Ms. Cummings laughed. "Right. It does seem that she is doing better already. But regardless, we still have to make sure that you have everything you need to care for her."

Electricity. Wasn't that what Maddie had been talking about? Charlotte pushed the thought away. "Nadine, can you show her what she needs to see?"

Part of Charlotte wanted to get up and make sure that everything in the house was in absolutely perfect order and there was no one thing that Ms. Cummings could find lacking in the care of the baby. But there was this other part of her, this small, dark part, that wanted to soak in this time in case Ms. Cummings decided that Amber could not stay there She wanted to build a memory, however small, of sharing with her. She had gotten this opportunity to see Amber, and she didn't want to waste it on a home visit.

Keep the faith, she told herself.

"Of course," Nadine replied.

Charlotte gave her mother-in-law a grateful smile, then turned her attention back to the baby she held in her arms. Truth be known, she had done her best to keep her faith, she had done her best to keep her spirits high and positive, but there had been times, mostly in the dead of night, when the darkness had crept over everything that the light of her faith kept alive. And in those times she had wondered if she would ever see Amber again.

Lord, forgive me for ever doubting, she prayed. *And, Lord, please make Your will be done, and please let Your will be that Amber stays here. I need her. And I think she needs me too. Amen.*

She half-listened as Nadine took Ms. Cummings on a tour of the house. She heard them in the kitchen, running water and clicking on the stove. She supposed to check to make sure it worked. Then the back door opened and closed again. After that, the pair came through the living room and up the stairs. Only their muffled voices reached her, but she knew what they were saying, Nadine was showing Ms. Cummings where Amber had slept while she had stayed with them. The crib she had bought at the garage sale, the changing table, all the clothes and other things that she had kept as a measure of faith, holding on to the hope that Amber would be back. But all Charlotte truly wanted to do was sit and hold this precious child. And correct whatever wrongs had been dispensed to her.

Amber took a deep, shuddering breath, then closed those remarkable blue eyes and fell asleep in Charlotte's arms.

She held one finger over her lips as Nadine and Ms. Cummings came back down the stairs. They walked softly over and sat down on the couch side by side.

"This is highly unusual," Ms. Cummings started. "But we find ourselves in a highly unusual situation. That is, Amber was doing just fine until you brought her to us. We cannot have her failing to thrive while in the care of DHS."

"So you're giving her back to us," Nadine said.

"We are allowing Charlotte to foster her for the time being. With the understanding that she will not take her across county lines and that she will not try to contact the birth mother in any manner."

"I don't have any idea who her birth mother is," Charlotte said. If she could've contacted her, she would've done so long ago. But since the girl had never come back to retrieve the baby, Charlotte could only assume that she had meant it when she'd walked away. That thought alone was heartbreaking.

"So why was she crying?" Nadine asked.

"We figure it was separation anxiety," Ms. Cummings said. She made a couple more notations in the file that was spread across the coffee table. "Best anyone can figure, she became attached to Charlotte in those two weeks and remembered her as her mother. Then, when Amber was taken from Charlotte, she experienced separation anxiety."

A knock sounded on the door a moment before Paul stepped into the house. "Everything okay?" he asked before he spied Charlotte in the rocker gently cradling Amber. His expression immediately softened.

Ms. Cummings stood. She turned to Charlotte. "Is this your fiancé?"

Paul gave a small chuckle and shook his head. "I'm just a neighbor." He pointed to his grandson holding his hand. "And this is Paul Daniel. We live across the hill there. I saw a car pull in and just wanted to make sure everything was all right."

He gazed again at Charlotte and Amber. "I see that it is." Then he squatted down next to Paul Daniel and pointed toward Amber. "See the baby?" he asked.

Paul Daniel stuck one finger in his mouth and nodded. His eyes were big in his little face as he gazed upon such a small creature. "You have to be really gentle with a baby," Paul continued.

Finger still in his mouth, Paul Daniel nodded as if he truly understood everything his *dawdi* was saying. Then Paul stood back up straight. "We were out looking for grasshoppers and saw the car. We didn't mean to intrude." He started toward the front door.

Nadine stood and followed behind him.

"You could never intrude, Paul Brennaman," she said as he pushed the screen door open and stepped out into the porch.

"You'll come get me if you need anything?" he asked, looking from Nadine to Charlotte and back again.

"Of course."

He gave a silent nod, then shut the screen door quietly behind him.

"Good neighbors," Ms. Cummings said as Nadine rejoined her on the couch.

Charlotte nodded. "The best."

Chapter Eighteen

"I wish you'd change your mind," Nadine said that following Sunday morning.

Charlotte shook her head. "I just want to stay at home."

It was a non-church Sunday for their district, but Charlotte, Amos, and Nadine had made plans to go over to Bishop Treager's district and attend church with Glenn.

"He's your fiancé."

She didn't need to be reminded of that. "I know, but that's not the point."

"Tell me again," Nadine said. "Because I sure didn't get it the first time."

"I haven't had time to talk to Glenn since they brought Amber back. It's only been a couple of days and yesterday he was at that auction all day. I think it would be a big shock if I just showed up at his church with a baby."

"It's not like he's never seen you with her before."

That was true, but even more truthful was the fact that there was more to it. She just didn't want to share yet. Was that so wrong? Did that make her a bad person? Or maybe she just wanted to be with Amber by herself. She hadn't had time to do that in the two days since she had gotten her back.

Maybe Amber needed a little bit of a break. She'd been jostled around since she had left Charlotte's.

Or maybe Charlotte was just making excuses.

"He's going to find out eventually," Nadine said.

Like she needed to be reminded of that either.

Nadine shrugged. "Suit yourself. Amos will be here any minute."

As her mother-in-law said the words, Charlotte began to feel like a chicken. Cowardice was not a becoming trait. Perhaps she should go. Perhaps she should show up at Glenn's church with this baby in tow, the baby she had told his children about, the baby that he hadn't told his children about. That was the main thing stopping her. She had wanted a baby so badly herself that she couldn't imagine that someone else might not, but thinking back over all the little things with Glenn . . .

At first, she had believed that he was just unaccustomed, and then she had watched him with his own grandchildren. He had been loving and kind, a typical caring *dawdi*. And she had told herself that he was just unaccustomed to Amber herself. Perhaps he hadn't given himself time to get to know her and love her. Or maybe he didn't want to for fear that she would be snatched away and his love would be left dangling in the wind. But it was Friday that got to her. Paul Daniel and Paul coming to visit because they had seen the car in their driveway when they were off in the field looking for grasshoppers. She wasn't sure she could ever imagine Glenn looking for grasshoppers in the field for no reason other than they were grasshoppers. That's when the doubts really started.

Doubts that she didn't want to face yet. "Nadine," she called as the woman started out the front door.

Nadine stopped with one arm bracing the screen door open and the other on her hip. "Don't say anything to him," Charlotte said. "Not about Amber. I'll tell him."

Nadine paused as if she was about to say something more. Then she gave a stern nod and let herself out of the house.

"I don't believe I've ever seen a happier baby." Ms. Cummings smiled at Charlotte.

She was glad she had stayed home the day before. She had needed that alone time with Amber. They hadn't done anything while Nadine had been gone, save sit on the porch and cuddle. They had eaten, played, and cuddled some more. It seemed to be just what Amber needed.

"I didn't realize you'd be by so soon," Charlotte said. "To check on her."

Ms. Cummings made a check mark in the file she carried, which was becoming quite commonplace, Charlotte thought. The woman gave them another wistful look. "We have to keep up on these things."

Charlotte supposed they did.

She wanted to ask when they might possibly hear anything about her being able to permanently adopt Amber, but she had only had her back a couple of days. Ms. Cummings would most likely come back and check again. If not this week, then definitely the next, and perhaps that time would be better.

The DHS worker pulled the strap of her bag over her shoulder and folded the file as if preparing to go. "You have our phone number and that emergency number as well," she said.

Charlotte nodded.

"Let us know if you need anything," Ms. Cummings said.

"We will," Charlotte replied, escorting the woman to the door.

A few more niceties were exchanged, and the woman left.

"Whew," Nadine said. "I don't know why, but that woman makes me nervous."

Charlotte took Amber back over and sat down in the rocking chair once more. "She's a bit high strung."

Nadine seemed to think about it a second. "Maybe that's it."

Or maybe Nadine knew just as well as Charlotte did that these home visits would be deciding factors in whether or not Amber got to stay.

Charlotte knew that Nadine had been concerned at first when they had found the baby, but it seemed she had gotten accustomed to the idea of Charlotte now having an infant to look after. And Nadine understood how important it was to Charlotte for her to have this baby.

They had stopped talking about things like her transferring all her attention from Jenna to Amber. It just wasn't the same thing. Jenna was all grown up now. She didn't need Charlotte. Not like she had before. And definitely not like Amber did now.

"Are you going visiting today?" Nadine didn't need to say where Charlotte would be visiting. They both knew perfectly well. Glenn.

"I don't have anything definite to tell him."

Nadine studied her for a moment, but Charlotte couldn't read the shadowy expression lurking across her face. She could guess though. "Don't you think it would be better if you told him that you have her, even if it is temporarily?"

"*Jah*," Charlotte admitted. But she wanted just one more day. Was that selfish of her? She wanted one more day to get Amber accustomed to being back. She wanted one more day of allowing the child to settle in, to realize this was her new normal. Then Charlotte would take her out, over to Glenn's, and explain the whole situation to him.

Jah, that was the answer. And if she worked it right, she might get his daughters together at the same time. They all seemed to be very supportive of her keeping Amber. Well, they had been supportive of her *caring* for Amber.

With the five of them on her side, perhaps Glenn would have no choice but to accept, maybe even begin to enjoy, the idea of having a little one underfoot.

"Tomorrow," she said. "I promise. I'll go to Glenn tomorrow."

Paul knocked on Charlotte's door just after lunch. He waited for her summons and stepped inside. "Hey," he said. "I came to see how you ladies are doing."

His heart melted at the sight of Charlotte holding Amber. Ever since he had known her, he had wanted Charlotte to be happy. Sitting there holding that baby, she was the happiest he had ever seen her. And he knew in that moment he would do anything to help her keep Amber.

Not just for Charlotte, but for Amber too. The baby who had been fussy and obviously crying on Saturday was cooing and gurgling, blowing bubbles on Monday. He knew it was no coincidence.

"We're all good," Charlotte replied with a smile.

"Except Charlotte's had a hard time putting that baby down." Nadine's voice was filled with teasing and censure, an odd combination to be sure.

"I just don't want her to believe she's going to be left behind," Charlotte replied.

Nadine chuckled. "You're going to spoil her rotten. Just wait until you're not able to take a shower because she wants to be held the entire time."

Paul could read the look on Charlotte's face, and Charlotte didn't care one way or another. She would be happy as long as she had Amber with her.

"I was going to ask if there was anything I could do to help, but it seems I found it." He crossed the living room and held his arms out to Amber. "Hand the baby over to me and go take a shower," he told Charlotte.

She shook her head. "No, I'm fine."

"You might not be able to take one until tomorrow," Nadine reminded her. "It's senior night, remember." She stopped and gave Charlotte a teasing look. "Unless you're actually going to put her in the carrier."

"Stop messing with me," Charlotte protested. "I just want to make sure she knows that she's not going to be abandoned."

It sounded like a pretty logical explanation to Paul, but

he had a feeling it was more in line with Nadine's theory of wanting to spoil the baby. Still, he had learned the hard way himself that babies were only little for a little while. And each moment had to be treasured.

He gestured back to Amber. "Hand her over." Treasure or not, parents still had to bathe.

"All right." Charlotte kissed the side of Amber's head, then handed her to Paul.

"Did she lose weight?" he asked.

Charlotte stood. "I suppose she did. They had her classified as failure to thrive. To me, that sounds like she didn't eat much while she was gone."

It was shocking to him that he could feel the difference in her from one week to the next. But he knew that if Charlotte had a say in the matter, she would have the baby back to weight in no time at all.

"If you're sure," Charlotte said, slowly inching toward the staircase. She was like all new mothers. She wanted to give all of her attention to the baby, but she still had to care for herself a little as well.

"We got this," Nadine said. "Now go."

"Okay." Charlotte inched a little further away.

"Go now," Nadine said, using a towel to wave her up the stairs. "And while you're up there, wash your hair."

"Bossy," Charlotte called in return.

Nadine just chuckled.

Paul shook his head at the two of them. They had come so far, since they had been in Wells Landing, and though Paul was happy for Nadine for finding a person she could love and even for Charlotte for finding Glenn to make her happy, he wondered what would become of their relationship when the two no longer shared a home.

"Is she eating?" Paul asked once Charlotte was upstairs and he heard the bathroom door shut.

"Better than she has been," Nadine said.

Paul placed Amber on the blanket under the mobile. He turned the crank that started the music, "Pop Goes the Weasel," or some sort of silly song. He stood back and watched as Amber laughed, waved her arms, and kicked her feet.

"You really care about her."

He tore his gaze away from Amber and settled it on Nadine. "She's a beautiful baby."

Nadine shook her head slowly, her gaze snagging his and refusing to let go. "Charlotte."

He started to deny it, thought about telling her that she was imagining things, but he wasn't in the habit of lying. And with as shrewd and observant as Nadine usually was, he was surprised she hadn't seen it before now. He wasn't very good at hiding his feelings. He never had been.

"She's very special to me." There. He'd said it. Well, part of it, and the world hadn't stopped turning. Life would go on.

"You should tell her," Nadine said. They stood side by side and watched Amber playing near their feet.

"What good would it do?"

"It might keep her from marrying Glenn Esh, for one." She said his name as if it tasted bitter on her lips.

"You have something against Glenn?"

Nadine looked back toward the staircase and sighed.

"Nothing other than I don't think he's good enough for Charlotte, and he thinks he's too good."

Paul did his best not to chuckle. "Fancy Amish."

"Exactly." Nadine cast another look toward the second-story landing.

"Are you expecting her back soon?" he asked.

"She's not going to wash her hair. Not without Amber asleep. She'll be back in a jiffy now."

"She's serious about this baby," Paul said with a smile.

"Very," Nadine agreed. "I'm just not sure Glenn is."

But Paul didn't have a chance to ask her what that meant as Charlotte was coming back down the stairs. She hadn't washed her hair.

"Told you," Nadine said where only Paul could hear.

He hid his smile, lest Charlotte start asking questions about what they had been talking about. One thing was certain. He wasn't ready to confess his feelings for Charlotte, and with her promised to marry Glenn Esh, he wasn't sure he would ever be.

"Chocolate chip cookies," she said sometime later. She had been so happy to see Paul today that she wasn't ready for him to leave. And she knew the one way to get him to stay was bribe him with cookies.

He groaned, but she could tell that she was wearing him down. It had been such a fun afternoon. Once she'd had her shower, the three of them had played with Amber, until Nadine had claimed she had a load of wash to hang and that she didn't need any help. Then her mother-in-law had disappeared, leaving Charlotte and Amber alone with Paul.

They had talked about the chances of her adopting Amber and when there might be word. How the home visits had gone and when there might be another one. They had talked about the important and the not so important, and she wasn't ready to see him leave.

"You watch Amber, and I'll bake cookies."

He shook his head, but he was smiling the whole while. "It's almost suppertime," he protested, but not ardently enough that she would change her mind.

She shrugged. "Then we'll have our dessert first."

He sighed and settled into one of the kitchen chairs to keep her company. Amber was sitting happily on the table in the car seat carrier, rattling a plastic set of keys and occasionally gnawing on the purple one. Then her fist. It didn't seem to matter to her either way.

Charlotte got out the butter and set it in the sunlight streaming through the window.

"You don't even have your butter softened," Paul protested.

She whirled around and propped her hands on her hips. "Paul Brennaman. I'm the cookie expert here. And you are the babysitter. Now babysit while I bake."

He widened his eyes comically. "Yes, sir. I mean ma'am."

She laughed.

"What do you think?" Nadine picked that moment to come back into the room. She twirled around in a circle so they could see her from every angle.

"Where are you going in that?" Paul asked, stifling a laugh. Or maybe he was simply choking.

Charlotte laughed, at his expression more than Nadine's outfit.

"A costume party." She gave him a look that said she hadn't figured him for a dimwit. "Sort of."

"But . . . but you're a cow."

"Of course I am."

He shook his head as if his eyesight was failing him. She had taken one of her black dresses and sewn white patches to it. A circle of pink with empty thread spools painted to match served as her udders. And tiny white horns on a plastic headband sat just to the front of her prayer *kapp*. All in all, the look was cute, fun, and ridiculous.

"That chicken place in town lets you eat free today if you dress up like a cow," Nadine explained. "So all the seniors are dressing up and going to eat."

Paul shook his head. "I still think it would be easier to just pay for the meal."

"Maybe," Nadine said. "But not nearly as fun."

"They're going to think that all the Amish old folks have dementia," Paul quipped.

"I don't care about that," Nadine said, "just as long as they feed me."

Charlotte laughed as a knock sounded at the door.

"That must be Amos," Nadine said. She grabbed her tail and started from the room.

"Have him come in here before you leave," Paul said. "We want to see what he looks like too."

"Sure," Nadine said and disappeared from sight. She

returned a few moments later, not with a cow-costumed Amos, but a confused-looking Glenn.

"Hi," Charlotte said as she saw him. She wanted to say something different, maybe something more, but it was the only word she could find.

Not only because she was surprised to see him, though she was. But also because she had forgotten their date.

"Are you ready to leave?" He said the words hesitantly as if he wasn't sure of them at all. Then his gaze fell to the baby. "She's back." The words held no infliction. They were part question, part statement. They simply were.

"*Jah*," Charlotte said, realizing the moment of truth had come.

"You're ready to leave?" he asked again.

Charlotte stuttered. "I—uh—"

Glenn shifted. "You forgot." His tone wasn't quite accusing, but it was on the way there.

"No! I mean, it must have slipped my mind. But it's all right."

He gave her a look that said he doubted that very much.

"I'll just—"

Another knock sounded on the door.

Everyone turned to look in that direction.

"That'll be Amos," Nadine said. She started for the living room.

Charlotte followed behind her, snagging her elbow before she could let Amos into the house.

"I need your help," she said under her breath.

"You need more than that," Nadine said in return.

"I can't take Amber bowling tonight."

"No," Nadine said emphatically. "I will not take her with us. You got yourself into this. You can get yourself out of it." With that, she opened the door.

Amos stood on the other side of the threshold. He had on all his regular clothes—well, his pants and suspenders—but he had put them over an English cow costume. It even had a hood that pulled over his head, complete with horns and a bright pink nose.

If she hadn't been so stressed, she might have laughed.

"Are you ready to go?" Amos asked. He looked from Nadine to Charlotte, then back again. He could tell something was up between then, but he wasn't going to be the one to ask.

"Let me get my purse," Nadine said.

Charlotte stood quietly by as Nadine gathered her bag and returned to the door, where Amos waited.

Nadine gave Charlotte a small tight smile. "I know you'll figure out something," she said. Then she stepped out onto the porch, leaving Charlotte alone to bite her lips and try to find a solution.

She supposed she had a few options, but the only one that would really seem to work would be to take Amber with her on the date.

And why not? Bowling alleys were known to be fun places for the whole family. Why shouldn't she take the baby she loved, the baby she planned to adopt just as soon as possible?

One thing was certain. She couldn't leave the baby with Paul. Amber was her responsibility. And she should be able to take her places. If she was going to adopt her—and she did plan to—then people needed to get used to seeing her with the baby. Maybe a night out together would allow Glenn to drop his guard and begin to adore her the way Charlotte did.

Charlotte made her way back into the kitchen, a bright— perhaps even too bright—smile pasted on her face.

"Shall we get going?" she asked.

Paul awkwardly stood, and she instantly regretted her words. She hadn't meant to make him uncomfortable, but it was inevitable, seeing as how she was uncomfortable herself.

"I guess I'll just—" He didn't finish the sentence, just trailed off with a flick of one hand. Then he pushed his chair back up to the table and walked stiff legged to the door.

"Bye," Charlotte said quietly; then the door shut and Paul was gone.

"What are you going to do with the baby?" Glenn asked.

And for the first time Charlotte wondered if he had ever said her name? She couldn't think of once. Not even once, though in all fairness it wasn't like Glenn talked about her all that much. Or maybe that wasn't being fair. Why didn't he talk about Amber? Ask Charlotte questions about the child's well-being?

It wasn't as if he wasn't a loving and caring man. She had seen him with his family. He might not be as all-in as Paul when it came to grandparenting, but he still seemed to be very interested in his grandchildren.

Just not Amber.

"We're going to take her with us," Charlotte said as if it were the grandest idea ever thought.

Glenn stopped.

He stared at Charlotte a moment. Then he switched his

gaze to the laughing, gurgling Amber. If that face couldn't convince him that she needed to go, Charlotte wasn't sure anything could.

"How did she get back here?" he asked.

It was a strange question, but Charlotte thought she knew what he meant by it. "The DHS worker brought her back here Friday," Charlotte explained.

"Friday?" That brought him out of the trance that he had seemed to have fallen under. "You've had her since Friday?"

Charlotte nodded. "She brought her back because she wasn't doing well in care. They wanted me to see if I could get her back to eating and sleeping regularly."

He turned back to the baby, his expression unchanged. "How long?"

"I'm sorry," she said, not understanding his question.

"How long are they leaving her here?"

"I suppose until they get my foster papers completely run through. Then they'll start the adoption."

"I see," he said. Though she wasn't sure she understood the tone of his voice.

She didn't have time to ask. A car horn sounded out front.

The noise startled Charlotte, and she jumped in place. Amber laughed as if she had performed the trick for her and her alone.

"That's my driver," Glenn said. He started toward the front door.

Charlotte grabbed Amber's bag and followed behind him.

* * *

Glenn didn't say a word to her all the way to the bowling alley. And Charlotte didn't know what to make of his silence. She figured he was a little upset that she hadn't told him about getting Amber back, but there hadn't been a great deal of time. It seemed as if there had been, when she'd said that they had brought Amber back to her on Friday, but that had been a day of adjustments. Then, Saturday, Glenn had been at an auction all day. Sunday . . . okay, maybe she had had the time to tell him on Sunday, but she hadn't thought that church would be the place to break the news to him. And now it was Monday.

Plus, they were Amish. It wasn't like everyone had a phone in their house or she could just jump in her car and buzz across town to tell him that Amber was with her once more. So really, he had a small right to be a little upset, but not a great one.

Glenn was a logical man. He would filter through it all and come up with the right conclusion. Of course he would.

When they arrived at the bowling alley, Glenn paid the driver as Charlotte took the carrier from the back seat of the car. That was another thing that had put distance between them on the ride over—literally. The car seat had sat between them, creating a wider gulf where the previous one had existed.

Time, she told herself. He just needed time. And he just needed to know that Amber was definitely going to be a part of their lives. Then he would come around.

And she had his daughters on her side. They would help him become accustomed to having Amber in their lives. She just knew it.

Satisfied that everything was going to turn out just the way God had intended it to, Charlotte walked into the bowling alley with Glenn and Amber.

Once Glenn opened the door, she could hear it, the crack of the ball against the pins. Someone had played a song on the jukebox, and a woman singing—if she really dared call it that—about a hump or something added to the noise. The mini-arcade was in full swing, and the *dings* of the pinball machines clashed with the *pew-pew* of the simulated firearms. A ball thumped against the lane, then cracked against the pins.

They had barely taken two steps inside when Amber began to cry.

"She's scared," Charlotte explained to Glenn.

He nodded. "Should I get you some shoes?"

"Size ten," she said.

Then he pointed in the direction where the other people they were meeting had already begun to warm up on their lanes.

Charlotte hastened her steps. She needed to get Amber out of the carrier for a moment and allow her to see that everything was all right. *Jah*, there was a lot of noise but nothing harmful. Just noise.

All eyes turned to her as she sat Amber on the plastic bench where they were sitting and quickly took her out of the carrier seat.

Charlotte gave everyone an apologetic smile, then cuddled Amber close, trying to calm her tears. But every time a ball cracked at the end of the lane, the baby jerked as if she had been shocked and the crying started once again.

Truthfully, it never stopped.

Monday nights weren't the busiest at the bowling alley, but the place was busy enough. Which meant that many more people staring at her as she tried to soothe the infant.

"She's just scared," Charlotte told the group, realizing as she said the words they were barely audible over the din of the crying. It seemed be getting worse instead of better. Or maybe it was just starting to get to her.

Everyone nodded sympathetically, though no one came over to offer assistance. No one questioned where the baby had come from. Perhaps they just assumed that it was her grandbaby and she had somehow been charged with watching her for the evening. Or perhaps there was simply too much noise for anyone to want to try and talk over it. Whatever it was, Charlotte continued to rock Amber, hold her close, even try to shush her, though she was certain the baby couldn't hear her over her own cries. Then Glenn finally appeared holding their shoes as if they might carry diseases.

"What's wrong with her?" he hollered over the racket of her sobs.

"I think she's scared," Charlotte replied, though not as loudly. There was already enough upsetting Amber; she didn't want to add her own voice to the list.

"Does she need to be changed?" he asked.

Charlotte shook her head and continued in vain to soothe the child.

"She was fine outside," Glenn pointed out.

And she had been. The crying had only started once they had set foot into the building itself.

Perhaps if she took her outside . . .

Glenn offered Charlotte a pair of the shoes he carried,

but she shook her head. Instead, she gently bounced Amber and nodded her head toward the door of the bowling alley.

I'm going to take her outside for a minute. She mouthed the words at Glenn rather than actually trying to say them where he could hear her. Her own hearing seemed nearly damaged by the amount of screaming Amber was doing. The longer the baby cried, the more it broke her heart. She had to get her to stop. Then she could worry about bowling or whatever.

Still shushing her and cooing and trying to make the baby realize that she was safe, Charlotte took her back out into the fading daylight.

It took a moment, but Amber eventually calmed down. Fat tears still clung to her dark, wet lashes as she hiccupped and got her breathing under control.

"See?" Charlotte crooned. "Everything's going to be okay."

Amber stuck out her lip and didn't look convinced. She shoved one tiny fist into her mouth and stared at Charlotte disparagingly.

Charlotte laughed at such a serious look. "I know, baby," she said. "But it's all better now." Thank goodness. Amber wasn't crying any longer.

Now she could take her back in and they could begin their evening of proving to Glenn—and perhaps all his friends—how wonderful it was to have a baby like Amber around.

Charlotte kissed that sweet spot on the side of Amber's chubby neck, then headed back into the bowling alley. She had no sooner cleared the second set of glass doors that led inside before the screams started once again. This time even louder than before.

"Okay, okay," she told Amber and stepped back into the parking lot. It took a little longer this second time than it had the first, but Charlotte finally managed to get the tears to stop.

"Why don't you like the bowling alley?" she asked the baby.

Amber gnawed her fist and stared at her impassively.

"Nothing's going to happen to you inside," she promised. "Glenn is in there. And all his nice friends. Let's go in and play, huh?" She started back inside, but once again Amber started squalling before they even reached the counter.

Charlotte turned and made her way back outside.

Thankfully, Glenn had noticed her and the trouble she was having. He came from the seats where he had just finished putting on his shoes and followed her out into the parking lot.

Charlotte gave his feet a pointed look. "You aren't supposed to wear those out here," she said once she got Amber to stop crying.

He sighed, more of an aggravated growl, and pulled off the multicolored shoes. "What's wrong with her?"

Charlotte gave a brief shrug, thankful that Amber had quit crying so quickly this third time. She had been afraid for a moment that she wasn't going to be able to calm the child. What would she do if she had to call DHS and tell them that Amber wouldn't stop crying?

She pushed the thought away. She was just being paranoid. But she wanted this baby with all her heart.

And she felt as if God wanted her to have Amber as well. Surely nothing of man could mess that up.

In God I will praise his word, in God I have put my trust; I will not fear what flesh can do unto me. Psalms something or another. The verse and the chapter weren't really as important as the message. This was God's plan. She just had to remember that.

"I guess you're not coming back in," Glenn said.

She shook her head. She hadn't really thought about it beyond this moment, but how could she go inside if every time she did, Amber squalled her head off? "It's too noisy for her, I think." Or maybe the sound of the bowling balls brought to mind the fireworks that had sounded when her mother had left her. Did sweet little Amber feel she was being abandoned all over again?

The thought was beyond heartbreaking.

"I'll call the car for you." He turned as if he was going back inside.

"Glenn," she said, effectively stopping him.

"*Jah?*"

"Will you come back out and wait with me?" She felt a little ridiculous even asking, but she had a strange feeling that if she didn't, he would go inside and never return.

He paused just a moment, then gave a swift nod.

She waited as he went back inside. She wished she had told him to get her diaper bag and the car seat, but she supposed she could send him back in for it while she waited for the driver.

He returned a few moments later carrying Amber's bag and carrier.

She smiled at him, though inside she could feel the

shift. Something had changed. Maybe not all at once. But slowly until it culminated into this moment.

"The driver is on his way," Glenn said. He sat the carrier on the metal bench next to the door and waited for her to get Amber settled before handing over the diaper bag.

Thankfully, Amber settled into her carrier as if she were home, smiling and gurgling once again.

"I was hoping that you would fall in love with her, just as I have," Charlotte said. She hated the wistful sound in her voice. There were things that needed to be said, and if she got too mawkish, she might not get through them without crying like a baby herself.

"It's not about loving her," Glenn said. His tone had grown a few sharp edges.

"I didn't mean that you couldn't, just that you don't."

He looked down at Amber, a faint smile whispering across his lips. "She's a beautiful baby," he said.

"But?"

"I've raised my children."

"And you don't want to raise more," she finished flatly.

He sighed. "Something like that. I mean, if it were our baby, well, I'm sure I would feel differently. But there are a lot of couples out there who want to adopt a child. Who need to adopt. She should go to one of those couples."

She understood where he was coming from. She had covered that ground herself, but she knew one thing if she knew anything at all. And that was that Amber had been left for her.

And she couldn't be with a man who didn't have that same goal. "So I guess that's it, huh?"

He hesitated, nodded.

The driver that had dropped them off drove up once again.

Glenn tried to hand her a couple of folded-up bills, but she held up one hand to stop him. "No. *Danki*," she said. It was nice of him, gracious, but she couldn't take any more from him. Not now.

"Charlotte," he started, but she shook her head.

"I'll be seeing you, Glenn Esh," she said. Then she ducked into the car to strap Amber's carrier onto the seat. When she looked back up, Glenn was gone.

Chapter Nineteen

"And you just left?" Nadine asked the following morning.

Charlotte nodded, then took a sip of her coffee. "Then I just left."

She had been in bed last night when Nadine had finally made it home. When she had come downstairs at two to get Amber a bottle, Amos had been snoring softly on the sofa. When she had come back down at six, Amos had been gone.

"And the wedding?" Nadine asked.

"It's off," Charlotte flatly replied. She knew she should have been devastated. Calling off the wedding should have broken her heart into a million pieces; it should have sent her into a tailspin of depression worse than finding out she was in menopause.

And yet it hadn't.

"I can't say that I'm not glad," Nadine said, reaching for another biscuit. "He wasn't right for you."

"He was perfect," Charlotte defended. And he had been perfect except for the fact that they had entirely different goals.

"He was too fancy. Driving around in a car all the time." She shook her head. "He just didn't seem like our kind of people."

She couldn't argue with that, so instead she grabbed up another biscuit for herself and slathered it with butter. She had taken the first bite of it when a knock sounded at the door.

"I'll get that." Charlotte stood and made her way to the front door, only halfway wondering who would be stopping by at this time of morning.

Amos maybe. Though he had only recently left. Or Paul. She hadn't seen him in a couple of days and they were due for a visit.

Except it was neither of them at the door, but a heavy-set lady with overly blond hair and bright pink lipstick. She held up a name badge for Charlotte to see. "Hello, I'm Regina Eldridge with DHS. I've come to check on you and Amber Doe."

Another visit? They were really being thorough. And after all the fussing everyone did about kids who fell through the cracks of "the system."

"*Jah, jah.*" Charlotte stepped back and allowed Ms. Eldridge to enter. "Someone from your office was just here yesterday."

Ms. Eldridge nodded as she stepped into the house. "We are particularly vigilant when an infant classified as failure to thrive is involved."

"I see." Charlotte said the words, but she wasn't sure exactly what Ms. Eldridge meant. It didn't matter. She had nothing to hide.

"Let's get started," Ms. Eldridge said. She put on a pair

of reading glasses, pulled out Amber's file, and went to work.

She trailed behind Ms. Eldridge as she did basically the same things that both the other workers had done. Switched on the stove, turned on the water and waited for it to get hot. Inspected every aspect of Amber's space.

Then she turned to Charlotte, her glasses perched low on her nose so she could see over them. "I see there is a fiancé."

Charlotte stopped. "*Jah,* uh, well . . ."

"Is he here?" Ms. Eldridge asked.

Charlotte sputtered. "No."

She looked around as if expecting him to pop out of a closet somewhere. "But he does exist."

"Of course." He had. She supposed she could say that he still existed, just no longer as her fiancé.

Ms. Eldridge flipped the file closed and removed her glasses before speaking. "I know that you want to adopt Amber, but I have to tell you that, as a single, middle-aged woman, you'll fall to the bottom of the list."

Charlotte blinked at her, certain she had misunderstood what the woman was trying to tell her. "What list?"

"For adoption. There are many young, married, two-income households who want to adopt infants like Amber. If you are not married, your chances of being selected to adopt her are not good," she said. "Not good at all."

"There has to be something I can do," Charlotte said just after lunch. She wasn't going down without a fight. She had too much invested in Amber, in God's plan for them all. She wasn't going to just give up and walk away. She couldn't. She owed as much to Amber.

"Surely it'll mean something that Amber thrives with you."

Charlotte flopped down on the sofa next to Nadine and rested her neck against the top of the cushion. She was careful not to crush the back of her prayer covering. The action was second nature to her. She had been doing it for as long as she could remember. That's how she felt about Amber. She had loved her for a few weeks, but she couldn't remember a time when she hadn't loved her. The little girl meant that much to her and more.

But without Glenn—or maybe she should say, without marrying Glenn—she might lose the child forever.

It didn't bear thinking about.

"There's a solution," Nadine said.

Charlotte cut her gaze over to look at the woman from the corner of her eye. "What if I've got it all wrong? What if Amber is not in God's plan for me?"

Nadine shrugged. "I stopped trying to figure out God's intentions a long time ago."

"How?"

"You have to realize and accept that He's in charge. He's in charge of it all and what He says goes."

She thought about that a moment. "Are you saying that I'm making what I want of God's plan?"

"I'm saying that we have no control over what God wills, but we have to listen to it all the same."

"How?" she asked again.

"Be still," she said simply as if that was the answer to everything.

* * *

Psalm 46:10 might be a very short verse, but it said a lot.

Be still and know that I am God.

The verse had been rattling around inside her head since yesterday afternoon.

Be still. Was that really her answer? She wanted to run around and search for what to do. Maybe go to the library or to the Child Protective Services offices. She felt like she needed to *do* something.

And yet here was Nadine telling her to be still.

So Charlotte had kept herself busy, taking care of Amber, getting things ready for puzzle night, and generally ignoring everything else. Not exactly being still, but she was fighting her own nature with this one.

Nadine hadn't said a word to her about it all day Wednesday, but Charlotte could feel her gaze upon her as she bustled around. Silently she thanked Nadine for keeping quiet. It was one thing to know what to do and another entirely to put it into action.

Be still.

It was about the hardest thing she could do. She was what some would call a go-getter. She made things happen.

Or maybe that was the problem. She had made things happen and they weren't the right things.

She was in the middle of taking cookies out of the oven—chocolate chip. Paul's favorite—when the thought hit her. She set down the cookie sheet and stopped right there, staring off at nothing as the thought descended upon her.

Had she forced things with Glenn? Had she made God's plan out to be what she had wanted it to be?

Was such a thing even possible?

She had no idea.

She turned away from the oven and sat down at the kitchen table. She bowed her head and began to pray.

Lord, I know not what Your will might be. But I am prone to guessing. If I have this wrong—

Was it possible that she had misread the entire situation? Not just that with Glenn? What if she wasn't destined to be Amber's mother?

No. That couldn't be right. Some things a person just felt down deep inside, all the way into their bones. Her being Amber's mother and raising the child was one of those things.

Wasn't it?

If I have this wrong, she began again, *please let me know. Please lead me in the right direction.*

And how would she know?

Please, Lord, she prayed. *Give me some sort of sign. Give me direction and insight. I want what's best for Amber. I want what's best for us all. But I can't work toward that, if I don't know what Your plan for us is. Please Lord, lend me wisdom and insight. Amen.*

"Charlotte." Nadine picked that time to come bustling into the kitchen. "What are you doing?" she asked. "You left the stove on." She hurried over and switched the knob to OFF. "Charlotte?" Nadine asked, quieter this time.

Charlotte opened her eyes, looked up, and gave Nadine a small smile. She prayed it looked hopeful, but it didn't feel like such on her lips. "*Jah?*"

"What are you doing just sitting there?"

Charlotte's smile turned into a frown. "I thought I was supposed to be still," she complained.

"You are," Nadine said. "But not when the oven's on and nothing is baking."

She was doing what she could. When she could. And once again she was doing it all wrong.

And where was her sign? How was she supposed to know what to do? Why wasn't God telling her these things? These were important issues. A baby's well-being, possibly even her life, was at stake. It wasn't like Charlotte was asking Him what sort of jelly to make or what color fabric to buy at the store.

She stood up so fast her chair tipped over behind her. "I don't know then," she all but shouted. She was amazed at herself and in a bad way. She felt as if she were watching from above, unable to stop herself from making a mess out of everything even as she knew that was exactly what she was doing.

"If you're so smart and you know so much, then perhaps you should figure it all out," she continued.

"What's gotten into you, daughter?"

But Nadine's words were spoken to an empty room. Charlotte had already left the kitchen. She heard Nadine's question, but she didn't go back to answer it. She might have if Nadine had sounded indignant or shocked. Instead her mother-in-law just sounded a little bruised, as if she had been hurt by what was happening between them.

Which should have made Charlotte turn right around and apologize. She should have gone right back into the kitchen and said she was sorry. That she was having a tough time trying to figure out God's plan and Psalm 46:10

wasn't helping one bit. If anything, it was confusing her more.

But she didn't turn around, She stomped up the stairs and made her way into her room. She resisted the urge she had to slam the door behind her. It would feel good to release some of the tensions and frustrations that she had swirling around inside her, but the noise would wake Amber.

She expelled the breath she had been holding since she had stormed out of the kitchen and slowly approached the crib.

She peeked inside and there she was. The very thing that had her tied up in knots. Sweet little Amber Doe.

Charlotte knew she shouldn't, but she reached into the crib and scooped the baby into her arms.

Amber stretched her arms above her head, arching her back as she continued to sleep. Then Charlotte settled down in the rocking chair next to the window and continued to hold the baby in her arms as she slept.

It was such joy. More joy than she could ever imagine feeling, holding the sleeping child. She wasn't sure how she would be able to let her go. And without Glenn in her life, that was surely what would happen.

Ms. Eldridge was right. There were too many two-parent families—English families with cars and electricity—who wanted to adopt a child. Why would they allow a middle-aged single widow the right to keep such a precious commodity?

"I'm sorry," she whispered to the sleeping child. She hated the thought, but that's exactly what Amber was to the state, the county, and the other powers that be. She was a commodity.

She kissed the top of her head, then laid her cheek on that downy-soft, rusty-colored hair. "But I promise, with everything I have, that I will take the very best care of you until that time. And if I have any say at all as to who gets to adopt you, I'll make sure it's the best family possible."

The truth was she wouldn't have any sort of say into who adopted Amber. If she did, then she would allow her own self to adopt the precious child. But she had to make that promise. Amber had grown to mean so much to her over the past few weeks. She couldn't imagine what her life would be like without her. The weeks that Amber had spent in foster care with someone else were like a distant, hellacious memory. One that she didn't want repeated. But until that time, she would care for the child as only she knew how and pray that God's will, whatever it might be, would be carried out for the benefit of the baby. It was all she could do. And that was something she had to accept. The sooner, the better.

But she couldn't put her down. She had come to accept one thing overall: that Amber was going to be taken from her and there was nothing she could do about that. There were higher powers—not nearly as high as God—that had control over such things. Those powers had the say, and if God didn't intervene, then Amber would go to live with a new family. Charlotte could only hope and pray that the family would be good for the baby girl.

Perhaps there was a lesson in this for her. But she had yet to figure out exactly what that was. Maybe, with time, she would be able to look back and see what God had wanted her to learn from all this.

But she couldn't set the baby down. Thank goodness

she had found one of those carrier things at a garage sale. She strapped on the contraption and carted Amber around on her chest from the time she woke up from her nap until everyone started to arrive for puzzle night.

Amos came first, bearing more of the savory pies that Esther had started carrying at the bakery. Then Jenna, Buddy, and the Lamberts arrived, followed finally by Paul.

Charlotte was happy he was there. It seemed like it had been a lifetime since she had seen him. She supposed it had only been a few days. But a lot had happened in that short amount of time. Perhaps that's what made the time seem like more than it was.

Paul held up a box of cheese-flavored crackers. "I was going to bring some of the pies again, but I—" He trailed off with a shrug, not giving a reason why.

"That's okay," Charlotte said, standing to one side so he could enter the house. "Amos brought some." She shook the box. "And we can have some of these with the cheese Jenna and Abbie brought."

Paul smiled as he pulled his hat from his head. But there was something off about his expression.

"Are you okay?" she asked.

He nodded. "Of course. What could be wrong?" he asked.

Everything, she wanted to say. *Anything.* But she had told herself that she was going to remain positive. In times such as these, when she was about to lose the most precious thing to her in that moment—or at least the most precious thing that needed her as much as she needed it— Charlotte had vowed to remain as positive as possible.

"Not a thing," she said instead, flashing him a smile to

reinforce her words. She had made a promise to herself and to Amber, and she was keeping it come what may.

"Hey, Paul's here." Buddy clapped his hands and grinned at Paul from his place at the table around the puzzle. "How's Obie and the dogs?" he asked.

"Fine," Paul said with a nod, but Charlotte saw it again. There was something wrong with Paul; she just couldn't put her finger on what it was.

Greetings went up all around, Nadine got Paul a plate, and everyone got down to work, eating, drinking, talking, laughing, and building the puzzle they had used as an excuse to get together.

"Mamm, you haven't put that baby down once," Jenna said accusingly.

"And good luck trying to make her," Nadine said with a chuckle.

Charlotte gave them both a *whatever* sort of look. "Nor do I plan to. I'm not sure how long I have left with Amber, and I want to make sure when she leaves here that she knows that one person in her life loved her."

Jenna wrinkled up her nose. "That sounds all well and good, but she's not going to be able to remember. She's a baby."

"I read an article at the doctor's office about how we can really remember everything that happens to us from the time we are born—maybe even conceived—but since we can't talk, we can't store the memories where we can get them back out of our minds." Abbie looked around to see what everyone thought about her revelation.

Nadine shook her head. "I don't know how much of that I believe. I mean, you're just a baby."

"I like the idea," Amos said with a nod.

"Of course you do," Nadine said dryly.

"Me too," Buddy chimed in.

"Well, just in case, I'm holding her all I want until they come and get her." Charlotte was so proud of herself for not allowing her voice to waver. She had promised to be less emotional about the whole ordeal. So far—today, at least—she had succeeded. Tomorrow was another day, and the actual time and day that they would come and pick her up was another matter altogether.

"But you are still planning on adopting her," Paul said, though his voice had taken on the soft edge of a question.

"Well, I was but . . ." She didn't want to say all her business out loud in front of everyone at puzzle night. "It doesn't seem like I will qualify for the adoption. I mean, there will be couples who rank higher than me on the list, and they will most likely have the first chance at adoption."

Buddy screwed his face into a frown. "That doesn't seem quite right since you found her."

Jenna elbowed him. "It's not like she's a puppy."

Buddy sighed. "I guess not." But Charlotte could see that it seemed that simple to him. Charlotte had found the baby so by all rights she should belong to Charlotte. If only Buddy were in charge of the placement. All her troubles would be settled in an instant.

"That doesn't seem quite fair," Titus said.

Paul and Amos nodded.

"You should know that fair doesn't always play a part in it," Abbie reminded him. Titus had spent five years in prison for an accident that he was not solely responsible for. Someone had had to take the blame, and it had fallen to him.

"I suppose you're right," he said.

Abbie held up both hands. "Somebody write that down. Time and date. Titus said Abbie was right."

Everyone laughed, including Titus. Charlotte had seen the two of them together enough to know that they enjoyed teasing each other. Perhaps it was one of the things that made their love so strong.

"But if you're married to Glenn," Paul started.

"Time to change the subject," Charlotte trilled, still patting Amber on the bottom as she rested one hip against the side of the table.

"Let's talk about ducks," Buddy said.

"Why?" Jenna asked.

"Why not?" Buddy returned.

"But why?" Jenna pressed.

"Because I like ducks," Buddy said.

Jenna seemed to think about it a moment. "Seems reasonable. All in favor of talking about ducks?" She raised her hand.

Several more hands went up, including Charlotte's. The vote was followed by much laughter, but not much conversation including ducks. But they had stopped talking about Glenn, and for that, Charlotte was thankful.

Chapter Twenty

He almost hadn't come tonight.

Paul looked around at the people gathered at Charlotte's table. He knew that Glenn had never shown up for a puzzle night before, but tonight could be the night that he decided to give it another try.

So Paul had almost stayed at home. He was doing his best to accept the fact that Charlotte and Glenn were getting married. That he, Paul, had waited too long to confess his feelings for Charlotte and now the opportunity was lost.

But Clara Rose had knocked on the door to his trailer just before seven and asked him what he was still doing home. When he told her, she said he was being ridiculous and needed to get himself over to Charlotte's.

His only excuse had been that he didn't have anything to offer them by way of food. Everyone always pitched in for the evening's snacks and he wasn't prepared for that.

Fortunately for him—or was it unfortunately?—Clara Rose was prepared. She handed him a box of cheese-flavored crackers and pointed toward Charlotte's house.

What choice did he have but to go?

Or maybe he'd wanted to, deep down, and Clara Rose's persistence had given him the perfect excuse to cave in and go.

No maybe about it. He did want to go to puzzle night. It was one of the brightest times in his week. He loved spending time with Charlotte. But he also loved spending time with the people she shared her life with—Nadine, Amos, Titus, Abbie, Jenna, and Buddy, of course. And little Amber.

The baby had come to be as special to him as his own grandchild. He looked forward to seeing her bright smile and the joy she had even though she had been left behind by the person who was supposed to love her most of all.

Perhaps that's why he was attached to her. Maybe he, like Charlotte, felt a certain obligation to see that she was happy since life had seemed stacked against her from the start.

Maybe that was why the Lord put Amber on Charlotte's porch. But that had nothing to do with him. Nothing at all.

But now it seemed as if something had happened between Charlotte and Glenn. Or maybe he was giving into some wishful thinking. She hadn't said there was a problem; she'd just done her best to change the subject to something other than Glenn.

Whatever it was, she had suggested that she wouldn't get to keep Amber and Paul wanted to know why. Perhaps he could go to Child Protective Services and give some sort of character testimony for Charlotte. Maybe that would give her the edge over the younger couples.

It wouldn't be a disservice to the baby. She loved

Charlotte as much as Charlotte loved her. No better match could have been made by man.

"I'll help," Paul said, picking up the cover to the puzzle board that Amos had made for them and placing it on the table.

The Millers and the Lamberts had already gone, and Nadine had walked Amos out to his tractor, leaving Paul alone with Charlotte.

Just the way he wanted it.

His gaze fell to the baby she still cradled in the padded contraption they had bought together at a garage sale when this crazy situation had first started. Amber was peacefully sleeping, no doubt lulled to dreamland by the motion of Charlotte's movements and the muffled sound of her beating heart. Amber's mouth moved back and forth as if she was nursing on something invisible. It was one of the first times he had seen her sleeping without her fist in her mouth.

"She's so precious," he murmured. Then caught himself. He sounded like a woman, but the girl was something special. Even he could see that.

Charlotte smoothed one hand down her little back and cupped her bottom. "She is at that."

"And you don't think they will let you keep her," he asked. "I mean, they brought her back to you that second time."

She nodded. Surprisingly enough, she didn't tear up in the way that he thought she would. "I was told that most likely Amber would be adopted to a two-parent family."

"But when you and Glenn marry—" He almost choked on the words, but somehow he managed to get them out.

Charlotte shook her head. "There isn't going to be a marriage with Glenn."

Paul's heart felt lighter than it had in weeks. Then the feeling was replaced with sadness for Charlotte. She seemed to be handling it all right, but he knew deep down inside she had to be heartbroken. She and Glenn had had a sort of whirlwind courtship. But now, she hadn't just lost the man she was going to marry; she had lost the child she loved as well. "Charlotte, I'm so sorry."

Her composure started to slip, and Paul felt terrible as tears rose into her eyes. She had managed all evening to stay in a good mood, to be brave and not break down in front of everyone, and then he'd had to go and do this.

He reached for her hand, but she smacked his away.

"Don't," she said. She closed her eyes and took a deep, seemingly calming breath.

The action made Paul want to mimic it. To bring some of that peace into his own being.

She opened her eyes once again. "And don't be sorry. It's all part of God's plan," she said.

And she believed it to be so. He could see it in her eyes. "If you need anything," he started.

She nodded. "I know where you are. But this is something you can't help me with, Paul. Though I appreciate you and your friendship more than you will ever know. It's something I've got to get through on my own."

And with that, she escorted him to the door and onto the porch, telling him, without words, that it was time for him to go home.

* * *

*The righteous cry out, and the LORD hears them;
he delivers them from all their troubles. The LORD
is close to the brokenhearted and saves those
who are crushed in spirit.*

Psalm 34, verses 17 and 18 turned out to be the best
verses she could have read. As much as she didn't want
it to be so, she was brokenhearted. She was crushed in
spirit, and she was doing everything in her power to keep
herself from sliding into an abyss of depression. Soon, so
soon, she figured they would come and get Amber.

Babies were in great demand for adoption. Everyone
wanted a baby. And there would be a family who would
suit her fine, and she would be gone. Until then, Charlotte had vowed to keep her spirits up, though it was
exhausting.

She had barely slept the night before with all the
thoughts in her head. She wanted to prepare herself for
the time when they would come and get Amber. She
wanted to be strong for the baby. She knew that babies
were sensitive to the moods of the people around them.
She didn't want to be anxious or too sad when they came
to get Amber. She didn't want the baby to feel that something was wrong. Or even that she was being abandoned
once again. She wanted Amber to be happy and to have a
healthy, loving life, and all that it handed her.

Even when that life was no longer with Charlotte.

Charlotte couldn't fathom why God wanted this from
her. Maybe to show her how precious life truly was.
Maybe to give her a bit of the second chance she had
asked for. Or maybe He just wanted her to know that she

could love another baby, but her Jenna would have a baby soon and that was when the rejoicing came in.

Maybe.

After she woke, Charlotte changed Amber's diaper and dressed her. Then she strapped on the carrier and cradled the baby close as she made her way downstairs to breakfast. She was going to continue to do everything in her power to make each day the best possible last day she would spend with Amber.

As much as she wanted to, she would not try to figure out what God was trying to show her. She would not question His plans or His motives. She would *be still*.

Nadine was already flipping pancakes when Charlotte and Amber walked into the kitchen.

"Good morning." Nadine half turned as she made her way to the stove to pour herself a cup of coffee.

"Good morning," Charlotte returned.

"You okay this morning?" Nadine handed her a plate with two pancakes and a couple of slices of bacon.

Charlotte set the plate on the table. Then she unstrapped Amber and placed her in the nearby carrier. "Of course. Why wouldn't I be?"

Nadine made a face as she set her own plate on the table. "I heard you stirring around half the night."

"I'm sorry I bothered you." And she truly was. But these were difficult times for her.

"It's all right. I was only concerned."

They continued to eat. Charlotte managing with one hand as she held the bottle for Amber to eat as well.

"What's on the agenda for today?" Nadine asked.

"I thought I would take a look at the paper and see if there are any jobs."

Nadine dropped her fork. "You're going to work?"

Charlotte shrugged. "Why not?"

"Because you don't need to, for one. And what about Amber?"

Charlotte gazed lovingly at the child, then turned her attention to Nadine. "You and I both know that Amber isn't going to be here for much longer. As soon as they get all the paperwork settled, she'll have a forever home. And I'll need something to do."

"That's why you want a job? Something to do?"

"I thought I might clean houses."

Nadine shook her head. "For the English? Do you even know how to run their appliances?"

Charlotte gave her a steady look. "I can learn." *And it will give me something to do when everyone is gone. I can't ask for more than that.*

"What about Cephas?" she asked. "Are you going to clear that with him?" There were a few members of their congregation who used electricity in their businesses, but Cephas might have a different view on the English conveniences like vacuums and steam cleaners.

"I'll cross that bridge when I get to it." Charlotte gave a decisive nod.

"Okay," Nadine said. "If you're certain."

"I am," Charlotte replied as a knock sounded at the front door.

"Who could that be?" Nadine asked even as she stood to go find out. "I'll get it," she said. "You need to burp that baby."

Charlotte smiled her thanks and lifted Amber from

the carrier. She braced her over one shoulder and gently rubbed her back.

"Paul's here." Nadine came back into the kitchen, Paul trailing behind her.

"Good morning," he said.

Charlotte nodded in return while Amber let out a burp worthy of a grown man.

The adults all laughed.

Charlotte cuddled the baby close, loving the smell of her, the sweetness and the innocence. She would miss her terribly when she was gone from her life. But at least she had now.

"I wanted to come by and check on you this morning," Paul said. He was hovering to one side as if he didn't want to get too close. In fact, he wasn't acting like Paul at all.

"Get yourself a cup of coffee," Nadine said.

"And sit down for a bit. We just finished eating," Charlotte told him.

"Are you hungry?" Nadine asked.

"I ate a little before I came over." Still, he hovered.

Nadine looked to Charlotte, but she could only shrug. Paul may have come to check on her, but he was the one acting strangely.

"I'll get you some coffee," Nadine said, pulling out the chair at the side of the table between them.

Paul still ignored it.

"What's going on, Paul?" Charlotte finally asked. "You don't seem quite yourself."

In fact, she thought he was beginning to sweat.

"Are you okay?" she asked again. "Is it your heart?"

"You could say that." His words sounded choked, as if he couldn't breathe on top of everything else.

"It is?" Charlotte stood.

What was someone supposed to do for a heart attack? She didn't know. The only thing she knew to do was run to the phone shanty and call 911.

Nadine set the coffee mug on the table. Then she grabbed Paul by the arms and pushed him into the waiting chair. "Wait here. I'll get an ambulance."

"No!" he cried before she made it to the kitchen exit.

Nadine stopped.

Charlotte stared at Paul.

Even Amber was watching intently to see what would happen next.

"I thought about this all night," Paul said. He stood, and Charlotte wondered the wisdom of that motion.

"*Jah*?" Charlotte asked, waiting for him to continue.

"And I've come to ask you to marry me, Charlotte Burkhart."

Chapter Twenty-One

She blinked at him as if he were speaking in a language other than English, or even Dutch.

"What did you say?" she asked.

"I came to ask you to marry me," he repeated. This time the words came easier for him.

Charlotte shook her head. "Why?"

"Because . . . because you need a husband so you can adopt Amber. I can be that husband for you. We get along just fine and have a good time together. Why shouldn't we get married?"

He had practiced his speech all night long. He had given great thought to what he was going to say, the argument he knew he would need to give. He'd covered just about everything, practiced it until he had it all down perfect. But now that he was actually in the moment, he could barely manage to get any words at all past the lump in his throat. And even then, they weren't the words he had rehearsed so diligently.

"Paul," Charlotte started. He knew right away from the tone of her voice that she was going to turn him down.

"Charlotte," he started, trying to circumvent any argument she could make.

She held up one hand to stay his words. "That is the sweetest thing anyone has ever thought to do for me. But I can't ask that of you."

"You didn't ask," he said. "I offered. That's completely different."

She shook her head. "It's still the same. You can't give up your life for me."

He frowned. "I'm not giving up anything." He was barely aware of Nadine silently leaving the room and giving them the privacy he should have asked for when he first came in. But he had never dreamed that Charlotte would turn him down. Wasn't this what she wanted more than anything? If she had a husband, she would jump back up to the top of the list to adopt Amber. Without one, she would have to give the baby up.

So why was she saying no?

"You don't love me. And I can't let you marry me just so I can adopt Amber. Or even worse what if we were to get married and they still won't let me have Amber. What would our lives be like then?"

The best! he wanted to shout. *Our lives would be a dream come true for me.*

But it was too late for that. He should have led with the fact that he loved her. Maybe that would have made a difference, but if he said the words now . . .

"I love you." There. Let her make of that what she would.

Her shoulders dropped, and she set Amber back in the car carrier. "Don't do this, Paul. I value your friendship above all else. Don't start lying to me because you think you know what's best for me."

"It's not a li—" He stopped. This was exactly what he had been afraid would happen. She didn't believe him. If he had told her first that he loved her, then she might have believed him. But now . . .

She only thought he was saying what she wanted to hear. Stubborn woman.

"I tried," he said, even though his heart was breaking in two. "I value your friendship more than you will ever know. It means the world to me. So why wouldn't I come to help my friend? But I think now . . ." He started for the door. "I'm sorry. Good-bye, Charlotte."

She watched him go, wondering if it all had really happened. It was too real to be a dream, but too surreal to be reality.

"What was that all about?" Nadine asked, coming back into the room.

"He's a good friend," Charlotte said.

"So marry him."

Charlotte shook her head and shot Nadine a look that clearly said she had lost her mind. "I cannot marry Paul Brennaman."

"Why not?"

"Why not?" There were a dozen reasons why not. And just as soon as she thought of one, she would tell Nadine.

"I'm waiting."

"I don't . . . love him," Charlotte finally said.

"Are you sure about that?"

Okay, she did love him. As a person and as a friend. But that wasn't the kind of love she was talking about.

"Of course, I'm sure. There are no romantic feelings between me and Paul. There never have been, and there never will be."

But the sound of his good-bye had her worried. It sounded like forever. Like she wouldn't be seeing him anymore after today. A life without Paul was not something she thought she could bear. And a life without Amber or Paul would be intolerable.

But that wasn't going to happen. DHS would come get Amber, and Paul would see that it all was for the best. And she would too. As long as she kept telling herself that, she might actually believe it. Then life would go back to normal. And hopefully, somewhere down the road, God's plan would be revealed. But she wasn't looking for it now. It was too early, and she was busy following the decree of "be still."

But one day they all would know.

Two weeks passed before the inevitable came. Two weeks of diaper changes, silly bubble baths, and midnight feedings.

Charlotte had gone to his trailer a couple of times to see Paul, but either no one answered or his sons told her that he wasn't home. Finally, she decided that she had hurt him in some way and it might take him a little time to heal before he would be ready to forgive. He knew where she lived, and she would be waiting for him when that time came.

Then DHS showed up first.

Yet another worker came to the house late Wednesday afternoon.

Wednesdays always filled her with a particular hope. That perhaps today would be the day that Paul would come back to puzzle night. And of course having friends and family over always lifted her spirits.

The car that pulled up into the drive was blue, one of the four-door models that seemed to be so common in the English world. Nothing about it seemed special or different, and when Charlotte saw it pull up outside, she figured they were there for another home visit, once again making sure that Amber was being well cared for.

The woman who came to the door was dark-haired and thin, wearing a dark skirt that just reached her knees and flat black shoes that could have used a good polishing.

"Cassie Edwards," she said, flashing them her credentials and proving that she worked for Child Protective Services. "I've come to pick up Amber Doe."

For a moment, Charlotte thought she had heard the woman wrong, and then the truth set in. She had come to take Amber away.

"Is that the baby?" Ms. Edwards asked, nodding toward the carrier Charlotte had strapped to her chest.

"*Jah*," she managed to whisper. She cupped one hand under Amber's padded bottom as if that would somehow protect her, protect them both from what was to come.

"Fine then." Ms. Edwards nodded. Waited.

Then Nadine tugged on Charlotte's elbow, indicating that she needed to allow Ms. Edwards into the house. Charlotte needed the prompt. She had somehow lost all her powers concerning social graces.

Charlotte swallowed hard and stepped to the side to

allow the woman to enter. In truth, she wanted to slam
the door in the woman's face or pretend that she didn't
speak English, anything to stall the inevitable. Anything
to keep them from taking Amber from her.

She had known that this time was coming. She had
even thought about it, imagining what it would be like.
How she would act. What she would say. She had heard
somewhere that, if a person was faced with a tough situation, pretending to go through it internally would make
it easier to handle. But now that she was here, in the
actual moment, she knew that nothing would be able to
adequately prepare her for losing the most precious thing
in her life.

"Why?" Nadine demanded. "Why are you taking her?"

Charlotte was glad that Nadine had asked. She herself
seemed to have lost her powers of speech. She wanted to
hear the woman say it, even though she knew what the
answer was going to be.

"We have a couple in line for adoption." Cassie Edwards
gave her a tight smile. Apparently, she had come to pick
up children before and had been warned that this one
might be difficult.

"Can you give us a moment?" Charlotte asked. She
needed a little time, a few minutes even to say good-bye.

Ms. Edwards looked as if she wanted to grab the baby
and dash away with her without even waiting for Charlotte to unstrap her. And definitely before she could wake
from the drowsy nap she had been taking while Charlotte
went about getting things ready for tonight.

Finally, she nodded and Charlotte made her way into the
living room. She needed to sit for a moment. She needed
to do . . . something. Anything. Nothing. She needed to

take Amber out of the carrier and hold her close. She needed to change the baby's clothes so the new couple would see how well she had been cared for. She needed to gather up her favorite things so Amber wouldn't be without them, the blanket that her birth mother had left for her in the carrier. The floppy bunny that Paul had bought her in town. The rattle made from plastic keys that Amos had given her.

Suddenly, tears filled her eyes. She could do this. She had to do this.

She blinked back the tears and lifted Amber from the quilted carrier. The baby stretched, blinked her blue eyes. She slowly opened them and focused on Charlotte. The sweetest smile Charlotte had ever seen spread across those chubby cheeks. Toothless gums grinning at her as if she was the most precious sight, instead of the other way around.

Charlotte's heart broke clean in two.

She raised Amber close to her, pressed her nose into the sweet-smelling crook of her neck and shoulder and closed her eyes, doing everything in her power to remember that moment forever. Even more heartbreaking than letting go was knowing that, with time, that memory would fade. It would lose its crisp, clean edges. It would lose all the details until it was just a time when . . .

But, for now, it was the most precious memory she had, and she would cherish it until time took it away.

"Would you like something to drink, Ms. Edwards?" Nadine asked.

Charlotte should have acted as hostess, but the niceties of polite society were the last things on her mind at that time. Thank heavens for Nadine. Once again, Charlotte didn't know where she would be without her.

"Just a water if you have it."

Charlotte looked up as Nadine frowned. "Of course we have it."

And some of the tension left her at Nadine's incredulous expression. It was amazing to them both how people could live so close to their Amish neighbors and yet not know a thing about them.

"Your house is nice," Ms. Edwards said, looking around as she took papers from the leather briefcase she carried. It was the open kind with two handles also made of leather. Her initials were embossed on one side.

"We like it," Charlotte said.

Ms. Edwards continued to look around. "How long have you had Amber?" she asked.

"A couple of months," Charlotte replied, though it seemed like she couldn't remember a time when she hadn't had Amber. July was just the other day and forever ago all at once.

"And you've fostered babies before?" Ms. Edwards placed the papers on the coffee table and set her case on the floor near her feet.

"No. Amber's our first."

Ms. Edwards blinked in what looked to be surprise, but she didn't reply as Nadine came back into the room carrying a glass of water for their guest.

"You have quite a lot of baby things for a first-timer."

Charlotte glanced around at all the baby stuff they had collected. It had been fun to gather the items to make Amber's life more comfortable. But she had also wanted to make up for the fact that the child had been abandoned on her doorstep. She had wanted to give Amber hope that the future wasn't as bleak as the present might look. She supposed material items weren't the way to prove devotion, so she had also done her best to love the child with all her heart. At least, in that, she had succeeded.

"All right then," Ms. Edwards said. "Let's get down to work here."

She went over all the papers that Charlotte had to sign. She wished nothing more than to put that task off on Nadine, but she herself had to sign. She had to take care of paperwork when all she wanted to do was hold Amber and relish the last moments she would get to spend with her.

The work that Ms. Edwards spoke of both seemed to take forever and was over in a heartbeat.

They examined Amber together, changing her clothes, checking for an abuse or trauma. Charlotte wanted to be offended that they would even dream that she would hurt that baby, but she couldn't muster up those emotions. She had more important matters at hand. Maybe tomorrow.

They changed Amber's diaper, put her back in clothes into something decidedly more English than the homemade dress that she wore, though Ms. Edwards did comment on the charm of the little pink *frock* that Charlotte had made for her. Gasping that she had made it herself and commenting on where she'd found the time between taking care of a small baby and all the other things an Amish woman had to do. Charlotte shrugged casually but was secretly thrilled with the compliments.

Then, all too soon, it was time for her to go.

"Wait," Charlotte said. She grabbed the diaper bag and started putting things in it, random things that she didn't want Amber to be without. Even her binky, which she never used.

"Mrs. Burkhart, that's not necessary," Ms. Edwards said. "Her new family will have all these things for her."

Charlotte stopped stuffing the bag. "What if they don't?" she asked. Hysteria was rising up the back of her throat. She had to keep it together. Not just for her sake but for that of Amber as well. It would do no one any good for her to break down and sob like a child. Or even worse, snatch Amber from Ms. Edwards's long, thin arms and run all the way to Paul's with her.

And that was what she truly wanted to do. She wanted to grab Amber and run away. She loved the child. More than she had loved anything since the moment Jenna was born.

And it was a pure love. She didn't have to love Amber. She wasn't her biological child, but she was her baby all the same.

"They'll have it," Ms. Edwards assured her.

"This." Charlotte raced across the room and grabbed up the floppy-eared bunny that Paul had bought for her. He would want her to have it. She just knew it. "Can she take this with her?"

Ms. Edwards sighed. "If you think it will make it easier."

"It'll be really good for her," Charlotte said with confidence.

"I was talking about you." Ms. Edwards gave her an understanding and indulgent smile.

Charlotte returned it despite the tears rising in her eyes. "Can I hold her one more time?"

Ms. Edwards thought about it a moment, then shook her head. "I'm not sure that's a good idea."

Charlotte nearly collapsed onto the floor. "Please," she whispered. "I'll take her to the car for you."

A myriad of emotions rushed across her face, but she relented, giving Charlotte a quick nod even as she reached for the child.

Amber slid into her arms as natural as breathing. Oh, how she was going to miss her. She wasn't sure her heart would be able to take it. When Daniel had died, she had felt the same way. And when Jenna had been hurt. Her heart had bounced back both times, but it had been a younger heart back then. And it hadn't been as cracked and damaged as it was now. Yet surely the good Lord would see her through. This was His plan after all.

She kissed the side of Amber's neck, then made the first step toward the front door. It felt like a death march. She was going to her own death.

She could do this.

She would survive.

Charlotte was barely aware of Nadine and Ms. Edwards following behind her as they walked toward the little blue car. Such a nonthreatening-looking vehicle that was sure to tear her life apart.

"This is going to be perfect for you," she told Amber, even as her own tears started to fall.

Goldie had come up next to her and started to whine. Somehow the dog knew that something big was happening. But Charlotte couldn't console her. Not with her own emotions still spinning around like a top.

"You're going to have a new mommy. And a *dat* too. You're going to love it." She sniffed and smiled though tears blurred her vision. She could barely see the smiling face of her baby angel. And she prayed with each word that she was telling her the truth. "And this new mommy and *dat*, they are going to love you very much and give you everything you could possibly want."

Amber cooed and reached up to grab Charlotte's nose.

Charlotte laughed and nibbled at the tiny little fingers. "But I hope you'll always remember us here. Remember me. And I hope you'll know somewhere inside yourself that you were loved here. Always and forever."

"Charlotte." Nadine spoke quietly behind her.

It was time. She could delay no longer.

"Have a good life, my angel." Her voice choked on the last word, but she managed to step back.

Ms. Edwards grabbed the plastic handle of the baby carrier. She hoisted it into the back seat of the sedan and settled it onto the plastic base with a decisive click. The sound held an edge of finality. And that was when she realized. She was never going to see Amber again.

She had no idea where the child might end up. Where she was going to live, or if anyone would know if she was being cared for.

But the words she would have used to ask Ms. Edwards those questions were all jumbled together, lodged in her throat and rendering her incapable of speech.

Her limbs seemed not to want to work any longer. Her tears the only part of her that could move. Nadine wrapped an arm around her waist and she was thankful for the support, though she wasn't able to say as much.

Ms. Edwards opened her car door, but stopped before getting in. She said something to them, something that sounded like a measure of gratitude. Nadine responded, but Charlotte couldn't. She could only concentrate on remaining upright while she waited for the worst to come.

Then Ms. Edwards got into her car and started the engine. A few seconds later, she was pulling down the drive.

Despite the support of Nadine's arm around her, Charlotte slid to the ground, grief paralyzing her very being.

Chapter Twenty-Two

She was acting like a ninny. Charlotte pulled herself to her feet. The Lord was her strength, and He would see her through.

"Charlotte?" Nadine's voice was full of concern.

"I'm all right,'" Charlotte said. Or she would be.

"Maybe I should call everyone and tell them puzzle night is off."

"No!" Charlotte straightened her spine. They were not cancelling puzzle night because something they had known all along would happen had happened. That was silliness on top of silliness.

"Charlotte."

"No," she said again, a little more calmly this time. "This is a hard time, and one thing we need more of in times like this is family."

Nadine nodded.

After all, could she really disagree?

"Are you sure she's okay?" Jenna asked just after everyone had arrived for the evening.

"I think so," Nadine said.

Charlotte pretended that she couldn't hear them. Jenna meant well, and her daughter's concern was precious to her. And she was all right. At least, she would be.

The Lord was her strength. It was something she would have to remind herself of in the coming days. But she would manage.

Even though she had never before experienced such heartbreak as losing Amber.

She had to believe that it was all going to work out for the best. That it was all part of God's plan for them all, even little Amber.

"Where's Paul?" Jenna asked. "Is he not coming again tonight?"

Now that was a heartache she wasn't sure she would ever recover from. She had hoped that by now he would be over whatever hurt he had suffered. She wanted to go to him, talk to him, but she wasn't able to bring herself. Not yet. Amber's leaving was still too fresh and might be for some time. But soon, she thought. Soon, she would do everything in her power to get her friend back. It was one thing that she had more control over than anything else in her life.

"I don't know," Nadine said. "We haven't seen him in weeks now."

Thank heavens she didn't mention to Jenna that it was after he had proposed to Charlotte. Jenna would want to know all the details of that, and as far as Charlotte was concerned, there were some things that she didn't need Jenna to know. Like the fact that Paul had proposed to her and she had turned him down. Those sorts of things she didn't understand herself, and until she did, it was better to keep them to herself.

"Are we ready to start?" Charlotte asked.

Everyone nodded. It was just the five of them tonight—Jenna, Buddy, Amos, Nadine, and Charlotte.

And for the first time in a long time, she felt like that fifth wheel that had no purpose.

"Gather round," she said. "I'll go get the snacks."

They all took their seats, and Charlotte made her way into the kitchen to gather their food for the evening.

Fifth wheel or not, she hoped that even after Nadine got married and moved out, everyone would still come over for puzzle night. It was the one joy she had left, and she desperately needed it. Even if everyone thought she was handling it all so well.

Paul looked up as a tractor chugged down his drive toward the main house. Since the drive curved a bit, he could see around the house he had lived in with Marie and around the side of the trailer he shared with Benjie and Adam. He was in the field staking out where he thought he would put the house.

Yes, he was going to build a house. Not for Charlotte. She had turned him down flat. In all fairness, he had messed up by not telling her first that he loved her. And when he'd tried to correct his error, she had not believed him.

But he was still building a house. He deserved it. His boys deserved it, and one of them could take it over when he went to his reward.

Still, he had thought that he would share it with Charlotte and even little Amber.

He had heard in town this morning that Amber had been taken away by DHS and placed into a new home where she would be adopted.

And he couldn't help but think that she could have been theirs. And now she belonged to someone else.

But he pushed those thoughts away. It made her sound too much like a stray puppy, and he didn't want to feel that way about the sweet little baby who had captured his heart without even trying.

The tractor stopped, and Jenna Burkhart Miller hopped to the ground. She waved at Paul.

He returned the gesture and went back to staking out the space he would need to level for the foundation.

He supposed Jenna was there to visit with Clara Rose. They were fairly close in age, were both pregnant, and surely they had even more in common than that, things Paul had no idea about that were all in a woman's domain.

He was glad for Jenna that she had a friend in Clara Rose.

"Paul Brennaman," Jenna called from the back of the trailer.

"She's in the house," Paul called in return. "Just knock."

Jenna frowned. "Who?"

"Clara Rose."

She shook her head. "I came to see you, Paul."

He stumbled; then he placed a stake in the ground where he had left off. He started across the field toward Charlotte's daughter. "Why do you need to see me?"

"What happened between you and my mother?" Jenna asked.

He stopped in front of her, waiting for her to continue.

She crossed her arms and waited for him to explain. So like Jenna, straight to the point.

"Nothing." But that wasn't true.

"I may have a simple brain, but I'm not stupid. Now something happened. And now you never come to puzzle night anymore."

He cleared his throat. "I think you should ask your mother about this."

"I'm asking you." Jenna propped her hands onto her hips, looking so much like her mother that Paul lost his breath for a moment.

Paul hesitated. One, he needed to catch his breath, and two, he wasn't sure what and how much he should actually tell Jenna. In the end, he decided on the truth and enough of it that she would understand why he couldn't come over any longer.

"I asked your mother to marry me."

Jenna's entire demeanor changed. Her shoulders relaxed, her eyes brightened, her mouth fell open. "You did? That's wonderful!"

"She turned me down."

Jenna's expression veered from elation to devastation. "Why?"

He shrugged. "I messed up. I told her that I wanted to marry her so she could adopt Amber."

"Why didn't you tell her that you're in love with her?"

"I don't know," he said, followed by, "How do you know that I'm in love with her?"

She pulled a face that reminded him of his sister-in-law Eileen in the happy years. "Everyone can see that you're in love with her."

"Your mother can't."

"And you're surprised by this?" Jenna scoffed. "There are none so blind as those who will not see."

Truer words he'd never heard. "Where'd you learn something like that?" he asked.

Jenna smiled. "Abbie," she said. "She's smart like that."

"I guess so."

"So what are you going to do about it?" Jenna continued.

"About what?"

"You've got to ask her again," Jenna said.

Paul sighed. "She doesn't believe me."

Jenna shook her head. "She *didn't* believe you. Who knows what she'll be able to see now?"

It was a gamble. And gambling was a sin.

Or did it matter when one was gambling with their heart on the line.

And how many times was he going to put it out there before he decided that enough was enough?

Again and again, he decided, as long as Charlotte Burkhart was the prize.

He had thought about Jenna's visit for two days. In fact, it was all he could think about.

But now it was Saturday and he could stand it no longer. He had to tell Charlotte again that he loved her. He had to lead with that. Let her know how much she meant to him. And from there . . .

Well, he supposed that if she still didn't believe him, he could just go home, no more lost than he already was.

So here he was, tromping across the field to tell her

that she meant the world to him. And if everyone else could see it, why couldn't she?

But as he started down the slight incline that led to her house, he could tell immediately something was wrong.

Something white was scattered along the yard. The pieces were stirring in the wind. Goldie tried to catch some, running this way and that as she danced about the yard.

On closer inspection, he could see that they were feathers. Hundreds and hundreds, perhaps even thousands, of feathers.

Nadine came around the side of the house toting a burlap sack and muttering to herself. There was no sign of Charlotte.

"Hey, neighbor," he called so as not to startle her.

She stopped and squinted in his direction. "Hey, Paul. Long time no see."

He nodded. "*Jah*. What happened?" He met Nadine in the middle of the yard. If he had thought it looked bad as he was coming over the hill, it was nothing compared to standing in the middle of the mess.

"Foxes." She spat the one word in disgust.

"Last night?" he asked.

She nodded.

"Where was Goldie?"

Nadine sighed. "She's taken to sleeping on the end of Charlotte's bed at night. Never seen a dog so worried about their owner in my life."

Worried? "Is something wrong?"

"See for yourself." She nodded her head toward the barn.

Charlotte came out of the barn carrying a yard broom

and a rake. "This is all I could find." She stopped. "Hi, Paul. Fancy seeing you here."

His heart skipped a beat, then returned to its normal rhythm. "Hi, Charlotte."

"You lose any chickens last night?" she asked.

"No."

"We lost every one of ours," she said with disgust.

Why were they talking about chickens like they were the most important thing that needed discussing?

"That's a shame," he said.

Nadine cleared her throat, drawing Paul's attention. "You have a little time to help us clean up? It sure would be appreciated."

"Of course." But he hadn't come to clean up. He had come to ask Charlotte to marry him. But standing knee-deep in chicken feathers didn't seem to be the right setting.

Goldie came up next to him and pushed her head into his hand, demanding attention. "Hey, girl," he crooned, stroking her between the eyes. She closed them in happiness.

"How've you been, Paul?" Charlotte asked, so polite, nearly formal.

"I've been good."

"We've missed you at puzzle night."

He swallowed harder than necessary, unable to find a proper response. He had missed puzzle night, but after she had turned down his proposal and denied that he could be in love with her, he hadn't been sure how to go back to the way things had been before.

See, Nadine mouthed at him.

But, as far as he could tell, Charlotte was Charlotte. Like nothing had happened.

And suddenly he understood.

She handed him the yard broom. "If you'll sweep up the feathers, Nadine and I are still tracking down the dead chickens."

He nodded and accepted the broom from her.

She started to turn back to Nadine when he spoke again. "Have you heard anything about Amber?" he asked.

She shook her head. "They're not going to tell me anything. That part of my life is over." She gave him too bright of a smile.

"But you must miss her," he said.

"*Do not grieve, for the joy of the Lord is your strength,*" she quoted. "That's Nehemiah 8:10."

"Uh, *danki*," Paul stuttered unable to think of anything else to say. "That's a real nice verse, but it doesn't change anything."

She took a shaky breath. "No, I don't suppose it does. But she's gone and there's nothing I can do about it."

"You need to grieve."

She shook her head. "Did you not hear my verse?"

"It doesn't mean bury all your feelings and pretend things never happened."

Out of the corner of his eye, he saw Nadine start to inch away, in the direction of the chicken coop.

"What about you?" Charlotte said. For the first time since he had come up, her voice changed. Her tone now sounded a little strained and not so unnaturally pleasant. "You just stopped coming to puzzle night like you didn't even know it was happening."

"I wasn't sure if it was."

"That's never stopped you from walking across that field before," she said.

"Well, you'd never told me that I didn't know my own mind before either. So there's that."

"I didn't tell you you didn't know your own mind."

He propped his hands on his hips and stared at her, his gaze unwavering.

"Stop trying to be the alpha dog with me," she said.

"You stop trying to be the alpha dog with me," he returned.

Goldie whined, then let out a bark from somewhere nearby.

They continued to stare at each other, neither one willing to back down.

"I thought you were my friend," she said.

"I thought you trusted me," he countered.

"How did I not trust you?" she asked.

It was getting hard to hold the same position, but he'd be a son of a gun before he backed down from her. Just like with Goldie, he had to show her that he was serious. He'd been easygoing about it for way too long. Now was the time to state his intentions and pray that God was on his side.

"I told you I loved you. And you said I didn't. How am I not your friend?"

"You stopped coming over. Just because I turned down your proposal."

"Did you just hear yourself?"

A shrill whistle brought both of their attention around to Nadine. She stood, one finger and her thumb in her mouth. She took them out. "You two need a referee." She shook her head, then turned to him. "Paul," she started. "Do you love Charlotte?"

"With all my heart."

"Are you her friend?"

"Forever and always."

She wanted to believe what she was hearing. She wanted to believe it more than she wanted to believe anything in the world. Including the hope that Amber would be returned to her.

"Charlotte," Nadine said turning to her. "Do you love Paul?"

Did she? Honestly, she had never given any thought to love, but these last two weeks without him had been the hardest she'd ever had to face. She had thought that it was because she had lost Amber, but when she had seen Paul again, she'd realized the pain had more to do with him than the baby. She loved Amber with her entire heart, but she loved Paul differently.

He shifted in place, uncomfortable since it was taking her so long to answer. "I'll just go now," he started, handing off the yard broom to Nadine.

"No. I mean, yes." She was messing this up big time, as Jenna would say. "No, don't go," she clarified. "Yes, I love you."

Just saying the words made her heart feel lighter. Somehow everything made sense now. Everything. Even losing Amber. Because she hadn't lost Paul, and that was the most important thing. He was the most important thing.

"I don't know why I haven't seen it until now," she whispered.

He smiled at her, looking so handsome, so Paul. "There

are none so blind as those who will not see," he said. "Jenna told me that."

"My Jenna?" Charlotte asked. The world had taken on that surreal quality again, as if life were not quite real. The feathers surrounding them, stirring in the Oklahoma breeze, didn't help. She felt as if she were standing in a cloud.

"*Jah.*"

"When did you see her?"

"She came to the house yesterday. Told me I needed to come over and tell you that I loved you again."

"And you did," she said in amazement.

"And I did." He took a step closer to her. "You're going to marry me, Charlotte Burkhart. And if you want to adopt a child, then we can adopt a child. I want you to be happy."

She smiled at him, moved a little closer to him as well, mindful, but not quite minding that Nadine was standing so close.

He swooped in and pressed a quick kiss to her lips.

Charlotte's heart sped up in response.

"There's more where that came from," he said with a mischievous grin.

"I saw that," Nadine called.

"I'm sure you did," Paul returned.

Nadine handed him back the yard broom. "No more kissing until this yard is cleaned up."

He stared at her even though he was still standing so very close to Charlotte. Close enough that, if he chose to, he could kiss her again.

"Paul Brennaman, don't try that alpha dog stuff with me either," Nadine admonished.

He chuckled, then kissed Charlotte on the forehead, and they got down to the messy business of cleaning up the chaos the foxes had left in their wake.

It took them over an hour to clean up the majority of the feathers. But they were like trying to chase down the wind. And in Oklahoma that was no easy task. Nadine had long since given in and stomped to the house, promising at least to make everyone something to eat.

Paul propped his hands on the wooden handle of the yard broom and called out to Charlotte. "You never did answer my question, Charlotte."

She stopped bagging the last pile of feathers they had managed to push together. "What question was that?"

"You never told me if you were going to marry me or not."

She smiled at him. "You never asked me."

"Will you marry me, Charlotte?"

She paused, stared up at the sky as if giving it great contemplation. "Let me think about it."

"What?" He picked up a handful of feathers and tried to throw them her way. They fluttered all around. She blew one out of her face, then picked up her own handful and tossed them back. He scooped up some more, and before she knew what was happening, she found herself on the ground on her knees tossing feathers into the air and doing her best to stuff them down the collar of Paul's shirt.

And that's how Cassie Edwards, DHS worker, found them a few minutes later.

* * *

"I can't believe it," Charlotte said. "Explain it to me again." She had been a little embarrassed to be found rolling around on the ground having a feather fight with a man when Ms. Edwards happened to drop in. But how was Charlotte to know that the woman would come back? How was she to know that she would bring Amber?

But Ms. Edwards hadn't blinked an eye. Charlotte supposed that, in her line of work, she had probably seen practically everything.

"It's not that complicated," she said. "The couple who wanted to adopt a baby changed their minds. They decided they didn't want first available. They decided they had to have a boy."

"And they can do that?" Charlotte asked.

"Of course. Just as you can turn down my offer," Ms. Edwards explained.

Charlotte closed her eyes and resisted the urge to pinch herself. What a day this had turned out to be. First the chickens, then Paul. And now Amber.

"No, it's just . . . why me?"

They had all gathered in the living room eating cheese and crackers and the grapes that Nadine had prepared for their snack. Amber was still in her carrier seat, looking around as if she knew she was home.

"It's unusual," Ms. Edwards said. "I'll admit, but when I was here last time, I saw how much you cared for the baby.

"I've been doing this for fifteen years and I've worried about every child I've ever placed. But I don't have any worries about leaving Amber here with you. Husband or not."

"She's going to have one of those as soon as possible," Paul said.

Charlotte felt her face heat up, and she figured she must be about as red as the giant box of Valentine's chocolate that Amos had given Nadine last year.

Ms. Edwards smiled. "I'm glad to hear that." She stood. "You know where to reach me if you need me for anything. Not that I think you will.

"We'll be in touch with court dates and such, but everything should go smoothly."

Charlotte stood as well. She wiped her hands down her apron. Her palms were sweaty, and she didn't want to shake the woman's hand like that.

They walked to the door together and said good-bye. She and Paul and Nadine stood at the threshold and watched as Ms. Edwards got into her blue sedan car and drove away. And still Charlotte couldn't believe everything that just happened.

"God is good," Nadine said.

Paul took up her hand and squeezed Charlotte's fingers. "Indeed He is."

Two months later

Charlotte woke with a start. Something was wrong, terribly wrong. Off, missing. She wanted to get up and check the stove and see if they had left it on, but they hadn't cooked today. Not since yesterday. They had cooked yesterday for the wedding they'd had today. She settled back into her bed, reached out a hand, and touched the man lying next to her. Paul.

She would have never imagined in a hundred years

that she would be married to her best friend. Adopting an English baby. And loving every minute of it. Yet here she was.

It had been a glorious day. Who said second marriages couldn't be as elaborate as firsts? And today had been a great party. The guests had arrived all morning, some English, most Amish. Buddy and Jenna had cleaned the discount dollar store out of balloons and had the colorful orbs tied to everything possible, from the porch railing to Goldie's new pink collar. They had even tied a few to the handle on Amber's carrier seat.

Amber.

Charlotte eased from the bed and tiptoed out and to the room next door where the baby slept, as peaceful as the angel she was. As beautiful as the salvation she had been.

Charlotte pressed a kiss to her sweet chubby cheek and tiptoed back out the door. The room had once been Nadine's, but she had moved in with the Titus Lamberts until her wedding next month. Charlotte had tried to convince Nadine that it wasn't necessary. But she had insisted, saying that Charlotte and Paul were starting a ready-made family, but they didn't need an old woman hanging around.

Charlotte eased back into her bedroom, *their* bedroom, and slipped beneath the covers.

"Where'd you go?" Paul asked, his eyes still closed. It had been a full day.

"To check on Amber."

"She okay?" he asked.

"She's perfect."

"*Jah*," he said, He settled a little deeper into the covers, then started to softly snore once again.

Charlotte smiled a little to herself and scrunched down to get more comfortable.

God's plan. It was a wonderous thing. How complete, how perfect. And a verse from Isaiah came to mind.

> *Behold, God is my salvation; I will trust, and not*
> *be afraid: for the Lord Jehovah is my strength*
> *and my song; he also is become my salvation.*

Jah, that was it. Her life in verse. Strength, song, salvation. A forever family. Forever in love.